BY MAX BROOKS

FOR YOUNG READERS

Minecraft: The Island

Minecraft: The Mountain

Minecraft: The Village

NOVELS

Devolution

The Zombie Survival Guide:
Complete Protection from the Living Dead

World War Z: An Oral History of the Zombie War

GRAPHIC NOVELS

The Zombie Survival Guide: Recorded Attacks

G.I. Joe: Hearts & Minds

The Extinction Parade

The Harlem Hellfighters

MINECRAFT™
THE VILLAGE

MINECRAFT™
THE VILLAGE

MAX BROOKS

1 3 5 7 9 10 8 6 4 2

Del Rey
20 Vauxhall Bridge Road
London SW1V 2SA

Del Rey is part of the Penguin Random House group of companies whose
addresses can be found at global.penguinrandomhouse.com

Penguin
Random House
UK

Endpaper illustration: M. S. Corley

Max Brooks has asserted his right to be identified as the author of this
Work in accordance with the Copyright, Designs and Patents Act 1988

First published in the US by Random House Worlds, an imprint of Random
House, a division of Penguin Random House LLC, New York, in 2023
First published in the UK by Del Rey in 2023

www.penguin.co.uk

A CIP catalogue record for this book is available from the British Library.

Hardback ISBN 9781529135121
Trade paperback ISBN 9781529135138

Book design by Elizabeth A. D. Eno.

Printed and bound in Great Britain by Clays Ltd, Elcograf S.p.A.

The authorised representative in the EEA is Penguin Random House Ireland,
Morrison Chambers, 32 Nassau Street, Dublin D02 YH68

www.greenpenguin.co.uk

To the children of war. May your children only know peace.

MINECRAFT™

THE VILLAGE

INTRODUCTION

This is Summer, Guy's more practical companion. I'm writing this part in order to give Guy more time to prep his kit for our next journey. Don't worry, it's still his story, although I'll be writing another bit later. I'll also be writing about all the new lessons we've learned from this adventure because, just like Guy's last two books, there was a lot to learn. And if you haven't read the last two books, well, that's what this introduction is for.

Just know that, a while back, Guy popped into this strange, blocky world with no memory and no idea how to survive. And he spent the first book on an island learning how to do just that. And I don't just mean figuring out fire or tools, but figuring himself out: how to think and act and, well, just be a fully "rounded" person, so to speak. And of all the life lessons he learned on that island, the last one was that he'd have to keep going. "Growth doesn't come from a comfort zone," he's fond of saying, "but from leaving it." So he set out to discover more about this world and, perhaps, the way home. He paddled across the sea, bumped into a new, frozen land, and eventually bumped into me.

Like Guy, I'd also popped blindly into "Right-Anglia" (or whatever it's called) and had to fight to survive. I didn't collect any earth-shattering revelations, though. As I said, I'm the more practical, no-nonsense type, while Guy tends to think and talk about everything. A lot.

Our initial meeting didn't go swimmingly at first. We had a devilish time learning how to be friends. But, through adventures in my mountain palace, and below it in the Nether, we became inseparable. That was why, when it came time for Guy to keep moving on, I made the difficult choice to go with him. And that's where this story begins, on the first steps of our new journey.

Over to you, Guy . . .

CHAPTER 1

"Are we headed in the right direction?"

Summer asked me this the moment we stepped out of her under-mountain fortress. It was a good question, and I wish I had a good answer.

"I don't know." I shrugged. "But this direction led me to you, so it seems as good as any."

We were heading due west, crunching over the snow-covered taiga with the frigid wind at our backs.

"Swimming this way brought me to my island," I continued, "and when I finally left, paddling this way brought me to you."

"Can't argue with that." Summer nodded, then, focusing on the land ahead, declared, "We've got a lot of ground to cover before nightfall."

Our plan for day one was to traverse this patch of taiga, then the forest, then camp at its edge before setting out across the

5

next taiga. Day two would end at the jungle, the farthest Summer had ever been from her home base, and beyond that was the great unknown.

It was a simple plan, and very doable provided we didn't run into any trouble. But it had started snowing, which cut down our visibility, hiding any early morning creeper or other night mob lucky enough to be sheltering in the shade of a lone tree.

That's why Summer didn't say anything more, not just because she was done pondering our decision (which she was) but also to concentrate on any potential hazards. Surface mobs weren't the only danger out there. There were also those patches of thin, camouflaged "snowtraps," like the kind I'd fallen through on my first night in this continent. Just thinking about it made me shiver; the covered hole, the freezing pond, the skeleton shooting from the darkness.

More of these natural threats had to be out there, along with the possibility of new ones. This world was always changing. It had happened at least twice since meeting Summer. New animals, new plants, and, in the case of the Nether, entirely new environments that had nearly gotten us both killed.

Had there been other, recent changes to the taiga? If there were, we wouldn't have seen them. We'd been so obsessed with "electrifying" the mountain with redstone lamps that we hadn't even been outside for a plunge in the nearby ice river. If the surface world had changed, we'd find out soon enough. Not that I was worried, though. I knew we could roll with whatever was out there. As I'd learned back on my island: when the world changes, you've got to change with it.

And I had, every time. The first change had gotten me the

means to make the shield in my left hand. And the most recent world-morph had gotten me the crossbow now clutched in my right hand. I'd grown to really dig this new weapon, and to prefer it over the older stand-up bow. First, I could leave it cocked, which meant no straining or slowing my pace to draw. Second, and more important for me, it wasn't a rapid-fire weapon. That might sound like a disadvantage, but at this point I was running out of arrows.

Why not just make more? Fair question, especially if you haven't found the last two books I've left behind for other lost adventurers, but just know that I don't kill animals for food anymore. I'd been too guilt-ridden since slaughtering my chicken flock back on the island. I'd tried not to think about that time, but recently I couldn't help it. My original supply of arrows was running out, and, as you might know—or might not, if you're new to this world—arrows can't be made without chicken feathers.

What would I do? Start killing birds again? Or share feathers from Summer's kills? I'd learned a long time ago that sometimes you have to compromise an ideal in order to save it, but I wasn't ready to make that particular compromise just yet. Conserving arrows with a crossbow would, hopefully, buy me enough time to make up my mind.

And I hope you aren't too annoyed with me for pulling you out of the story to go off on what seems to be a totally random tangent. Trust me, it's not. Just like I did, you'll see how important this moral quandary will be later. But, that morning, all that mattered were the dangers right in front of us. And fortunately, there weren't any.

No new mobs, no new plants or animals, and, thankfully, no old threats like a carpet of thin "please fall through me" quick-snow. We reached the igloo where I'd first met Summer without incident, then continued on into the forest that bordered the white waste.

We stopped at the sweet berry bushes, which had appeared after the last change, and had a quick, flavorful snack. We'd brought plenty of food with us, but, as a general rule, it was always better to live off the land when possible. Personally, I was glad that Summer filled her belly with berries, because otherwise she might have turned her hunger on the next food source that ambled by.

"Mooo."

Cows. The herd I'd met before, just like my best friend Moo from the island. Yes, maybe it wasn't very original naming my mooing friend Moo, but Summer had named me Guy because I'm a guy. Simple, yeah, but meaningful, like when I named Summer after her warm, summer breeze laugh—and those are just first names! Just wait until later in this story, when we dig into some people getting their last names.

But that's not for a while. Right now, what mattered were the cows in front of us and the other animals behind them.

"Baaaa."

"Hey, flock," I said to the sheep, "been a while." I was pleased to see that they were all here, including Chippie, the brown lamb I'd helped spawn by feeding his parents when first meeting them. Fewer sheep would have meant more wolves, and since we'd eliminated the original pack a while ago, I was happy to see the new changes hadn't brought more.

Okay, side note, I know you're not supposed to mess with the balance of nature, right? Take out animal A that eats animal B, and soon animal B has multiplied out of control. But that's in our world, right? Here, the fact that this herd hadn't grown on their own showed that I'd actually preserved the balance by removing the predators. "No need to thank me," I said to Chip, "and I'm glad there aren't any new changes to the wildlife around here." I looked up as a white fox skittered past. "I was thinking, since we already have polar bears, this world's next change might give us grizzly bears, or . . . what are those mythical ape creatures that are supposed to lurk in the woods? Yetis, or Bigfoot?"

"Don't be so paranoid," Summer scolded between berry bites.

"Just waiting for the other shoe to drop," I replied, then let out a snorting giggle. "Get it? Bigfoot? Shoe?"

Everyone just looked at me: Summer, cows, and sheep.

"Tough room," I said with a shrug, "which I guess is our cue to keep going."

"Just a moment," Summer interjected and turned to climb a small hill.

"Where are you going?" I shouted up to her, waving my hands at her back. "We're burning daylight."

"Won't be long," she called over her shoulder.

I was about to keep pressing, wondering why she'd taken this sudden detour, but then I noticed the snow had stopped, and as she reached the top of the hill, I realized what she was up to.

Summer was looking behind us in the direction of her mountain and moving slightly back and forth. It's a weird quirk of this

9

world that faraway objects are always obscured by mist. One minute you don't see a thing and then, just a step forward, it's suddenly there. That's what Summer was doing, crossing and retreating over the exact line where her mountain disappeared.

"She's saying goodbye," I told Chippie, "like in that one book or books? Or maybe it was a movie, because I distinctly remember how crazy talented the actor was in that scene."

"Bah?" asked the little brown sheep.

"Oh, right," I replied. "You probably haven't seen it. It's a magical fantasy about little people going on a big adventure, and in this early scene, that brilliant actor says something like 'If I take one more step, it'll be the farthest from home I've ever been.'"

"Bah."

"Yeah, I guess it's not exactly like what Summer's going through," I told Chip. "She isn't technically leaving her home so much as setting off for her real one. But that mountain's meant everything to her. She hollowed it out, furnished it, gave it heat and light. It's kept her alive and safe for so long, and now she's leaving it all behind . . ."

"Bah." Chip's retort clenched my stomach.

"Waddaya mean 'if' she leaves it all behind? She's comin' with me. We agreed. She—"

"Bah."

I sighed. "Good point. I did keep making up reasons not to leave my island, and when I did, I almost turned my boat around and headed right back. And, now that I think about it, Summer and I almost ended our friendship because she was too scared to leave her comfort zone."

I looked up at my friend, alone on the hill, eyes fixed on the east, on the past.

"I gotta go talk to her," I told Chip. "Make sure she doesn't get cold feet, remind her that growth doesn't come from a comfort zone, but from leaving it!"

"Moo!" That was the cow, butting in on our conversation.

"Who asked you?" I snapped defensively. "And what am I supposed to do? Just let her back out now?"

"Moo," insisted the cow, sounding just like my island friend Moo, and just as wise.

"You're right," I grunted. "Friends respect each other's life choices." I turned away from the hill, giving Summer a true moment alone. "The only way she was able to leave was because she made the decision on her own, and that's the only way she's going to be able to keep going. Her life. Her choice."

"Well, that's comforting."

"What-oh-hiii . . ." I spun to face Summer. "I was just, uh . . ."

"Yes, I know," she said flatly. "I could hear your entire conversation from up there, and yes, I was saying goodbye."

"Oh, w-well . . ." I stammered.

"C'mon, then," she chirped, marching into the woods. "We should reach the other taiga before dark."

"Uh, yeah, totally," I mumbled in tow.

"And Guy," she said, without looking back. "Thank you."

I didn't respond. I knew she needed silence. Summer's not big on the whole "bare your soul" kinda thing. Which I totally understood when first hearing about how she'd started out in this world. Like I wrote in the last book, I don't know if I would have survived; spawning on the frozen taiga, living on zombie flesh (without a milk chaser), and having to fight every day just to get through to the next one. She didn't have the luxury of feelings. She'd had to shellack her heart with a thick coat of toughness. So I didn't press, didn't prod, didn't try to get her to talk about how she was feeling. I was just relieved that she was coming with me.

And that relief evaporated just a few minutes later.

"We can't go on."

We were almost at the end of the forest. She was a little ahead of me, standing at the top of a shallow ridge.

"What? Why?" The words came out in a high, frazzly yip. I couldn't control myself this time. I thought we'd settled it. Why had she changed her mind so quickly?

"Look for yourself," she said with a beckoning, blocky arm.

I scrambled up next to her and saw that it was the world, not her mind, that had changed. The next taiga was gone, replaced by a barrier of high hills. We stared for a moment, silently awed by the steep slopes dotted with dark spruce trees and bright patches of snow blocks.

"No luck making it across before dark," mused Summer, then, looking around for the best location to bed down, asked, "What do you think? Igloo or cave?"

"How about a log cabin?" I suggested. "It's comfier, would make a better landmark for any possible travelers coming up behind us, and"—I opened my arms to the trees around us— "we agreed to stretch our pack loads with the resources around us, right?" I was referring to our long-term strategy of living off the land whenever possible. Because, even though we carried everything from food to tools to extra supplies like torches and blaze rods, there was no telling when our finite inventory would run out.

"Couldn't agree more," said Summer, nodding, and reached for the latest addition to this ever-changing world, her netherite axe. It was a new material, or . . . alloy? Isn't that the right word? Mixing different metals into one? That's what we did with gold ingots and scraps of this mysterious ore from the Nether. Following the instructions in the book we'd found in the Nether bastion, we'd learned how to make a smithing table to combine the netherite scraps with Summer's diamond axe. The result was a tool that let her harvest wood like a machine.

"Should have all we need in a jiffy," she called over the sound of chopping trees, "so why don't you get to work on our chimney?"

Now it was my turn to use a Nether souped-up tool.

This was the enchanted pickaxe I'd found in that same ruined fortress as the netherite. Not only was it as fast and efficient as Summer's axe, its shimmering sheen hinted that, somehow, it was possible to either find more enchanted items, or, maybe, stumble on a way to enchant them myself. Either possibility would have to wait for a later date. Right now, I was just grateful for how quickly and easily it tore into the stone of a nearby hill. About a minute later, I had more than enough cobblestone for the cabin's chimney.

"Not bad," said Summer, placing the first layer of our seven-by-nine walls. "We should have the rest up in no time." And we did; first the walls, then the single door, then the shallow, angled roof of spruce planks.

"I'm gonna go hunt for some sand," I said as we fixed the last few planks into place. "You know, for window glass."

"I'd give that a miss if I were you," Summer argued. "Not the safest move so close to sunset."

"Safety's what I'm thinking about," I countered, "'cause if we're shut up in this wooden box with no way to see out, how are we gonna know there isn't a creeper waiting for us tomorrow morning?"

Summer considered this silently, then asked, "What about trapdoor windows?"

"Hm?" I didn't get it.

"Using trapdoors in window frames," Summer explained. "Just flip them up to keep out the cold and down whenever you want to see out."

"That's a good idea." I nodded, then, as the idea churned, said, "No, like, a *really* good idea."

"Thank you." Summer climbed down the ladder we'd fixed to the outside of the chimney and, with me in tow, went back into our nearly finished cabin to get to work on the windows.

"You've got me thinking," I said, cutting out the window frames.

"Oh, really?" Summer mocked. "You? Thinking?"

"Ha ha," I flat-laughed. "But seriously, what we're doing with these windows, using something old to make something new, plus these sudden hills, it's all got me thinking about how the world change might mean new items."

"Possible," Summer answered, fixing the trapdoor windows in place, "and as soon as we have the time, I look forward to some experimenting."

"Don't we have time now?" I set a netherrack cube in the fireplace, ignited it with my flint and steel, then stood closer to chase away the chills.

And wow, were those chills chilly. This world might not let you freeze to death, but the tight muscles, stinging eyes, chattering teeth, and burning numbness in my ears, nose, and fingers were definitely not fun! "Ugh," I groaned, as the flames shook the last frosty bolts from my spine. "The cabin's done, the sun is setting. There's nothing left to do."

"Except sleep." Summer placed her bed against one of the side walls. "I don't know about you, but I do *not* plan on tackling that ruddy great incline tomorrow without a proper rest."

"No argument there," I conceded, and placed my own bed opposite hers.

"Night, Guy," she said, slipping between her blankets.

"Night, Summer," I replied, preparing to rest my head.

Only I didn't. I couldn't. It was just too tantalizing to think about new crafting combos. And for that matter, what about the other two world changes before this one? Neither of us had done any experimenting those times. There'd been too many tasks and challenges before leaving. But now . . .

Just a few tries, I silently promised the crafting table, laying down materials as Summer blissfully snored behind me. *Maybe I can finally craft a sweater, or even a long-sleeved shirt! Just one or two random mash-ups before turning in.*

Yeah, right.

Five minutes and more than a few dozen mash-ups later, I let out a "Whoa!" that should have, but didn't, wake the sleeping Summer.

It was a simple combination: a collection of sticks, logs, and coal, but mixed up together, they made one of humanity's earliest achievements.

A campfire!

Like torches, it was cool and dormant when carried, but set in the fireplace, it blazed to life. And like torches, this fire never died! Warm and bright, and smelling so much better than the . . . well . . . shall we say "bathroomy" odor of burning netherrack.

"Summer!" I called. "Check this out!"

She didn't stir. I thought about shaking her awake (if this world would let me do that) or even going as far as chopping up the bed beneath her. She'd be mad, no doubt, but this breakthrough was too important not to share! Or was it?

Did a campfire mean there were more inventions waiting to be discovered, or was it just an old puzzle we hadn't been lucky enough to unlock before now?

"There must be more," I told my sleeping friend. "I just gotta keep trying!"

Which I did, and while I'd love to tell you that the night yielded amazing discoveries like ray guns or jet packs, what I really got were a series of new workstations that, for the most part, didn't seem immediately useful.

Some looked like different versions of what I already had: a square, barrel-looking version of a storage chest, a stone version of an anvil, and a superpowered furnace, which I got by placing an original furnace on a crafting table and surrounding it with iron ingots and smooth, double-cooked stone on the bottom.

Others looked like slight upgrades to what I'd already built, like a workbench that combined wool and dye into various banner things and a stone table with a circular saw that could shape stone into fancier stone.

"Nice, nice," I ho-hummed, reciting a line from a movie I'd watched once, "not *thrilling*, but nice."

I kept going, throwing everything I had on the crafting table, and came up with two more workbenches that I couldn't do anything with. The first seemed like another storage bin, but without a lid, and without the ability to store anything, while the second one looked like a crafting table but with bows, arrows, and targets instead of the usual tools.

Okay, time out. If you've been living in this world for a while and already know how to use all these specialized appliances, good for you, but cut me some slack, okay? It's not like I had a library to walk me through everything. It was trial and error, or, by this point, it felt like a trial *of* errors.

I was ready to call it quits and admit to Summer that all my efforts had landed me somewhere between "whatever" and "c'mon, man!" when my last blend of wood and paper got me what could only be a map table.

Not only did it expand an existing map with only one more sheet of paper, I could now, finally, make a copy! This was huge, especially for other castaways like you! Chances are, if you're reading this book, it's because you found it by following the copied maps we've been leaving along the way.

"Not bad," I hummed, "not a bad night's work."

"Well, you've been busy."

I spun to see Summer holding up a cubed fist, gesturing to the room full of new items. "And you'll have to tell me about all these wonderful new concoctions . . . later."

She walked over to one of the windows and flipped down the trapdoor. "But for now, let's yomp up those hills."

I didn't realize it was morning already. I'd been too distracted to hear the dawn-burning zombies (this world's version of roosters). "Yeah, totally," I said, slipping the map copy into that barrel box. "Let's roll."

I was a little sleepy, I admit, but the morning's chill woke me right up.

We left our cozy little cabin and started up the rugged slope. It was slow going, and not just because of the terrain. Forests at dawn are always dangerous. Too much shade, too many hiding mobs. We climbed slowly, cautiously, and with weapons at the ready. We didn't know it yet, but there was a whole new threat out there, and it had nothing to do with mobs.

Just before reaching the summit, I smelled something odd but familiar. Odd because it had no business floating through this icy, dry wind, and familiar because I'd first smelled it on the support beams in Summer's kitchen. It was pungent, leather.

"That wood . . ." I started to say, and held my nose to the air.

"I smell it, too," Summer confirmed, "just a few more steps."

As my eyes poked above the summit, my square jaw fell practically to my knees. Massive trees, four blocks thick, towered above a canopy of shorter siblings. Vines—yes, they had to be vines—grew up their skyscraper trunks or else fell in webbed curtains from brilliant green foliage.

"Yes," Summer answered my unspoken question, "that's the jungle."

I couldn't wait to explore it, to finally leave this teeth-chattering, nose-stinging, permafrosty shiver-fest of a climate way behind me.

"Let's go!" I called and took off down the slope. I thought I was being careful. I made a point of looking for mobs. I even mentally patted myself on the back for choosing an open path of clear, bright, slightly more powdery snow.

One step. That's all it took.

I fell. Not through the snow, but into it!

I was engulfed, chilled, choking. I looked back up for Summer, but couldn't see anything beyond white . . . darkening, closing in! My vision was tunneling! What was happening to me? I couldn't be . . . no . . . this world's cold is just a discomfort. It can't be . . .

Panic. Drowning my thoughts as the frozen water drowned my body.

I thrashed, punched, yelled for Summer. I fought to breathe, to move. I kicked, trying to jump, climb, swim back to the surface. The shivering, up my spine, across my chest, shook me like an invisible hand. I could feel the cold penetrating my lungs, gripping my heart, then . . . suddenly, it was gone. I was . . . warm? How? Was this special snow? Did you just have to push through the initial chill to get to this nice, warming calm? Because I did feel calm now, and slightly drowsy. I didn't want to fight anymore, didn't want to do anything but sleep. It was a wonderful feeling, like being wrapped in a soothing, safe, pale blanket.

Just a quick nap. Just a few minutes to wrap myself up in this wonderful peace. That's what I was thinking—but I wasn't thinking, not really. I couldn't. My mind was numb, shutting down, incapable of warning me that I was freezing to death.

CHAPTER 2

"Guy!"

Summer's voice. Distant. Muffled.

"Guy, where are you?!"

She was above me, was growing louder along with a constant, quick crunch.

"GUY!"

A flash of sunlight—blinding, shocking. I blinked hard, slurred, "Suuuu . . ."

"Guy!" Her face in mine. Warm breath, eyes meeting. "Guy, wake up! Snap out of it! Wake up!"

"I . . ."

Frozen, my lips, tongue, brain.

Summer closed her eyes, sighed. "I'm dreadfully sorry about this." A punch, hard, right in the nose.

Sharp, fast pain.

"Hey!" I was back, present, and shivering wildly.

"Follow me!" she shouted and tunneled furiously into the white wall behind her. "Hurry!"

I tried, staggering a half step behind her. But my legs were still lead-like, and my vision was barely an ice-encrusted circle.

"Th-th-the . . . s-s-snow . . ." I chattered.

"Fight it, Guy!" she shouted between shovel strokes. "You've got to fight it!"

"Th . . ." Whatever I tried to say, she cut off with, "Don't talk! Just follow me!"

I tried. I fought. But if you can imagine one of those cartoons where someone is trying to pilot a giant robot, then that was my spirit kicking and cursing the robot's sluggish controls—and all the warning lights were flashing red. Vision tunneled, life force sapping. How many seconds before the cold would finally win?

Move! Follow! Fight!

Light! A square of open air.

Summer was through, and a second later, so was I! Sunlight above, the jungle below.

CRACK! Summer's fist on my back, knocking me down the hill.

"Keep going!" Her voice behind me, her body shoving me forward.

I stumbled, hobbled, reached the bottom of the hill, and then was suddenly, gloriously warm!

If you're new to this world, this is going to sound crazy, but I'm not lying when I tell you that one second I was so cold that I felt like my legs were going to snap off, and the next, I was bathed in hot, humid air.

"Whouuuu . . ." I wheezed, long and deep, then flapped like a landed fish as the cold pulsed out of me.

"Well, that was rather unexpected," breathed Summer, "and thank heavens it was at least close to this steam bath of a biome."

"N-no kidding," I chattered, still in shock over the temperature shift. I reminded myself that just because the rules don't make sense to me doesn't mean they don't make sense.

"I suppose we'll really have to be on our guard," she continued, scanning the lush vegetation around us, "now that the new change seems to have turned the land against us."

"But you've been here, right?" I asked. "You've explored this jungle."

"Not quite . . ." Summer hemmed. "Not *all* of it per se, more like poking around the edges for a bit."

"Define 'edges'?"

"About here?" Summer was standing at the base of a tree that sprouted the same cocoa pods I'd seen in her kitchen. "Long enough to nick some of these before popping back to the mountain."

"Right," I said with a nod, gripping the crossbow tighter. "So you're saying we've got nothing but uncharted lands in front of us."

"I'm saying"—Summer turned to face the jungle—"that who dares, wins."

This was her people's version of my own personal lesson—that with great risk comes great reward—and as we plunged into the green maze, I tried not to obsess over what those risks might be.

What lurked in the jungles? Snakes? Poisonous plants? And what about disease? Weren't nasty plagues always crawling out of the sultry, overgrown corners of my world? They lived in water, in bats, and especially in insects like mosquitos. This world had always been bug-free, but maybe that changed along with the introduction of death-snow.

Not that I wouldn't have minded just the slightest tingle of that snow now, because, after only a few minutes of this march, I was already suffering from another extreme temperature swing. The heat. The humidity. It reminded me of the time beneath my island, when I first discovered the waterfall/lava cave. That experience had been uncomfortable enough, but now, the slimy, salty, eye-stinging sweat fest was made infinitely worse by the trek. The ground was covered in bushes, or, to be more specific, tiny, one-log trees that made sure no two squares were on the same level. Up and down, pant and sweat.

"Wouldn't that just be my luck?" I grumbled. "Tortured by overheating just in time to catch a disease that makes me doo-doo myself to death."

"What was that?" called Summer over her shoulder.

"Oh, nothing," I mumbled self-consciously, "just enjoying the scenery."

"It is rather spectacular," said Summer with the first hint of enthusiasm she'd shown since leaving her mountain. "Well worth the steam bath, don't you think?" I didn't, and I couldn't, for the life of me, understand how Summer could be so chipper. There was that toughness again, that can-do spirit that laughed in the face of discomfort. *Weirdo.*

"I reckon we'll keep this up till about midday," she chirped cheerily, "then climb one of those massive trees for a spot of lunch, some cool breeze, and a quick look-see."

"We can climb these?" I glanced up at the nearest cloud-teasing pillars. "Wouldn't it take forever to make a ladder?"

"No need," said Summer. "You can climb the vines."

That was a relief, as was the idea of a cool breeze. But thinking about it seemed to make my present ordeal even worse.

"I never thought I'd miss the dry heat of the Nether," I said, stopping to strip off my armor.

"I wouldn't do that," Summer warned. "A little more comfort isn't worth a lot less safety."

"But how can I be safe," I argued, "if I'm too distracted by feeling like butter in an oven?" I gestured to the uneven terrain and said, "And it doesn't exactly help, having to do step aerobics over this greenery."

"Then let's go through it." Summer paused, got out two iron ingots, then crafted them together into shears. "I came up with these long before I ever discovered any sheep," she explained, turning to the nearest cube of leaves, "and for the longest time . . ."

Snip.

". . . I thought they were hedge clippers."

"Nice!" I fell in behind her as she sheared our way forward. Slow and steady, with leaf blocks popping into our packs. Sometimes a tunnel, sometimes a trench. Not that I wasn't still swimming in my own sweat, but at least I wasn't drowning in it anymore, which gave me a little extra headspace to appreciate this fascinating biome.

I noticed more cocoa pods and patches of watermelon. And there were apple oaks mixed in among the jungle trees.

"Nice to know we can live off the land," I said, "and not have to dip into our rations."

"I was just thinking the same thing," Summer agreed, but she stopped suddenly when both of us heard . . .

"WEEP."

It was a short, quick little sound, kind of like a bat, but not quite.

I looked down, expecting to see new, jungle versions of silverfish, while Summer looked up and said, "Birds!"

Birds!

Brilliant, multicolored parrots flitting around from tree to tree. There was a bright green one, and blue, and a whole rainbow version with a red head and yellow-blue striped wings.

"Beautiful," I said, feeling suddenly comforted by this form of airborne life. The lack of birds—other than chickens—had made this world feel just that much more alien. Back home, birds were everywhere, even in cities. I can still remember the soft coo of fluttering pigeons, how I used to enjoy tossing them breadcrumbs.

"Nice to have birds," I said to Summer, who, without missing a beat, added, "Especially for dinner."

"Oh, c'mon!" I scoffed, which brought out Summer's signature laugh.

"Just winding you up."

"Consider me wound," I sneered, and I was trying to think of a zinger of a comeback when something darted by to my left. It was fast, small, and behind the leaves.

I spun, crossbow cocked, and caught a flash of spotted yellow.

"Don't worry," said Summer, "it's just an ocelot."

"Right." I suddenly remembered reading about the small jungle cats, and how Summer had mentioned she'd seen them here. They were supposed to be harmless (at least to us) and, if I remembered it correctly . . .

"Can't we feed them?" I asked, not taking my eyes off where I'd last seen the ocelot. "Didn't the manuals say giving them fish turned them into housecats?"

"Why on earth would we want to do that?" she challenged.

"To have animal friends?" I said in my best "duh" tone. "You should try it sometime, you know. If it wasn't for Moo, I totally wouldn't have made it on the island." And quoting one of my most precious lessons, I said, "Friends keep you sane."

Summer starting walking again. "With you, that's debatable."

"Hardy-harr-harr," I scoffed. "You can joke about it, but I know what you really mean . . ."

"Of course you do." Summer kept going, forcing me to keep up.

"Yeah." I continued with a confidence that could only come from one of my brilliant insights, "You like to play it all tough, but I know you're just trying to protect your heart from being hurt. You don't want to worry about an animal friend in case something . . ."

Summer stopped, and for a second, I wondered if I'd hit a nerve.

"What's that?" she asked, beckoning me to come up beside her.

She'd sheared through the last few leaf blocks to the bank of a large, shallow pond, and as I looked where she was pointing, I saw what had ended my astute monologue.

Across the pond was a large grove of what initially looked like sugar cane. Only they were darker, and so much higher than the normal kind.

"You haven't seen this before?" I asked.

Summer shook her head.

We waded across the block-deep pond and cautiously approached the nearest stalks. Raising my axe, I half expected them to grab me or maybe shoot some kind of poison. After nearly being killed by snow, I was now ready for anything.

The first stalk crumbled with my chop, falling at my feet just like sugar cane. But they didn't turn to sweet white crystals in my hand, and when I held two of them together, they appeared as a ghostly image of a wooden stick.

Bamboo! It had to be. Ironically, on my island, that's what I initially thought sugar cane was. And now, here was the real deal.

"I think I know what this is," I said to Summer, who was looking at and pointing to something wandering among the stalks.

"And I think I know what that is."

A bear, and not just any kind. Black and white with a short, stubby tail and an instantly recognizable face.

"A panda bear!" I couldn't contain myself. "How awesome-tastically cool!"

"Steady there," Summer cautioned, "don't go rushing in for a quick cuddle. Who knows what this world's version is capable of?"

"We will soon," I said, striding happily toward it. I could see her point about the different rules of this world, as well as my own personal lesson about never assuming anything. And yes, given that I hadn't read anything about these animals in either manual meant that they'd probably just spawned, which meant I had no idea what I was dealing with.

But, c'mon, it's a panda bear! Don't tell me you wouldn't want to make friends!

"Hey, Pal," I said, holding up a bamboo stalk, "you're supposed to like these, right?"

The animal was large; maybe not as big as the polar variety, but still big enough to ruin my day.

"C'mon," I said, edging closer, "let's make this the first nice moment I've had today."

The bear turned its ringed eyes toward me, shuffled closer, and . . .

CRUNCH.

It took my offering, then sat—actually sat, a wonder for this world!—on its big flat butt to enjoy the meal.

Then, as if there wasn't enough cuteness, it finished the snack and rolled in the grass like an oversize puppy dog.

"Will ya look at that!" I crowed in expectation of Summer's praise.

I should have known better.

"I wonder how panda tastes."

"Summer!"

As she laughed, my annoyance ramped back up to excitement. "We gotta find another one," I said, looking around. "We gotta breed more and make, like, a whole family. Tell me that wouldn't be so . . ."

My words trailed off. Something had caught my eye. Just beyond the frolicking fuzzball was a color that didn't belong here. Gray against the rainbow green background. And as I squinted through the bamboo curtain, I could make out that these drab blocks were definitely arranged in a structure.

"Over there"—I nodded with my chin—"is that a house?"

"Looks more like a temple," said Summer, "and if it's the kind of temple in all those adventure films, then we'd best be on our guard."

Her words filled me with vague memories of a grizzled, whip-armed action hero. "You've seen those movies, too?"

"We're from different countries," Summer snorted, "not different planets."

"Feels that way, sometimes," I muttered under my breath.

Making our way through the bamboo, we got close enough to get the full picture of the mossy, vine-covered construction.

It was about as wide as my island home. The square ground floor supported an upper story topped by a pyramid roof with four short columns at the corners. It looked deserted, no movement or artificial light. And as we peeked inside the doorless entryway, all that greeted us was an empty room.

There was no furniture, no chests filled with goodies. Only two sets of narrow steps that led up to the next floor, and a broad, central staircase between them that disappeared downward into darkness.

Summer, as usual, led the way, motioning for me to take the upper right staircase while she took the left. We crept to the second story, saw that it was as empty as the first, then, ever so slowly, made our way down to the basement.

As the stairs ended, so did the natural light. Summer placed a torch on the floor, showing us a claustrophobic two-block-wide hallway that ran perpendicular to the steps. To the right was just more hall that looked like it turned to the right again. But on the left, we faced a dead end, with three levers attached to the nearest wall.

"Let's check to the right first," suggested Summer, "before we go mucking about with those."

We turned, headed for the corner, and placed another torch.

At first, all we could see was another hallway. No mobs, no obvious danger, and if this were any normal situation, we'd just plod forward without delay. But there was something about the levers, and maybe the images from our world's scary movies. You know what I'm talking about, right? That scene in every adventure movie, where the dumbest dude in the group says, "I think we're safe now" right before falling through a hole in the floor. We must have both seen scenes like that because our mental caution alarms were clanging.

"One more for safety," said Summer, and using her hyper-reach, she placed another torch farther down.

"There it is!" she hissed, as we stared at what seemed to be a faraway face. It was at the end of the hall, one square in size. Two round dots above a central, larger circle.

"That's a dispenser," I declared, "loaded with who knows what."

"I quite agree," said Summer with a nod and, glancing back over her shoulder, added, "and I'll wager those levers are the key to disarming it."

Which is what we tried to do, flipping the sticks in all kinds of combinations. I'm not sure what we were expecting, some light or sound that signaled safety? We didn't get it, and after a few frustrating minutes, Summer finally threw up her cubed fists. "This won't do." She huffed, stomping back down the tunnel. "Don't know why we even bothered in the first place . . ." Positioning herself to the left of the dispenser's firing line, she added, "If it shoots anything less than a ghast's fireball, we shouldn't have to worry about—"

"Stop!" I cried, freezing her in place. "Ahead, down, to your right!"

She hadn't seen it. She'd been looking straight ahead. But from where I was, a couple of steps behind, I noticed one of those iron loop things recessed into the wall. "That's the trigger!"

Summer's eyes followed my directions. "Well spotted." From the loop, I could see her gaze trace across the stone floor. "And there's the rest of it."

Squinting hard, I made out a couple lengths of spider silk.

"Tripwire." I sighed. "Good thing we dodged that."

Why did I have to say that out loud? Because just as the words left me, Summer punched up the first block of string—and an arrow shot from the dispenser to bury itself in her shoulder.

"Not . . . quite . . ." she winced.

"I'll do the next one," I volunteered, and punched up the second square. Nothing happened this time (which I felt a little guilty about).

"Lemme go first," I said. "If there's another booby trap, it's only fair I take the hit."

"Very gallant of you," Summer said, stepping behind me.

We inched forward, snail-pacing right up the dispenser. "Stand back." I pulled out my pickaxe, smashing the kill box out of the wall. Not only did it fly into my belt, but so did its load of eight arrows. "Sweet," I said, grateful to replenish my dwindling stock. "This is turning out to be as lucrative as a treasure chest."

"I wouldn't go that far," said Summer, looking to our right.

I turned my head and saw, right past another trip line of redstone, an actual treasure chest sitting under another dispenser.

"Hang back," I said, knocking up the redstone. This time it didn't trigger the trap, but, just like last time, the dispenser held a cache of arrows. "Just keeps gettin' better," I said as Summer opened the chest.

"After all that?" Summer motioned to a few gold and iron bars. "This is it?"

"Maybe not." I looked back down the hallway. "Maybe there's still something to do with those levers. If they aren't attached to the booby traps, then it's gotta be something else."

"Like tripping a giant boulder?" Summer's eyes circled the room. "Or closing the walls to squash us?"

"Or," I countered positively, "the real treasure, like, I don't know, a magic gold statuette or"—my mind flashed to another movie—"ever see the one where a dude and lady go on this jungle adventure and find a giant emerald?"

"I might have." Summer walked past me. "And I'll be more than happy to discuss it later"—she turned back for the stairs—"after we block up the door and windows."

"Wait," I said. "You're not—"

"It'll be dark soon," said Summer, nearly to the steps, "and we don't want to get caught out in the open."

"We're not staying here," I argued. "I can barely breathe." As if the choking heat of the jungle wasn't bad enough, it was truly suffocating in the temple.

"Oh, stop whingeing," chided Summer. "It's just for one night."

"Yeah, but why suffer that one night when we don't have to."

"You've got a better idea?"

"As a matter of fact"—I led her up the stairs, out of the temple, and over to the nearest tall tree—"I do." She stared up at the canopy as I continued talking. "Remember when you told me how we could climb these," I said, grabbing a vine. "Well . . ."

Yeah, it was kinda scary, shimmying up that crazy tall tree. But this was my idea, and I had to sell it to Summer. *Please don't fall, please don't fall.* I sweated, knowing that if I took a tumble, I'd either die or be so embarrassed that I'd wish I had. I'm proud to say that Summer was never the wiser, even when I reached the bottom of the canopy and called confidently down, "Ya waitin' for a formal invitation?" A few dozen fist chops got me up to the top of the trunk, where I shifted to punching out a staircase up into open air.

A breeze! Cool and dry. That was the advantage of this world's permanent east wind. The snowy hills behind us were blowing their frosty air our way. *This almost makes up for you trying to kill me,* I thought silently, then closed my eyes to soak in the natural air conditioning.

"Not your worst idea." That was Summer, right behind me. I

turned to see her filling in the staircase with some of the leaf blocks she'd sheared from our trench. "Just in case the odd zed head tries to climb up after me."

Always thinking practically. That's Summer for you. Even zombies or skeletons could never make it up here now, and spiders couldn't walk up and under the leaf top toward us. We were safe. We were comfortable. There was nothing to do now but enjoy the sunset and the spectacular view.

"The jungle's smaller than I thought," I said, sweeping my cubed fist across its edges. It was bizarre to see that what had taken us half a day to cross would have been barely a few minutes in open taiga. Or whatever that new terrain was up ahead. "Is that more snow?"

"Hard to tell." Summer peered just below the sinking sun. It was definitely lighter, and devoid of trees, but the color seemed a little bit darker than the snow behind us. "I suppose we'll know tomorrow," she said, plunking down a crafting table. "And I'd say it's time for that handy new mapping table you've discovered."

"Good idea." I combined four woodblocks with a couple sheets of paper. "We're about at the edge of this map now, so we should also start thinking about crafting a new one." *And copying this one*, I thought, *for any new travelers behind us.*

"Just a moment." Summer started sticking torches to all four corners of the treetop. "Don't want any baddies suddenly spawning on top of us."

"Can't be too safe," I concurred, getting out the ingredients for a new map.

Okay, compass first, so one pinch of redstone and four ingots of . . .

SMASH!

Something hit me, hard, in the shoulder.

I stumbled sideways and spun around, reaching for my sword.

Nothing! No spawned zombie, no climbing spider.

"What the . . ."

"Guywatchout!" Summer's panicked warning, too late.

Hit again, this time in the back of the neck. Fangs, sharp and cold, and a raspy hiss.

"Up there!" Summer ran next to me, pointing her bow skyward.

At first all I saw were stars, small, pale and slowly moving in the same direction . . . except for a handful heading toward us! I could discern a couple of tiny green pinpricks circling among the white dots.

FRP-FRP. The sound of flapping, leathery wings.

"That one!" Summer pointed her bow at an approaching face. It was dark and narrow, the eyes growing larger every second.

But the raspy "Hhhhhaaaahhhh!" was cut short by the WHIP of Summer's bow. The arrow struck as the eyes darted upward with a sharp, pained "Caaaah!"

In the dim torchlight we could see its whole body now: a bluish, bony, batlike creature that was now clawing for altitude.

"You got 'em!" I whooped, reaching for my crossbow.

"For all the good it did." Summer nocked another arrow. "See if you can spot the other ones."

Gulp. *Other ones?*

Crossbow up, I scanned the sky. There was the one Summer'd hit, circling for another dive. But the others . . .

There! A second pair of eyes, growing, descending.

Come and get me. I aimed with calm, cool concentration. So concentrated, though, that I completely forgot how close to the edge I was.

"Guy!"

Too late. A third knocked me forward.

Falling! Darkness!

Splash!

The pond! We were right above it; that one lifesaving layer of water.

"Hhhhaaahhh!"

The second, or maybe third, creature, diving on me again.

"Not this time!" I barked, lining up my shot.

Aim, breathe, easy on the trigger . . .

Flck!

The crossbow sprang. The creature hissed in pain. I watched it climb up and away, but froze when I saw another one diving right behind it!

No time to reload! Duck? Shield?

It was almost on me, flat eyes pinning me in place . . . and something behind it? A flash of diamond, a sword!

"Caaaah!" Smoke!

Summer! Leaping from the tree, slicing the bat-thing in mid-air! Turns out this jungle did have an action hero.

"You rock!" I gasped as my savior splashed down next to me.

"Too . . . many of them," she panted in reply. "To the temple!"

I almost put up a fight, arguing that we could easily handle the other airborne threats. But then my eyes, and sanity, came quickly back down to earth.

Summer wasn't just talking about those new threats above us, but all the regular, earthbound mobs. I could see them now, skeletons, zombies, and the glowing, blood-colored eyes of spiders.

"The temple!" I repeated, splashing right behind her as something jumped into my pack. It was a piece of soft, wet, brainlike substance from the bat, and while I barely acknowledged it at the time, I'd literally owe my life to it much later.

Flp-flp. Those wings again, flapping close. I didn't look behind me, just traded crossbow for sword.

"Hhhhaaaahhhh!"

I turned and swung, catching it right in the face.

"Aw yeah!" I crooned, but got a skeleton's arrow for the encore.

Now, in case you forgot, I didn't have any armor on. I'd taken it all off earlier in the day, and there'd been no time in this attack to put it back on. Bottom line, another couple arrows, or even zombie punches, would spell bye-bye for this guy!

"Don't stop for anything!" Summer must have sensed what I was thinking, that I was considering a pause to armor up. "It's right there!" She was right. I could see the faint torchlight flickering just behind the leaves.

But that last dash, up and over and around everything in our way. And all to the nightmare symphony of zombie groans, skeleton clacks, spider hisses, and now this new flapping rasp.

We were nearly there, just one more small tree trunk to dodge. But it wasn't a tree trunk.

Blinking . . . crackling.

Shield!

I raised the iron-and-wood barrier just as the creeper exploded.

Unhurt but dazed, ears ringing, I looked every which way for the light. Where was the temple?

"Keep going!" Summer, shoving me in the back, drove me forward.

Head and vision cleared to see the confines of mossy stone.

"Block it up!" Summer was already stuffing leaf cubes in the doorway. "The windows, all of it!" I didn't care that plugging the windows cut off the last gasp of fresh air. Nothing like fear of death to get your priorities straight.

I was frantically filling the last window frame and about to say, "I think we're safe now" when, wouldn't you know it, I fell through a hole in the floor.

Thankfully, it was only into another room and, thankfully, the only thing in that room was another treasure chest.

"Hey, Summer," I called, sticking a torch to the wall. "You gotta see this!"

"Hmm . . ." Summer's face appeared above me. "Hard to believe we missed it."

"Maybe we didn't," I proposed. "Messing with the levers might have opened it."

Summer nodded and hopped down next to me. "Hopefully they disarmed any booby traps around the chest."

I hadn't thought of that, and quickly slipped into my armor.

"Let's see what . . ." Summer opened the chest and said, "Here now, what's this?"

Looking over her shoulder, I saw that the chest held a worn stone shovel, a couple bars of iron, and, of all things, a large green gem.

"An emerald!" I cried. "Just like in the movie!"

Summer, unimpressed by the cinematic coincidence, examined the lustrous jewel with a more practical eye. "Must be rather useful, like diamonds, but even stronger."

"Let's find out!" I shouted, reaching for my crafting table.

"After a good night's rest." Summer took out her pickaxe and knocked out an exit to the staircase. "Which we'll need to face the jungle tomorrow."

"Yeah, totally." I nodded as she headed upstairs. "Just a few quick combos first."

This time I meant it. Because, unlike the other night, there were limited possibilities. If this emerald was a diamond substitute, then all I could make was a shovel, which turned out to be impossible. I tried thinking of other potential combinations, other materials to add, but I'd gone so many nights without sleep that my brain felt as tough as oven-baked bricks.

"Tomorrow," I yawned, climbing the steps to place my bed next to Summer's. "I'll figure it all out tomorrow."

CHAPTER 3

Another nice thing about this world: you can always sleep. I mean, yeah, if there are monsters around, forget it. But unlike back home, where I would have been way too stuffy and uncomfortable for slumber, here the sandman knocked me right out.

The next morning, after telling Summer about the emerald crafting dud, she just shrugged with a resilient, "No worries, I'm sure the answer is out there somewhere."

We breakfasted, packed our gear, knocked out the leaves in the doorway, and said goodbye to that sweatbox of a temple. After a stop at the treetop to collect the rest of our gear (and to make a map copy), we headed for what appeared to be the end of the jungle. In the morning light it didn't look exactly like taiga—more tan than white—but I didn't care. I was just glad to be moving on.

Don't get me wrong, this biome was really pretty, and we'd

learned a lot, but I was more than ready to ditch the steamy, grossly humid wetness of it all. And the wetness was in full wet mode now because we'd woken up to rain. Heavy, warm drops ran under our armor, soaking our clothes, pooling in our boots. We could barely see in front of us while every squishy step felt like my feet were wrapped in slimy sponges.

Dry. The word, the feeling, kept floating through my brain. *The heat wouldn't be so bad if I could just be dry.*

What's that expression? Be careful what you wish for?

After a few minutes of shearing through leaves and vines, we were nearing what had looked, last night, like the edge of the tree line. We knew we were getting close because the air around us started to change. Moisture levels were dropping, and fast. But the temperature remained the same, which confirmed that whatever was up ahead wasn't taiga.

"Hm." That was Summer, stepping ahead of me to peer forward. "Well, this is something new."

Having broken through the last green barrier, we found ourselves staring at a desert.

Sand and sandstone stretched out into hills and valleys. And no rain. The shower literally halted right at the last verdant squares.

"Again with the constantly changing land." I gawked at the waterless wasteland. "Snow, then steam, and now this."

"It never stops surprising me," added Summer. "And no, in answer to your next question, I have not seen anything like it before." She set down her crafting table and started placing iron bars on it. "And while dying of thirst might not have been a danger before"—she handed me an empty iron pail—"your recent bout with frozen water should be a warning to bring the liquid kind."

"Good thinkin'," I said, following her back to the pond. Even if the heat wasn't life threatening, a cool drink might be as welcoming here as in the Nether. And filling buckets (unlike bottles) would give us the ability to make more water as we went.

But would it? I began to wonder as we filled our containers. That was before these recent world changes. Was a desert new? And if we poured water in a hole, would it just evaporate like in the Nether? I kept these questions to myself, not wanting to dampen the mood.

And for a little while, that mood was pretty good. What had been rain now morphed into an overcast sky. Gray above, and dry sand below. It felt nice, comfortable and pleasant . . . until the sun came out.

Wow!

I'd never really missed shade before. Sunlight had always been my friend. Warm, moderate. In this world, you could even look right at it without hurting your eyes. But now . . . even though it didn't look any different than before, the sheer intensity was like a blowtorch from the sky!

It felt like every exposed patch of skin was frying—my arms, my face! Ever done that trick with a magnifying glass, catching the sun's rays to set a piece of paper on fire? That's what the back of my neck felt like—that piece of charring paper!

Why, I mentally moaned, flashing back to that first time on the taiga, when all I'd wanted to craft was a wool sweater, *why won't this world let me craft a wide-brimmed hat!?*

"Detour," Summer declared, sidestepping the stone-rimmed pit of, get this, lava.

"Oh, good," I griped, "just what we need, more heat."

"At least it's a dry heat," Summer twittered back.

"Yeah, I guess." I wasn't sure about that, but I didn't want to be a wet blanket, either.

Ah, a wet blanket, shade and moisture. Wouldn't that be, literally, so cool.

I tried to focus on the land around us, to make mental notes of anything interesting. As if to argue with me, all the land gave back were a few brown, dead, scrubby-looking bushes, and short, green columns that had to be cactuses . . . cactuseses . . . cacti? You know.

And there were bunnies. Just like in the taiga. Little sandy-colored hoppers bouncing across the baking sand. And just like their dumb arctic cousins, I saw one spring off a sandstone ledge to land with an audibly painful "eep."

"Silly little blighters," laughed Summer, "don't have enough sense to get out of the sun."

Neither do we, I thought, noticing that the sun was at its highest.

The temperature had climbed considerably since the morning. It was now way hotter than the jungle, or the Nether. I think, barring the occasional close contact with lava, this was the hottest I'd ever been.

"Water break?" I suggested, stopping to reach for my bucket.

"Not yet." Summer trudged forward, not even stopping to look back at me. "We just got here."

"And I feel like eggs in a pan."

"Only a little longer." Summer marched on. "Just over that sand dune."

I didn't argue. I didn't want to seem like a wimp. I kept my mouth shut and trudged behind her up to the small hummock. But when we got there, she kept going.

"Summer," I called, "I thought we—"

"That next dune." She pointed to a distant, higher rise. "We'll probably see the end of the desert from up there. Every biome seems to be barely a day's walk. We might even see one of those . . . what do you call them? Oasis thingies, with palm trees and a pond to splash about in."

She was making sense. But I didn't think sense was driving her on. The sun was getting to us both, and it was bringing out our basic nature. While I wanted to stop, think, and figure out a new way of dealing with the problem, Summer just kept marching, kept attacking. Why else would she deny taking the very water break she had promised we'd take?

I tried to keep the peace—that was also my nature—but when we reached the small hill, saw that there was only more desert in front of us, and I watched her continue to march on, I barked, "That's it!" I got out my shovel. "We're not just stopping for water, we're stopping."

"Oh, Guy," Summer huffed, "don't be so—"

"Summer." I tried, really hard, to soften my tone, to not let the blazing temperature turn us against each other. "I can barely see or think or function in this oven, and I know you feel the same way. So let's just take a breath, have a drink, and figure out a better way to—"

"Rubbish," Summer said, striding down the dune. "It can't be that far. All we need to do is press on."

"But we're not here to just 'press on'!" I shot back. "We're here to explore. Remember? The whole point of leaving your mountain, just like when I left my island, was to try to find a way home." I swung my arms out to take in the vastness of the desert. "For all we know, that way is right here! There could be a portal, or . . . I don't know, a buried book on how to make a portal in a temple just like we found in the jungle." My arms came together, facing her, imploring. "I get that you want to win this battle with the desert, but it's not a battle. It's an opportunity we can't afford to ignore."

She stopped at that, not turning, but giving me enough encouragement to "press on."

"Remember in the Nether," I reminded her, "when you built that snow-insulated cabin, the 'Ice Cube'? You told me that you couldn't function on deep range missions without a comfortable forward base. Well . . ." Another sweep of my arms. "Our mission won't get any deeper than this, and if we don't have one of your forward bases, how successful can that mission be?"

A new tactic, quoting her back with an extra coat of praise. Would it work?

Summer didn't respond at first. Didn't speak, didn't move. That was the first time since coming to this moisture suck of a sand trap that I felt a bead of sweat run down my cheek.

"Right then"—she pivoted toward me—"let's get to it." I could see that something was in her hand, a stack of leaf cubes from the jungle, and as I scampered down the hill, she started building four columns in a ten-by-ten pattern. "You handle the pond," she said, tossing me her water pail, "and I'll get us some proper shade." I could see where she was going, and it was a perfect plan. If this desert didn't have a natural oasis, why not build one?

In a couple short minutes, she'd constructed an open-air shelter (what's the technical term? Pergola? Arugula?) while I dug a one-block-deep, five-by-five pit and filled it with two buckets of water, which multiplied to fill the hole.

"Fancy a dip?" Summer stripped off her armor and splashed in.

"Ohhhh," I groaned, waist-deep in cooling, liquid awesomosity. "This is the life."

"Thanks for standing up to me," Summer said with a tinge of embarrassment. "I know I can be a bit tornado-ish at times."

"Wouldn't have it any other way," I said, lifting a pail to wet my whistle. "We're a good team, you and me, and together, we can handle anything."

"Including our first night on this solar cooker." Summer rotated in a slow, intel-gathering circle. "How do you feel about a hut at the top of the hill? Easy to defend, high enough for the evening breeze, and if we just compress sand into sandstone, we'll have all the building materials we need."

"Oh, super," I chirped in a mock Summer-esque accent.

She laughed, punched the water in an attempt to splash me, then got back out and climbed to the top of the hill.

"Guy?" Her voice was serious now, which immediately got me right up there with her. "What's that?"

I squinted in the glare, following her southwest gaze. It was so small we'd missed it the first time. A short, rectangular structure, too far away to tell if it was artificial or natural.

"Let's check it out," I said and, re-armoring for anything that might be out there, we headed out across the seething sand. It was artificial, we deduced halfway there. Three-by-three, open in the middle, and as we got close enough to touch it, we found the center floor cube filled with water.

"Looks like a well," observed Summer, which prompted my witty response of, "Well . . . if you say so."

For some reason, she didn't laugh. "Doesn't seem to be anything more than what it is." She walked around it quickly, examining every cube. "No levers or buttons for a trapdoor." Getting out her shovel, she dug out a few sand blocks beneath it. "And no secret passages, either."

"Except water," I offered, taking a drink from my bucket then refilling from the middle cube. "Which is probably why somebody built it, you know, to let travelers like us tank up."

"But where were those travelers heading to?" Summer began another slow, rotating scan.

"We can search for that tomorrow," I said, noticing the afternoon sun. "We should get back and get to work on that sandstone hut."

Summer nodded, and we left for the oasis. The temperature was dropping—not a lot, but a welcome change from the noonday broil. I could feel my eye muscles relaxing, my skin going from "seared" to a mild "toasted."

Looking around, I couldn't help but take in the subtle beauty of the place. Yeah, I mean it. The simplicity of the sand, the scarce twigs and cacti. Don't ask me where I saw this, but I know in some movie, a dude in white robes once said he loved the desert because it was "clean." I couldn't help but agree now, appreciating this ocean of sand.

"You know," I said, looking around, "the desert's not such a ba . . ."

Something . . . to my left.

I stopped, faced due south.

"I see it, too," said Summer as we gazed at a far-off, distinctly odd-shaped hill. It was easy to miss, which is why we had on the way to the well. But from this angle, it looked like a pyramid made of sandstone, right at the edge of the mist. And just a few steps closer, that mist parted to reveal two stubby towers at either end. Another temple?

Now, if I'd been alone, it would have been the perfect time to mentally mark this location on the map, head back to base camp, build the hut, have a nice dinner and a full night's sleep before coming back here the next morning. But what do you think happened?

"Tallyho!" cried Summer, practically skipping toward it.

"And here we go."

Closing the distance, we saw that the twin rectangles held open doorways, and, climbing the stepped side, we saw another pair of doorways opening on the opposite side of the top of the structure.

"Careful now," said Summer, cautiously peering through one of the entrances. The top turned out to be a separate room, with nothing but holes in the ceiling and floor. I looked through the latter and saw a larger, darkened chamber below.

"Nothin' movin'," I reported and got an excited "C'mon then!" from my partner. Leading me through one of the towers, we planted torches along the descending staircase. Solid sand greeted us at the ground floor, which meant some digging until we came to doorways at our right and left. The right held more sand (probably the buried main entrance) but the left opened into the main chamber I'd seen from above.

As we entered slowly, Summer with raised bow and me trailing to plant torches, we found this room to be much larger, and supported by enough pillars to hide an army.

"Okay, mobs," I called, eyes darting from the darkness ahead to the potentially trip-wired floor, "I know you're in here, so let's just get it over with already, okay?"

I think I was expecting one of those dudes wrapped in bandages. And why not? The desert temple? Tell me you wouldn't expect the same. But we didn't find anything, not even any booby traps.

"Any levers?" Summer asked. "Trapdoors?"

"Squat," I answered, lighting the last pillar, "and no chests."

"There has to be something," she said impatiently. "Why else would this place exist?"

"There might be nothing"—I shrugged—"if the rules for deserts are different than the rules for jungles."

"I refuse to believe that," she grumbled, retracing our steps to look for hidden levers. "There has to be something somewhere. We're just not looking hard enough."

"What's there to look at?" I countered, taking in the sandstone room. Mostly sandstone, that is. The floor beneath us had some kind of pattern embedded in it. Orange blocks formed a checkerboard star in the middle of the room, with a single blue square in the middle of the star.

"What do you think that is?" I asked and got out my pickaxe to examine it. But as soon as the blue clay came free, we both gasped at the real find underneath.

A pit! Too deep and dark for us to see the bottom.

"Woah-ho," I breathed, "there's our secret room." Since the pit looked much wider than the single open square, I backed up to a spot just beyond the pattern and started picking. As predicted, the first block came up to reveal more sandstone. "This is the edge," I declared, as more sandstone flew up into my pack, "Shouldn't take too long to pick out a staircase down there."

"Or"—to my surprise, Summer held out her bucket—"we could try this." She poured it into the open block. "How about a waterfall lift?"

Lift? Did she mean elevator?

Off my obviously confused silence, she explained, "Remember that time you told me about your first house burning down? And how the only way to escape was flushing yourself out of the toilet? Same principle here."

And without waiting for my response, she stepped right in and disappeared beneath the blue.

"Summer, wait!" Holding my breath, I dove into the water—and into my fears of drowning, heights, and the general unknown.

I fell slowly, gently, as the dim light above me faded.

How long was the way down?

My mind flashed back to the time on my island when I'd waged a one-man war against the mobs of the mineshaft—

specifically when I'd detonated a multi-TNT bomb above the zombie spawner, and brought down not only the gravel roof but the entire ocean above it.

How long before I'd lose my nerve, bolt back up to the surface?

Courage. Calm. You can do this.

Light! Summer was using her hyper-reach to place torches on the chamber walls. Through the liquid curtain, I could make out the smooth sandstone sides around us, and . . . yes . . . the floor! Coming up soon. We'd have plenty of air to make it. Nothing to worry about.

Summer saw it, too, glancing down in between torch placements. Then, for some reason, she stopped with the torches and kept her eyes locked on the floor. Had she seen something? What? I couldn't tell from my position above her. Suddenly she was looking at me, trying to shout something through the water. Then she was swimming up, pushing me, forcing me out of the column. Our heads broke the water as I heard her yell, "Juuump!"

Falling, sideways, scraping the wall on my way down.

Striking the bottom and saved by the thin layer of expanding water.

Summer dropped in front of me, shield raised, waiting for . . . what?

I didn't ask, but raised my own shield as well. A tense second or two, and then I heard her exhale.

"I think we're okay," she said, lowering her personal barrier.

"What gives?" I asked, stepping next to her.

Summer turned to place a couple of torches on the wall behind us, then said, "Look there." She was pointing to the center of the floor, right where we would have landed. It took a moment, but then I saw it. A raised square, barely a minicube thick.

A pressure plate!

"Better shield yourself again," said Summer, holding up her pickaxe, "just in case this booby trap is booby-trapped."

"Oy," I exclaimed, which prompted an impatient "What?" from Summer.

"Oh, nothing," I answered, forgetting that, back home for her, it was "Oi," which was an attention getter and not a versatile expression of stress. "Just get it over with," I said, cowering behind my shield.

A single pick released the pressure plate, and released a dual sigh of relief. But that momentary relief dissolved as we picked out the floor beneath the now-floating trigger.

TNT! Nine whole blocks of it, arranged just like the megabomb I'd made to blow up that zombie spawning chamber. If we'd set it off . . . would the water have saved us? I don't know, and I hope I never find out.

And even though my brain knew that TNT needed a detonator to go off, my stomach couldn't settle as I watched her punch up the explosive cubes. "Not a bad haul," she purred through the bomb collecting, "in addition to all the other goodies." Her square eyes flicked to the four chests recessed into each wall. Goodies was an understatement. Besides the bones and zombie flesh (yuck), we found gold bars, gold nuggets, iron bars, iron nuggets, redstone, a couple of diamonds, and . . . cue the trumpets . . . another emerald!

"That's gotta be it!" I announced, hoisting the green gem

aloft. "All we needed was another one to unlock the crafting recipes."

"Well, let's get to it!" chimed Summer as we stepped back into the watervator.

As before, Summer was a little bit ahead of me, and as before, she saw the danger ahead first.

Poking my face above the surface, I watched her shooting at a couple of shambling meat bags.

Nightfall! The sun had set while we were below.

"Seems we've run into a new variety," she said, finishing them off with more flaming arrows. "Did you notice how one of them was dressed?"

"Sorry." I shook my head. "By the time I got a good look, the one you were talking about was smoked." I thought I had heard something, though, a slight difference in the moan?

"No matter," she chirped as the second puffed away to join the first. "Let's get to fortifying before any more show up."

Using the sand we'd cleared from the hallway, I blocked up the main chamber's doorway. I was about to seal up that hole in the ceiling with leaves when one of those little halfling-zombies dropped through it onto my head.

"Ghaaaa," it gurgled, with a well-placed sock to the stomach.

"Thanks," I oofed, slicing it away with my sword. "I'll finish you in a second." Turning to close the skylight, I took another hit in the behind. "Fine," I snapped with a sword-swiping turn, "you first." Another swing, another "ghaaaa!" and the room was clear.

"Looks like we've got ourselves a proper forward base," said

Summer. "Easily defended and, with a few modcons like a cold shower, we could stay here for quite a while."

"I am inclined to agree with you," I said, setting down a crafting table.

"You're not going to . . ." Summer began.

"Just a few combos," I promised.

"Of course." Summer gave a resigned sigh before setting down her bed. "Just don't blame me if you're all bleary-eyed for tomorrow's ranging."

"Night, Summer," I said dismissively and placed both emeralds on the table.

This is gonna be so awesome!

Super tools, new devices. This had to be the key.

And it was . . . to total frustration.

"Really, guys?" I whined to the two gems. "Really?" I'd tried all the tool and weapon recipes, along with a few random mixes. Zip-zilch-zuck. Is zuck a word? It is to me, as in, this night truly zucked. And it didn't help that it was still way too oven-y in here. I should have figured that sandstone would have absorbed the sunlight of the day, and was holding in its heat like a battery.

We need some windows, I thought, using the crafting table to make a couple of fenceposts. *One on either side for some cross-breeze should ventilate this place and also keep the shortzees out.*

Spruce bars in hand, I knocked away a block of west-facing wall. Woof, that air was chilly, and I mean really frigid. In a few minutes this temple would be as chilly as the noonday taiga.

"First too hot, then too cold," I said to the two emeralds, "and unless you can be used to craft a thermostat, I'm stuck with sandstone-stored warmth."

I pocketed the gems, got out the sandstone block, and was about to replace it, when I suddenly froze—and it had nothing to do with the air. Something was shining, far off in the darkened desert. Something that looked exactly like my magical pickaxe. It was only there for a second before it disappeared into the night.

I didn't think. I ran to the front entrance, tore away the sand cubes, then charged up the staircase to the roof of the pyramid. From this vantage point, I could see it again, glimmering like a zigzaggy star. Definitely an enchanted object, the first I'd seen outside the Nether. This was huge! This meant that magic items were everywhere now, and I could gather more! If only I could see what exactly it was or what kind of mob possessed it.

"What I wouldn't give for a pair of binoculars!" I told the desert wind.

"Ssssp," came the answer.

Ah, nuts.

The spider was halfway up. I swung, I hit. It tried another pounce. I finished it with another sword strike. "This is getting too easy." I laughed.

"Ssssp . . . Ghuuuh . . . clickety-clack." They were all out there—more spiders, skeletons, and, of course, zombies. But, as Summer had hinted before, most of these were different. Of the seven converging on my position, at least five of them were dressed in tan tatters that matched the desert. And was their skin brown instead of green? I didn't stick around to find out.

"Okay, I get it," I announced, "dinner is served and I'm the main course."

Instead of staying to fight, I jumped through the top skylight into the pyramid's upper chamber, sealed it and the two doorways behind me, knocked out the leaf block in the floor, and dropped into the main chamber.

"Summer, you're not gonna believe this!" I told my sleeping buddy. "The surface world's got magic stuff now!" All I got was a slow, almost zombie-esque "hghghghg" in response. Summer doesn't know she snores, by the way, so this is gonna be a heck of a surprise if she reads this.

Setting down my bed, I could only pray that the bounty didn't evaporate with the dawn.

CHAPTER 4

I sprang out of bed the next morning and had everything packed before Summer could finish. "What are you—"

"Enchanted item!" I squeaked, rummaging through my belt. "I saw it last night, out in the desert!" My hand closed on a Potion of Speed.

From belt to hand to mouth. GLP!

"C'mon!" I shouted, tearing the sand door down and rushing out without waiting for her. "Before it disappears!"

Racing across the tan expanse. Squinting, hoping.

Just a few more seconds. Just a little bit closer.

I couldn't see any mobs ahead, or even the flames of them burning in the sun.

But there was something . . . a bunch of somethings.

Structures? Short and small, rising above the uneven sand?

Another minute and I was there. Standing in the middle

of . . . houses. About half a dozen of them: flat-roofed, single-storied, and made of sandstone, or a sandstone and red clay combination. The doors were open, and through them I could see beds in three of the buildings. Those were definitely houses.

The fourth had what could be an automatic door, if one of the three buttons above it worked. I should have been thinking about booby traps. For all I knew, one of those buttons could set off a temple-like TNT bomb. That thought came to me only after I pressed the middle button and walked inside. I didn't find anything but another bed, and a chest holding nothing more than a loaf of bread.

Breakfast. And still fresh after who knows how long.

I walked outside, and over to a larger, twelve-by-twelve building with short towers at its corners. This one was doorless, and I might have gone in to investigate, but the building behind it had a tighter grip on my curiosity. Maybe it was the second story that got me. Or the fact that it had five doors, three below and two above, which made it look important.

That turned out to be the only interesting feature. The ground floor contained a water-filled cauldron while the upper floor was completely bare. Stepping out onto the balcony, I could see a couple of gardens, ripe wheat and carrots growing in raised dirt rows separated by water trenches and surrounded by sandstone blocks. I noticed a few piles of what looked like harvested wheat blocks, all compacted together, next to the gardens, along with the same open wood bins I'd accidentally crafted back in the forest cabin. What was the connection with growing crops?

And what was this open-air building next to it? With its

shaded roof, sandstone fence, grass floor, and central, raised enclosure that held two cubes of water . . . Was this some kind of animal pen?

I walked over to another strange hut sitting in the middle of all the others. Sandstone blocks held water that encased a column. Another well? A broken fountain? And what was that contraption fixed to the north side? Gray material holding a piece of bell-shaped yellow metal. Was it actually a bell? I couldn't resist ringing it.

Ding!

Nothing happened. No one answered back.

I shouldn't have been surprised. All the buildings looked like they'd been long abandoned. Each had chunks taken out of them, and had cobwebs growing thicker than a mineshaft in their corners. The whole scene made me sad, because it wasn't a mineshaft or a temple where people worked or worshipped before heading home. This *was* home. This was a village. People had lived here, raised families, laughed and cried, and come together in a community here. And now they were all gone.

When? To where? And why?

Did they just move on? Find somewhere nicer? I think I'd heard stories about places like this from where I'm from, ancient desert towns that didn't used to be desert but were abandoned by their inhabitants when the climate changed. Was that the case here, as well as the temples and mineshafts? Did the folks who built them just leave? Or did they die out? I hoped not. That would be too depressing.

I suddenly missed Summer, thought about running back for her.

I should have waited, I thought, feeling painfully alone. *I shouldn't have just run off to try to find that . . .*

"Ooogh!" A nearby sound, a gurgle. Zombie!

The enchanted item!

I'd totally forgotten, distracted by this new discovery. I ran outside, looking every which way.

"Ooogh!" Past the village! A shambling corpse. It was that new type, the desert variety with tan clothes, brown skin, and a lower, huskier groan.

I didn't stop for a closer look, or consider that maybe this sand-born subspecies might have some new trick up its rotting sleeve. I should have, though. It might have saved me from what happened next.

I sprinted toward the sound and soon saw why I hadn't seen it earlier. Beyond the village was a river, snaking through a shallow canyon. I rushed down, sword in hand, eyes flicking side to side.

I struck, hard enough to send it tumbling into the river.

"Ha," I sneered, ready for it to climb back up. "No problem."

"Oooogh." Behind me, another husky groan.

Teeth, dry and cracked, crunched into the back of my neck.

Pain shot through me, and then . . . hunger!

I hadn't felt anything like it for months, not since my first desperate days on the island, when I'd been forced to live on zombie flesh. But the poison the mob's bite carried made me ravenous! Back then I'd had pails of Moo's milk to counteract it. But now . . . I had nothing to help, just the need to eat, to devour, to fill the growing hole.

"Oooogh!" I turned to face reaching, rotted fists. My sword

waled on the leathery flesh like a kitchen knife through beef jerky.

I didn't celebrate its smoking death. I had to eat!

Cookies from my pack! Scarfing, gorging.

"Grgrgrgl!"

That wasn't my stomach. It was coming from the river.

I looked up to see where I'd splashed the desert zombie, but it wasn't there anymore. Something had replaced it: a bloated, greenish-blue, waterlogged version was floating slowly toward the bank.

"What happened to you?" I asked as an arrow flew over my head to strike it between the eyes.

"I was going to ask the same thing."

"Summer!"

"For heaven's sake, Guy . . ."

"I know!" I held up my arms in surrender. "I got a little hypnotized by magic stuff."

"Did you at least nab it?"

"Nah." Eyes down, head shaking. "Musta been on a mob that burned before I got here. But"—I swung my arms up toward the village—"I did find this."

"And quite a find." Summer turned back toward the houses. "Have you had time to explore it all?"

"Not yet," I confessed, "but we'll have all the time we need, because tell me this wouldn't make the ultimate forward base."

"Hmmm . . ." Summer considered the village, her head turning to assess each building. "We could clean up the cobwebs, patch up all the holes."

"Maybe even put a sandstone wall around the whole thing,"
I suggested. "You know, so we can walk around safely at night."

"And place torches about," added Summer, "so no mobs
spawn within the wall."

"Exactly!" This idea was sounding better and better. "Just like
I did on my island!"

"We really could have quite a decent time here," Summer
ruminated, as much to herself as me, "living off these gardens,
ranging out daily in all directions."

"And at the end of the day"—I gestured to the river—"we've
got a cool swim waiting for us."

"Yes . . ." Summer turned back to the river, then added softly,
"Or . . ."

I knew what she was thinking, because I was thinking the
same thing. "We could take the morning to explore, come back,
and spend the afternoon fixing everything up."

"Quite." Summer nodded, bounding down the bank. A couple minutes later, we boarded a pair of boats and rowed slowly
up the blue highway.

"So much nicer than walking," I said. "Faster, smoother."

"I think," Summer began, "that back home, in my country,
we've got a lot of little rivers like this, or canals, and I think . . .
people used to use them quite a bit for everything: trading, traveling, living."

"That'd be pretty sweet," I said, imagining life on a house-
boat. "Can you remember anything else about where you're
from?"

"Not really." Her voice quivered slightly, then strengthened
with, "Better to focus on the here and now."

I didn't answer, letting us lapse into silence. We'd nearly ended our friendship because Summer had been so insecure about home. If you haven't read the last book, it's a pretty intense part. She was, is, so scared to find out who she is and what her life is like in that other round, soft world. I get it. We all have different fears. And while she could jump off a cliff or charge happily into a whole horde of zombie pigmen, the idea of discovering her other self was more terrifying than all of those dangers combined.

Me, I'll stick with being scared of the here and now. I'm not saying I wasn't nervous about what was waiting for me back home. Specifically, something had begun to bother me, which I'll tell you about later on. But that something, as well as all other future worries, wouldn't be worth spilled water in the Nether if we didn't focus on what was in front of us.

And, for the moment, what was in front of us was more of the same. Bare dunes, cacti, the occasional dead twig. And the river wasn't much to write home about, either. It was similar to the one outside Summer's mountain, minus the ice. I saw clumps of wavy green grass on the bottom, and every so often, a school of dark red salmon. The water itself was a welcome asset, and not just for the transportation. Eventually, as the sun got higher and hotter, we'd be able to stop for both a drink and a swim. We could even build another canopy, like with our first oasis. Did Summer have any leaf blocks left?

It was around noon, just about the time I would have suggested stopping, when Summer abruptly called out, "Tree!"

Ahead of us, at a bend in the river, was definitely a tree, but the closer we got, the stranger it looked. The trunk was crooked, something neither of us had ever seen. And the color was off; gray, like stone, with muted green leaves that were almost brownish when compared to birches, spruces, oaks, and especially the brilliant jungle variety.

Rowing closer, we noticed that the air was getting cooler. Not crazy cold, like a taiga wind, but it was definitely dropping from that scalding hair-dryer-in-your-face blast to a milder, almost pleasant breeze. By the time we beached our boats and climbed up the bank to the tree, something truly bizarre had happened to the climate. It was nice! Not too hot, or cold, or wet, or dry. Maybe a smidge warmer than my island, but, like the little blond girl in that home invasion story, I uttered a relaxed "just right."

The smells were back, too. Did I mention how sterile the desert was? Sorry, should have done that. Like the taiga, it had made my nose unemployed. Now it was working again, taking in the scent of trees, grass, and soil.

And poking our heads out of the canyon, we saw how the land matched the air. A rolling, brownish green grassland was dotted with these crooked trees that were sparking memories in both of us. It was something about their shape, something unique and distinctive.

"I've seen this place," I said, struggling with the foggy image, "someplace on our world."

"So have I," said Summer, "I'm sure of it. I don't live there, I'm sure of that, too. But I have been to a place like it. I think it's called a 'savanna,' except the animals don't match." She was referring to the grazing cows and sheep.

"Yeah," I agreed. "I feel like there should be more exotic types, like giraffes and zebras."

"Zeh-bras," Summer tried to correct.

Okay, this part is just between us, okay? I don't want Summer to read it. I'd been wondering how we could come from different parts of our world but still share a similar language. And I think I've got it figured out. My people must have invented that language, whatever it's called, and Summer's people are still trying to catch up. That's why she uses those weird words and pronunciations. Makes sense, right? But, like I said, I don't want Summer reading this because I know the truth would hurt. How good a friend am I?

"We might find some zee-bras or zeh-bras," I said, motioning inland, "if we keep on going." It was midday, right when we should have turned back. But the lure of the unknown, the excitement of finding this new biome (and maybe a "zeh-bra" or two) was enough to drive us on.

Keeping the river in sight, we set out across the savanna. I probably should have been more on my guard. If exotic new animals did live here, there might also be dangerous ones like lions and tigers. Do tigers live in the savanna, or am I thinking about someplace else?

Whatever. I should have been on the lookout for trouble, but it was just so nice. The cool breeze, the smell of the earth, the beautiful squiggly trees whose diagonal growth allowed us to see deep orange wood beneath gray bark.

They would make a beautiful house, I fantasized as we came to a large field surrounded by tall hills, *and this place would make a much better base.* Temperate climate, plenty of room to grow crops, and we'd still have the river as an exploration expressway.

The idea was so clear in my head that I could actually picture what a house would look like. Right there, up ahead in that wide open pasture ringed by high hills, with a few sheep and cows peacefully grazing, I imagined . . .

No . . . that wasn't my imagination!

"Hey, Summer," I blurted, quickening my pace. There they were, real houses! Different from the ones in the desert, though. These had slanted orange wood roofs while the walls were either made entirely of gray logs, or mixed with some kind of mustard-colored blocks. Stone or clay? I could see one of the houses up on stilts above a small pond.

And there was a bigger pond right in the middle of town. Set in the center of the water was a fountain; or rather, a well, two of them. Raised cubes of water next to each other, connected by a joint awning with a hanging bell in the middle. I didn't need binoculars to see that, unlike the desert village, all these dwellings looked intact. No holes. No spider webs.

I should have taken that as a warning sign, along with the garden crops that were clearly not ready for harvest. If I hadn't been so excited, I might have put these pieces together. But no. Why think clearly when you can act impulsively?

"C'mon!" I said, about to take off at a run. "This base is move-in ready!"

"Stop!" Summer jumped in front of me. "Take cover!"

Feet and heart stopping, I turned and followed her behind a shallow rise. "What did you see?"

She peeked over the top. "Locals."

"Whuuu?!" I poked my head up beside her.

Little, far-off figures were milling around the buildings. Not zombies, not Nether piglins . . . "Humans!" I gasped.

"Not sure about that," said Summer. "Humanoid, more likely, in that they seem to have all the outside human parts: legs, arms, head—"

"Yeah, but just look at them. They look like us."

"But are we human anymore?"

"You know what I mean!" I was practically vibrating with excitement. This changed everything! This world had people! No more stumbling around in the dark. No more trying to piece together answers from abandoned ruins and long-lost books. Finally, there were people we could talk to. People who could just tell us what we needed to know, and they were right here!

"Stay down!" Summer must have guessed my next action. "We don't know if they're friendly."

"Oh com—"

"Guy," Summer cut me off, "what's that lesson you keep quoting?"

I sighed. "Just because someone looks like you doesn't automatically make them a friend."

I'd learned that one the hard way, back on my island, when the first "human" I'd met turned out to be a poison-throwing witch. This could be a whole village of them, and even if it wasn't, who's to say they wouldn't just attack us on sight?

"They don't look like witches," I said, taking in their brighter clothes. "I don't see any purple robes or pointed hats."

"They might be a different variety," she postulated. "This is a whole new biome, after all, and these might be a surface-dwelling, day-walking, savanna sort."

I couldn't counter that. I had no evidence either way.

"What do you think we should do?"

Summer didn't answer immediately. "Watch them for a bit," she suggested. "Didn't you do that on your island? Build an 'observation bubble' to study the mobs from a distance?"

She was making sense, even if it was cautious, buzz-killing sense. We didn't know anything about these people; how many there were, if they were armed, and especially, if they were friendly or foe-y.

"I guess we could hollow out this ridge," I said with a resigned exhale, "and use some river sand for windows."

"If only this world let us craft binocs," Summer muttered.

"I was thinking the same thing," I said, reaching for the shovel in my pack.

"Down!" Summer hissed.

We ducked.

"What?" I whispered, then, realizing that my whisper's high pitch was actually louder, I switched to a soft, low-toned, "What do you see?"

Summer got out her bow. "One of them's coming this way."

The villager wore a red shirt, whitish pants with what looked like a green skirt or apron, and a wide-brimmed hat—the kind of wide-brimmed straw hat I would have killed for in the desert. But the face . . . the high forehead and big, dark nose that dropped over where the mouth should be. That was a witch's face.

"Get down," Summer whispered sharply.

"She . . . he . . . they don't see me," I countered, watching them roam aimlessly among the grass. "And I don't see any weapons."

"You don't see witches carry potions," Summer pointed out, "until it's too late."

"Touché," I granted, "but they're all alone."

"They have a whole bleeding village behind them."

"Then we just take off." I pointed to the other villagers, who were spreading out in different directions. "We can beat it back to the boats and be outta here before the rest of them can catch up."

Summer gave me a sidelong, doubt-filled glance, then, nocking an arrow to her bow, said skeptically, "It's a big risk."

"But with a big reward," I countered.

"Don't you have a lesson about curiosity?"

"Yeah, but it's about careful curiosity," I volleyed back, "and I think we've just discovered a new lesson." Another glance at the approaching villager. I couldn't see a weapon, or even an aggressive stride. Instead of heading right for us in a charge, they were just lazily zigzagging in our general direction. "When making first contact, always come in peace."

"But don't let your guard down," added Summer.

"Fair enough." I nodded, mentally tacking the addendum to the end of my new lesson. "Just try to stay out of sight. If they see a weapon in your hand, it might cause the exact fight we're trying to avoid."

"Be careful"—Summer drew her bow—"and good luck." As

she raised just her head, I could see that the villager couldn't see her bow. Ever the tactician, she was making sure that they knew I wasn't alone while at the same time not advertising her weapon.

"Here goes nuthin'," I said, and with a big, brave breath, I got up in full sight of the villager. "Hey there!"

They didn't see me, too busy looking down at the ground.

"Hello, sir/ma'am/buddy!" I called louder, taking a few nervous steps forward. "I . . . uh . . . come in peace?"

They looked up. Our eyes met.

"Uh, me friend? Me . . . my name is Guy . . ." I noticed their arms were folded tight, like a witch — or, I reminded myself, just a normal person in my world who isn't totally comfortable.

"I don't mean any harm," I said over the drum solo of my heart. "I just wanna talk. Okay?"

They took a step toward me. We were now within hyper reach. I braced for an attack, a splash of potion. "Do you understand?" My voice was quivering. "Can you speak?"

"Hrrh. Hrrh."

"Come again?" I asked, hoping I'd misheard.

"Hrrh." Their voice was high, nasally.

"Are you . . . actually speaking?" I asked delicately. "Or, are you, like, about to sneeze?"

"Hrrh."

And I thought Summer talked funny.

"Hrrh," I responded, hoping it was a greeting and not a challenge.

"Hrrh," nose-breathed the villager again.

Were we getting somewhere?

"Hrrh" from me.

70

And another "Hrrh" in reply.

"Ohhh . . . kay . . ." I said slowly. "While this has been a stimulating conversation, I think we're gonna need some other way to communicate."

How did people do that in my world? How did individuals who didn't understand each other connect? Hand gestures? Hadn't this exact situation been why folks back home had invented them in the first place? Hadn't the most common physical greeting from my people, the handshake, been a way of showing the other person that you weren't carrying a weapon? *If only*, I thought, frustrated that I couldn't unclench my fists. Those were weapons, too! Balled-up hands were humanity's first clubs! And if I pointed just one of them in the villager's direction, wouldn't that be a nonverbal threat? *Of all the times I needed to open my hands!*

But wait, I could! My left hand opened whenever I wanted to craft something. If I tried that, with nothing to craft . . .

"Okay now," I said, stepping perilously close. "I'm just gonna open my left hand, okay? That cool?"

"Hrrh."

"I'll take that as a yes."

I stepped closer, raising my left arm. The fingers opened and . . .

"Guy!" Summer, behind me, her voice high and loud, her bow creaking to launch an arrow. "Be careful!"

CHAPTER 5

"No!" Instinctively, I shielded the villager with my back. "Don't shoot!"

Summer had assumed that the villager's approach meant hostility. But as I opened my left hand, the familiar four-square crafting grid was replaced by two horizontal panels. The left side of the first panel showed a carrot, and right below it, a bushel of wheat. Both had the number 20 below them, and to their right, light gray arrows pointed to a couple of emeralds.

"Do you want to"—I rummaged for some carrots in my pack—"trade?"

As soon as the orange roots came out, the villager produced an emerald from their clasped hands.

"You do!"

I gave twenty carrots and got a sparkly green gem in return.

"Summer!" I spun to show her the prize. "They're friendly! They want to trade."

"Blimey," she breathed, running down next to me. "This changes things a bit."

A bit?! What is it with her and understatement?

"More carrots!" I cried, but before I could reach for another bundle, the villager had wandered away.

"Short attention span," commented Summer. "But let's see what some of the others might want."

She charged off, reaching the next villager before me. This one wore a red shirt, white overalls, and a short brown cap, and when Summer opened her hand to trade, I could see two emeralds offered in exchange for eighteen white or black wool cubes.

Summer swore one of her weird, insectoid swears, then huffed, "All I've got is three red blocks for an extra bed."

"And I got three yellow for the same purpose," I lamented. "But"—the figurative light bulb blinked on—"you've still got those shears!"

"The sheep!" Summer turned and ran past me, shouting as she went, "You're a ruddy genius, Guy!"

"I know," I said, sauntering a few steps behind.

It didn't go exactly as planned. Too much use clearing a path in the jungle had worn the shears down, and they snapped after a couple snips. But between crafting a new one and using a few extra wool cubes from our store of spider silk, we soon had enough to sell.

"Here you go," she said, bouncing over to the wool-wanting villager.

TLING!

Another green gem glimmered in Summer's hand.

"Funny how they both want to pay us in emeralds," I noted, "especially when they don't seem to be very useful."

"Maybe that's the point." Summer stared intently at the jewel. "Maybe this is a bob."

"Who's Bob?" I asked.

"No, not a person." Summer shook her head. "I mean quid." And off my silence. "Pounds?"

"What, like a measurement of weight?"

"Oh, good lord." Summer gave an exasperated sigh. "Money!"

"Oh." I nodded, finally understanding. "Dollars."

Were emeralds this world's currency? Maybe she was on to something. "Let's see what you got?" I walked up to a villager in a drab olive shirt.

"Hrrh." This one just looked at me blankly, arms refusing to unfold.

"What?" I asked. "I say something wrong?"

"Hrrh."

"I'll handle this," said Summer, pushing in front of me. "I'm terribly sorry if my friend offended you, but we'd love to see your wares and maybe work out some sort of arrangement."

The villager just stood there. "Hrrh."

"Oh, come now"—Summer held up her emeralds—"there must be something you want."

"Hrrh."

"C'mon," I said, heading for a fourth villager, "that store's open."

Summer muttered something about another kind of hand gesture (which I do not understand and will not repeat) as we approached the villager in a brown brimmed hat. "Hey th—" I said, but couldn't finish before they took off. "Hey!"

"Not your fault," said Summer, pointing to the setting sun. "We'd better get indoors." All around us, villagers were heading for their homes. We could hear doors slamming as we made for the closest hut. It was occupied, as we saw movement through the slats of the savanna wood door. That was the case for the next one, and the one after that. All the houses had a villager tucked snugly in their bed. My mind pictured a flashing sign from our world: "No Vacancy."

"The raised one," Summer said decisively, taking off for the hut on stilts; then, before I could even reach it, ran back down the steps with a harsh, "Too cramped! Just three open squares!"

"That's enough for one bed," I said. "You take it."

"You really think I'd just leave you?!" She scoffed as the sun disappeared behind a western hill. "Time for a proper burrow!" And that's what we did, heading for the shallow hill outside of town. By the time we reached it, both our shovels, and the mobs, were out.

"You dig!" shouted Summer. "I'll fight!" An approaching hiss was cut short with the sound of her axe. Much as I wanted to, I didn't turn to help. I kept digging, first through dirt, then through stone. Switching to my enchanted pickaxe, I winced as an arrow struck my armored back.

"Sorry," called Summer, "won't happen again." And it didn't. The next TWANG of a skeleton's bow was quickly followed by the

THUNK of its arrow hitting her shield. I kept at my work, picking in near total darkness. The dirt and cobblestone flying into my pack told me I'd hollowed out a cramped little compartment.

Jumping in front of her, I shouted, "Switch with me!" and placed the first soil block at the entrance.

Creeper! Right in front of me, blinking, vibrating, barely seconds from exploding!

The second block slammed down. Sealed in. Safe.

"Lucky those bombers don't blow after we're out of sight." That was Summer, placing a torch on the floor.

"You know it," I replied with a relieved sigh that came all the way up from my toes.

"Leave it for tomorrow," Summer said as I continued picking out our hidey hole. "Let's get some rest."

"Rest?!" I was incredulous. "How can you rest at a time like this?" I had a whole night-long conversation ready to go. "We've discovered a village! People! The Village People! V-I-L-L . . ." I think I was reciting lyrics from a barely-remembered song, which wasn't remembered at all by Summer.

"Night, Guy," was all she said before climbing into bed.

As I slipped between my own blankets, another song floated up from deep-buried memories. This had been the one that had come to me on the island, that seemed to follow me through all our adventures. And while I still couldn't remember these lyrics, either, it seemed more appropriate to make up new ones.

"And you might find yourself, in a whole new biome, with a whole new group, and they may finally tell me, well . . . how did I get here?"

How did I get here? And how can we get home?

Hope, curiosity. Questions and fantasies spawned through my brain just like the mobs spawning out in the night. But just like we'd shut those mobs out with a dirt wall, this world walled off my spawning thoughts with sleep.

THUNK-THUNK-THUNK.

I awoke to that sound the next morning. Square eyes opened to see Summer picking away at the surrounding stone. "Care to help me with a proper shelter?"

"Can't we do that later?" I pouted, putting away my bed. "We've got so much to learn from the villagers!"

"I don't think they're going anywhere," said Summer. "So why not get ourselves properly settled first?"

"Got me there," I replied, taking out my magic pickaxe. If this was going to be our new base, we'd need the bare essentials. I dug out a modest bunker while Summer set down the "Fab Four" (her term) of crafting table, furnace, storage chest, and brewing stand.

"We can add and upgrade as we need to," she said, stepping back from the appliances. "Now let's get socializing!"

We practically skipped down the late morning slope toward the village (which, from this angle, we could see sat at the end of the river) and were immediately greeted by a friendly "Hrrh."

"And salutations to you, too," Summer said to the villager in the brown hat. "Are the shops open?" Presenting her left hand revealed a trade of ten coal for an emerald, or three emeralds for . . . was that a fish in a bucket?

Right after Summer traded her coal, I paid my three jewels for the bucketed brown swimmer. Well, at least I hoped it would swim. The bucket in my hand held nothing more than a frozen image. "What are you supposed to do with that?" asked Summer.

"Beats me," I said with a shrug. "Keep it as a pet?"

"Or breakfast." She tried not to laugh at my exasperated huff.

Protectively, I backed up to the pond.

"If it doesn't take off"—Summer stifled a giggle—"it's going in the pot!"

It was alive! As soon as I poured it in the water, the liberated fish swam happily down and out of sight.

"Maybe you're right," I said, "about it being a pet."

"Then why don't we recapture it," suggested Summer. "We could build a glass fish tank in the shelter."

"Too confining," I argued as the little brown fish came back to the surface. "At least here, he's got room to frolic."

Summer shook her head and chuckled. "Always the animal lover."

Justifying her taunt, I responded, "He looks lonely, all by himself."

"Can't be helped." She held up her axe and teased, "Unless you want to put him out of his—"

"Summer!" I chided and strode back over to the villager. "One fish partner, please." This was a two-part trade, paying thirty coal for three emeralds then turning those emeralds right around for another bucket of fish.

PLING!

The sound was so loud that I actually retreated a step.

Something was happening to the villager. Pink, swirly bubbles began rising all around them. "What the . . . you okay?" I asked.

"Hrrh!" said the unchanged villager. Unchanged on the outside, that is. Summer must have sensed that something was happening beneath the skin, because she stepped forward to offer a trade. Bingo! Now there were two additional trade slots. Fifteen raw salmon got us an emerald, while another emerald and six raw salmon got us six cooked salmon.

"Will ya look at that," I mused. "A whole new level."

"Eh?" Summer gave me a curious side glance. "You mean like a video game."

"No, no, no," I protested, seeing where she was taking this. Back in the Nether, we'd argued about what this world of ours really was. Summer insisted we were trapped in a video game while I believed, and still do, that it's a world made to look like a video game in order to help us learn life lessons. It was kinda like the arguments people have on our world about religion and the afterlife and all that, and just like those arguments, there was no proof who was right.

But that didn't mean I wasn't gonna stick to my guns. So, in response to her teasing tone, I held up my cubed fists and said, "Not like a video game, just the language of it, okay? The more you learn, the more advanced you get. Just like us. You could say that everything we've been learning keeps bumping us up to new levels of wisdom. Right?"

Summer gave a low, languishing, *I'm not sure I agree with you but by all means continue* "Mmhmm . . ."

"Same for these folks," I continued, glancing at the newly advanced fish-seller. "The more they trade, the more they learn, and the more they learn, the more they can do, just like us."

This time, Summer's "Mmhmm" sounded more convinced,

although her tone soured as she gestured to the villager. "Seems like all this fisherman's learned is to give us a rather shabby deal."

My head snapped over at Summer. "What did you just say?"

Summer shrugged. "Just that we're not getting a worthwhile—"

"No, no," I cut her off, "not about the deal. What did you just call this villager?"

"A fisherman," Summer said. "That's the job."

"Whoaheyho . . ." I cocked my head, feeling the roots of my hair prickle.

"What?" Summer spread her arms. "What are you on about?"

I didn't answer. My head spun round to find the next villager. There! The wide-brimmed hat. The first one we'd met, who was now working in the garden. Working!

"Check it out!" I said to Summer, watching the hrrh-ing figure punch up a bushel of ripe wheat and seeds, then replant some of those same seeds.

"Are you a gardener?" I asked the villager. "A farmer?"

As if answering my question, the villager stepped over to the upright, open barrel next to the garden, put the rest of the seeds in, and then, before our eyes, removed a pinch of white bone meal.

"That's not a barrel!" I declared. "It's a bin! A . . . whaddaya-callit? Compost bin! Where organic trash turns into fertilizer!"

"Hrrh!" said the villager, clearly applauding my observation.

"Which definitely makes you—"

"A farmer," Summer completed my sentence. "Which doesn't exactly seem like anything worth writing home about."

"It isn't!?" My head felt like a creeper ready to blow. "Look around. Look at all these people. Their different clothing, their different jobs. This is . . ." The word rocketed from the back of my brain. A powerful word, as life changing as fire and tools. "Specialization! Which is totally different from us! We've been doing everything all at once, every job, every skill. And that's why everything takes so long for us. But here, with everyone focusing on just one job, they're able to advance much more quickly. That's how our world works! Instead of everyone just crawling forward by having to do everything for themselves, breaking off into specialized jobs allowed us to advance from the stone age to the iron age, to the industrial revolution, to . . ."

"Mmhmm." Summer could not have been less impressed. "So, people here specialize, too. So what? That's what you do in a community."

Community.

The word hit me like a lightning bolt.

"Summer." I felt sick, but in a good way. "You got it!"

"Got what?"

"It!" I took a deep breath, tried to corral my thoughts. "The reason we're here! The reason the . . . mystery powers designed this video game–looking world."

"Or just video game," Summer jabbed.

"Whatever!" I groaned. "It all makes sense now! Why we started out alone, then found each other, then found this village!"

Another breath, a mental drum roll.

"First, we had to learn to live with ourselves. Then, we had to learn to live with a friend. Now . . . bum-bah-bahhh! We have to learn to live in a community!"

I don't know what I was expecting. Fireworks?

What I got was Summer's flat, dry response. "I gather this means more of your lessons?"

"Exactly!" I trumpeted. "And not just regular lessons, or friend-lesson Fressons. These will be community lessons! Communessons . . . no . . . that doesn't sound right. Society lessons! Sesessons! No . . . And I guess a group lesson would sound like 'Agresson,' which would definitely not be—"

"Oh, for Nether's sake!" blurted Summer. "Just call them 'Vessons,' will you? Village lessons? Will that satisfy your need to be the next . . . whatever his name was? The bloke who wrote all those fables, whose name sounds like an electronic soaking tool."

I squinted with confusion. "I-mop?"

"Of course not," Summer scoffed. "E-mop! That's it. E-mop's fables. Just call them Vessons so you can get on to writing the next book of E-mop's fables."

"Deal!" I was practically dancing on air. "Vessons they are! With the first one we learned yesterday about first contact, and the second one we just learned right now."

Doing my signature victory dance (hop-spin-hop), I said, "Specialization moves everyone forward!"

"If only I could applaud," Summer replied sarcastically. "Now, if you don't mind, E-mop, can we please get on with helping our new neighbors specialize?"

"You're right!" I danced again. "The more we trade with them, the more skilled they get, and the more skilled they get, the more stuff they'll have to sell!" I turned back to the farmer. "Still open for business?" The trade slots appeared, and while I still didn't have enough carrots, Summer was rolling in them.

PLING!

As the pink bubbles faded, we stared at two new offerings of either four apples or four bread loaves, for one emerald.

Another Vesson, I thought, watching Summer buy some apples. *Trade is a universal language.* You want something, I want something, let's help each other out. That must have been why language was invented in the first place; not for fun or entertainment, but as a genuine survival skill. "Okay, tribe, here's how we're gonna live through this week. You pick berries, you watch for lions, you light the fire . . ." and so on. From grunts and hand gestures to specific words and sentences. What a leap that must have been; the power to plan, to share ideas. Everybody understanding everybody else, feeling connected, allowing the tribe, the community, to act as one.

And if two tribes met that didn't understand each other, they could still communicate by trade. Food, tools, whatever both sides needed to help them survive. Just like now! We might never understand each other's words (well, our words, their hrrhs) but did it matter if we could exchange stuff we both needed?

And emeralds are as much a leap over barter as words are over grunts.

Summer must have been on the same exact wavelength, because after sharing her apples with me, she said, "Funny, you know, reintroducing ourselves to money."

It was funny, but not in a laughing way. When we'd been

alone, there'd been nothing to buy. Everything we'd needed had to be harvested or crafted with our own two hands. And then, when we'd met each other, sharing personal property was based on mutual trust and understanding.

But here, in this complex community, with strangers like Summer and me showing up, we'd all need to agree on what these emeralds were worth. And that agreement was the only thing that made it worth anything. I could see, now, why that kind of stuff was so convoluted and headache-y on our world. Some countries might not value another country's money, or how much you could buy with that money might change day to day. It was enough to make you dizzy. But, at the same time, when everything worked as planned . . .

"It's kinda like magic," I suggested, "when you think that, through buying and selling stuff, you can transform emeralds into anything, and anything back into emeralds."

"And bloody simpler than trying to cart around all sorts of trade goods," said Summer.

"But isn't money supposed to be the root of all evil?" I asked. "I don't know where I've heard that, but I know I've heard it a lot."

"I think I have, too," pondered Summer before crunching down on a newly bought apple. "But bless me if I can think of why."

I was trying to think of it, too. "I know I went a little nuts for the gold and diamonds under my island. But that was just left-over greed from our world. I didn't understand why I did that then. I still don't." I munched on my own apple. "Especially now, when you think about how useful money is for this village."

"Maybe we don't need to think about it all right at this moment," suggested Summer, which couldn't have sounded more attractive to me. I know I thrive on feeding my brain, but after so many Vessons in such a short time, my noggin was well and truly stuffed.

"Agreed," I said and, realizing I was standing next to the bell, announced, "Class dismissed."

DING!

As soon as I rang the bell, all chaos broke loose!

"Hrrh! Hrrh!" Villagers went crazy, running everywhere, in and out of houses, bumping into us, actual beads of sweat flying from their high heads.

"What did you do, Guy?" Summer asked accusingly.

"How the Nether should I know?" I shot back. "This bell must be some kind of alarm!"

"But what are they so alarmed about?" Summer asked.

"That?" I gulped at what was clunking around the corner.

CHAPTER 6

It was huge! As tall as a house, and nearly as wide across its massive metal shoulders. It was made of iron, a humanoid robot with long, swinging arms and red, evil-looking eyes.

"I've got this!" Bow raised, Summer shoved me out of the way.

"No, stop!" I babbled, shoving her back. "Look at it! Look at how it's behaving."

I gotta say, I'm pretty proud of how I reacted in that moment, keeping the peace by keeping my cool. Somehow I managed to observe that, as scary as this iron giant was, it wasn't attacking the villagers. And the villagers didn't seem to notice it. They just kept skittering back and forth as the silent goliath trudged slowly through them.

"Oh . . ." Summer lowered her bow. "I see what you mean."

"What do you think it is?" I asked, to her and the world.

"A machine of some kind," she answered, "or . . . perhaps an armored suit, with one of the villagers driving it from inside."

My head suddenly flooded with memory fragments: cartoons of people operating everything from robot lions to fighter jets that transformed into warriors. And wasn't there a book about soldiers who wore powered suits of armor to fight giant insects?

"As insanely cool as that idea might be," I said, "I think you were right the first time."

"About it being filled with wheels and gears and whatnot?"

"Probably. But it doesn't explain where it came from."

"Must have happened when you rang the bell. An alarm call that summoned it to protect the village."

"That would make it the army."

"Or the police."

"Yeah, but . . ." Something was scratching at the back of my mind. ". . . If the bell's what brings it to life, then why didn't one appear when I rang it in the deserted village?"

Summer gave that a moment's thought. "Either it won't work without villagers around, or the two things are completely unrelated." Another contemplative pause. "For all we know this iron copper could have been here yesterday just out of our sight."

"Then what does the bell do?"

"Judging by their reactions," Summer reasoned, "we're spot on about it being a threat warning."

The gnawing at the back of my mind was now crawling to the bottom of my stomach. "But what is the threat?" I noticed the villagers had calmed down by now, as the robot continued its clanking patrol. "It can't be the regular mobs, or else we would have heard it ring last night." I looked out across the horizon. "There must be something else out there."

"Well, until it shows up for a visit"—Summer bounced away, clearly not sharing my concern—"let's get back to the business of business."

Who could argue with that? There was no sense in wondering, and worrying, about something we hadn't yet discovered. Especially when we were right in the middle of so many actual discoveries.

I was more than ready to go back to trading with the villagers. What I wasn't ready for was Summer making a beeline for one of the shacks. "Come on then," she said, fist barely a minicube from throwing open the door. "Let's see if these chaps have any chests or—"

"Hey now!" I held up an arm. "You can't do that."

"What?" Her voice was tinged with honest confusion.

"Barge in there like it's an abandoned temple."

"No one's home," Summer argued, opening the door.

"Yeah, but that's not the point!" I argued back fruitlessly.

She was already inside and, following her, I saw that she was right. The room was empty, and other than the storage chest to my right, the other objects were a complete mystery. The first was on the other side of the room, directly opposite the storage chest, and it looked like . . . what are those things on stage that have speeches, or sheet music? Podium? Lectern? Whatever. There it was, and next to it, extending all along the wall, were stacks of multicolored blocks that seemed like bookshelves.

"Is this place—" I started to say, but was interrupted by Summer announcing, "A library, or a bookshop."

She'd opened the chest and, looking past her, I could see every storage slot contained a different book!

"Books make the world bigger," I breathed, repeating a lesson from my island.

"Finally, some decent treasure," Summer agreed, pulling out a volume labeled "wildlife."

"Dude!" My arm shot out between her and the chest. "That's not cool! You can't just take someone else's things. Remember how mad you got at me when I rummaged through your storage chests without permission?"

She couldn't argue with that. But, somehow, she found a way. "I'm not taking anything, Guy. I'm just borrowing it." Then, with just the slightest hint of condescension, added, "That's what you do in libraries."

I was going to say something, and I'm sure it would have been bitingly witty, but, with impeccable timing, a villager wearing a brimless red cap and glasses over their pronounced schnoz came hrrh-ing in.

"Finally, some service," Summer mock-sighed. "Do we need a library card to check these out?"

"Hrrh."

"Didn't think so." She tucked the book in her belt. "Have it back in a jiffy."

"I'm not convinced," I protested, knowing full well that she was right. I was being stubborn, okay? I'm not proud of it, but, if I hadn't been, what happened next might not have happened. "Let's make sure. We all cool, buddy?" I asked the librarian, and held out my trading hand. I wasn't really expecting anything other than a response similar to yesterday's green-shirted resident. There was no way I could have possibly guessed at what the librarian showed me next.

The first offer was twenty-four sheets of paper for one emerald. And the other one . . .

"Summer," I whispered, heart pounding. "Summer, look!"

Seven emeralds plus what looked like a blank book got us . . .

"An enchanted book!" she whispered.

"We can buy magic items." And then, in a louder voice, I shouted, "We can buy magic items!"

"Brill!" chimed Summer. "I wonder how it works, what spell it has."

"Let's find out!" I said, rifling through my pack and belt. "And all we need are seven emeralds, which we've got, or can get, no biggie . . ."

"And a blank book." Summer's voice seemed to cool on that.

"Which we can make!" I continued with unbridled enthusiasm. "What's in a book? Paper, right?" I looked through one of the fencepost windows. "There's sugar cane growing down by the river. We can harvest it, or replant it to grow more. Either way, we'll have plenty of paper toot sweet."

"But that's not all." Summer's even tone finally brought me back down to earth.

"Skin." I suddenly felt my own start to prickle. The first book I'd made had needed the scrap of cow hide from Moo's creeper-killed friend.

Sensing my angst, Summer said, "We can always use rabbit fur. That's what you used to make your second journal, right? The one of our adventures in the Nether? The one that you left in the mountain? You made that second book out of all the rabbit fur I'd collected from my hunting trips. I can just do that again, go out into the desert, harvest more hoppers for stew that I'll eat, and you won't have to watch."

"Yeah," I said, "and if I feel too bad about it in the end, I don't have to use the spell, it can be for you. But . . ." Now I really felt it. Churning stomach, swimming head. ". . . if, for some reason, he"—I nodded at the librarian—"won't accept a book made from rabbit fur, and will only take . . ." I glanced out the door, to the grassland, to the grazing cows who looked just like my dear friend Moo. "If the only way to get the book is to kill a cow . . ."

"Then we won't." She was clear, confident. "It's just not worth it." Summer to the rescue! "I know I wind you up a lot about eating animals, but I hope you know how much I respect your love of them, especially cows. And if the price of that magic book is the life of one, then that price is simply too high"—she held up her fist—"for either of us."

"Thank you, Summer." Nose stinging, eyes watering, I bumped her fist. "I think I get it now. About money being the root of all evil."

It's not the money itself; it's what people are willing to do for it. And I get that, to some extent. I have to admit that the whole process of buying and selling was kind of exciting. I get the rush people feel when they go shopping for fun. It's not just about the stuff they buy, but the feeling you get from buying it. And then the selling, the having money just to have it. I guess I can understand why people piled it up to feel good about themselves, or used it to compare themselves to others. Wasn't there a dude back home who once said money was "a way of keeping score"?

Like life was a game and his money made him the winner? But how far was he willing to go to win the game?

Probably a lot farther than Summer. That guy, and too many people like him, were willing to do just about anything for money, no matter who they hurt and what they broke. That guy would probably burn down the whole world just to brag that he had the most emeralds.

"Money isn't evil," I said sadly. "It's what you'll do for it."

"Don't lose heart, Guy," Summer said, "we'll find an honorable way to get that magic tome." She turned to the librarian, saying, "And I think I have a way to do it."

"Really?" With lifting spirits, I followed her out into the village square.

"The more we trade with these villagers," began Summer, "the more they advance, right?"

"Right." I nodded.

"And the more they advance, the more things they have to sell, right?"

"Right . . ."

"So, if we can just bump up the librarian with enough paper sales, the next advance might let us buy a blank book, or even another magic book for just emeralds!"

"Right!" It was a solid plan, the first P in the Way of the Cube! And if you haven't read about our previous adventures, then this is a major moment. Back on my island, when the only goal was not dying, I realized I needed a method, a philosophy of life to help me organize my actions. Over time, and with plenty of mistakes to learn from, I collected the six P's:

Planning: What do I need to do?

Preparing: What stuff do I need in order to do it?

Prioritizing: What do I need to do first?

Practice: Self-explanatory.

Patience: Never easy.

Perseverance: If it doesn't work immediately, either keep trying, or try tweaking the plan and preparation until it does! Either way, perseverance is a direct shoutout to my very first lesson: Never give up!

Ironically, I realized that if I could fold those six P's together, they'd look like a cube. That was where the name came from, and "The Way of the Cube" has guided me ever since.

"How's your paper cache?" asked Summer, ticking off the second P.

"Pretty low," I said sourly. After making two mapping tables, a copy of our first map, and a second one for these new lands, we only had enough for one complete trade, which got us one emerald, but not to the next trading level.

"A minor setback," said my undaunted partner, "which will soon be rectified with planting more sugar cane."

Those were the next two P's, Preparation and Prioritization!

"To the river!" she declared as we bounded down the bank. There were three stalks growing nearby, each one three blocks high.

"All too easy," I said, knocking them down for replanting. The next P, Practice, was a cinch! We could plant sugar cane in our sleep. No tools, no prepping the land. And no need to dig irrigation ditches because, duh, the river was right here! All we had to do was stick them in the sand.

"Nothing left to do," I said proudly, "but sit back and watch them grow."

Which we actually did, for at least a minute. Standing there, silently, remembering we now had to deal with the fifth P of Patience!

Why is that one always so hard?

"You know . . ." I said, mentally pivoting to another plan, "while this crop takes care of itself, why don't we keep trading with the other villagers to help them grow."

"Excellent idea," said Summer. "One of them might have some paper to sell, or even a blank book!"

"Now yer talkin'!" I crooned and bounced back up to the village.

We saw the farmer first, pacing up and down the little garden. "Next," I said, as we were both nearly carrotless.

"What about wheat?" proposed Summer.

"What about it?" I asked. "We didn't pack any."

"We didn't need to," Summer said, glancing away. "There's practically a whole lorry load over there." She was referring to the compressed bushel blocks near the garden.

As she made for them, I called, "No, wait. That's not ours."

"Yes, but"—she was almost there—"it'll be all right."

"No, it won't!" I insisted, shifting my stance nervously. "And don't tell me we're just 'borrowing' it this time, 'cause we're not. We're stealing someone's property and selling it back to them."

"Oh, Guy." Summer laughed. "You're always so worried about getting in trouble."

"With good reason!" I said, pointing to the clanking, scary robot. "Breaking a rule is bad enough, but we could be breaking the *law!*" And at her silence, I added, "And the difference between a rule and a law is its enforcement."

"But what if they don't have any laws?"

I froze in place, head cocked to the side. "Huh?"

"It's so obvious," continued Summer. "Back on our world, we have laws to keep people from misbehaving. But here"—she looked out at the villagers—"I don't see any misbehavior."

I gestured again at the robot. "Maybe they're just afraid of old Officer Steel Fist."

"Or," Summer sounded completely convinced by her own logic, "maybe they simply want to do what's right. Look, I don't know what makes people act badly back home. Maybe we're taught to, or born with the urge, but whatever it is simply doesn't exist here, and therefore, there's no need for laws."

Before I could answer, or even think of an answer, Summer punched up a block of wheat and showed me the stack of nine stalks. "See? Nothing." I jumped, bracing for trouble. No response from the villagers, and, most importantly, no response from the ore ogre. "See?" she repeated, going over to one of the houses and knocking a clay block from the wall. "Nothing."

I couldn't believe it. Nobody did anything. Was Summer right? Was this a society without laws? But weren't laws what made a society? How could you have one without the other? Did these people all live together peacefully, sharing possessions and homes without any disagreement just because of their own innate morality? Of all the strange things of this world—hyper-healing, instant crafting, magic, and monsters, and even selective gravity—by far the most alien was people doing the right thing just because it was the right thing to do.

I could see how, back on my world, a guy had once written a song imagining people living like this. And it was nice to imagine. But in reality, all it took was one—or, in our case, two people with completely different morals to ruin everything. Could we take all their stuff in their homes, or even burn those homes down because we could?

I suddenly felt a weight on my shoulders, like my armor was made of lead. "Summer," I said, swallowing, "if you're right, and we can do anything we want because nobody's gonna stop us, then . . ."

"Then we'll just have to treat them the way we'd want to be treated." Summer placed the knocked-out clay block back in the house. "I won't damage anything else, and I'll replant and replace all the wheat I use."

"I know," I said, "and I'm sorry if I let you think that I thought you wouldn't."

"Let's just leave the philosophy and get on with the business at hand." She punched up another two wheat blocks, then walked the stalks over to the farmer. The result was one emerald, but no new level.

"Just have to keep trying," she chirped indomitably and rushed off to gather more wheat. Back and forth, with mounting

96

emeralds—and frustration, as I mentally calculated how long it would take to grow enough wheat to replace all those blocks. I was halfway through planning our industrial-size farm when Summer uttered an exasperated, "Oh, bother!"

"What's up?" I asked, noticing that she still had a few more wheat blocks to go.

"The shop's closed!" She huffed and, looking at her trade slots, I saw that the arrow had a big red X through it.

"Hmm," I hmm'd, as she lowered her arms in disappointment. "We must have run out of demand."

"Eh?" Summer side-glanced me quizzically.

"Isn't that the whole thing with trading?" I asked. "Supply and demand? For trade to work, you gotta hit that sweet spot of having what someone wants in the amount they want it."

As if to back me up, the farmer gave a "Hrrh" in reply.

"We're on the supply side and, at least for now, there's no more demand." I noticed that all the other trading slots were still open. The farmer was still buying carrots, which we didn't have, but . . .

"Why not switch from supply to demand?" I suggested. "Let's buy some food!"

A few emeralds later, we were swimming in bread, apples, and the triumph of a new level!

Two more trading slots gave us the chance to either sell four whole watermelons for one emerald, or use three emeralds to buy eighteen cookies.

"Sweet!" I crowed. "On both counts! We've got packed watermelon slices we can plant and then sell for emeralds to buy more cookies!"

"But still no books or paper." Summer sounded more determined than disappointed. "We should keep trying for higher levels."

"I'm with you," I agreed, "but with a wrinkle. It seemed like it was more expensive this time since it took more trades to keep growing." I glanced at some nearby villagers. "It might be cheaper to try getting some of the others to grow."

"Good thinking." Summer brandished her shears. "I'm off to do a bit of sheep shearing."

"And I'm . . ." I noticed the other villager with the brown hat and said, "off to sell the fisherman some coal."

We parted ways, and I headed for the house on stilts. "Hey, buddy," I said, fishing the stacked black lumps from my pack. "I'm not sure why you're interested in buying coal, maybe to cook what you catch or something, but, anyways, here they are."

I was feeling pretty good, losing my law-breaking anxiety. *Maybe Summer's on to something*, I thought, getting to within hyper-reach of the fisherman. *Maybe I do worry too much about getting into trouble.*

And that was when I got in trouble.

Okay, so, you know how there are the two sides of the brain, and how they control your opposite hand's motion? Well, for a moment, just a moment, I mixed them up. It had happened before, when I'd accidentally socked an island sheep, and it was happening now, in slow motion, as my fist swung out to clock the fisherman right in the honker.

"Oh!" I gasped, as the fisherman took off with an angry "Hrrh!"

"I'm so sorry!" I called at a run. "I didn't mean to! Here"—
I reached in my belt for emeralds—"lemme make it up to y . . ."

The hands. Big. Metal. Balled into clubs as they swung into
me like monstrous wrecking balls.

I saw white, felt my bones crack, then opened my eyes to see
the ground shooting away.

"Guy!" Summer's voice, distant, fading.

I was a cannonball, propelled by shock and pain, and the
knowledge that there was, at least, one law in this village:

You could break stuff, you could take stuff, but you could
never, ever, hurt people.

CHAPTER 7

"Oooof!" I hit the ground hard, my bones feeling like eggs in a dropped carton.

"Run, Guy!" shouted Summer as my scrambled brain tried to reassemble.

SMASH! Another behemoth blow sent me sprawling. This time I took off, hobbling out of the village.

How far would it chase me? Like creepers and spiders, or as doggedly determined as zombies? I couldn't stop to check. I couldn't afford another hit. I made it to about the middle of the pasture before slowing just enough to listen. No clanks. No hints of pursuit. I turned to see that all was clear. I'd apparently out-run the tin hulk's jurisdiction, and the only figure running after me was Summer.

"Guy!" Her hand was out, offering a healing potion.

"Thanks," I said, chugging the brew, "I needed that."

"I'm so dreadfully sorry," she panted, contrite eyes refusing to meet mine.

"Nah," I argued as my battered body began to re-knit itself. "It was an accident."

"Yes, but it might not have happened if I hadn't been so cavalier about law and order." She shook her head. "I think I was just using idealism as an excuse to get what I wanted."

"Why, Summer," I said with mock shock, "you're not getting self-reflective on me, are you?"

Summer laughed. "That'll be the day!" And she playfully punched my healed shoulder. "Still, I feel awful about your little tumble, and I think I know a way to make it up to you."

She took off running again, back to the village. "Don't worry," she shouted, clearly reading my mind, "I don't need any covering fire."

Laughing at her clairvoyance, I put away my crossbow and watched as she slowed to a walk right by the iron enforcer. It didn't attack, didn't even notice her. "No guilt by association," she called back to me, then disappeared into the library.

"Well, that's something," I said to a nearby cow. "At least the cops here don't punish someone just because they look the same as the criminal."

"Moo," answered the munching cow.

"Yeah," I agreed, "there's gotta be a Vesson in there somewhere . . ."

But before I could come up with one, another, more pressing thought crossed my mind.

"What about me?" I swallowed. "What exactly is my punishment?"

The cow gave a soft "moo."

"You're right," I said with a nod, "it did look like the death penalty. Kinda harsh for just hitting someone, and now that I've escaped, it looks like I've been sentenced to . . . what do you call it . . . banishment? Like when an Old West sheriff runs a dude out of town. Does that mean I gotta stay out forever? How long do I have to pay my debt to society?"

I was pulled from these anxious musings by Summer's reappearance across the field. Something was in her hand, and as she approached at a run, I saw it was another book. And as she came to a full stop in front of me, I read the cover's title: *Enchanting*. And below that one angst-banishing word, the subtitle read, "How to Create and Enchant Items."

"OhmagodSummer!"

"I had a hunch," she said in her typical deadpan, "after I saw the magic book for sale."

"Which we don't need to buy anymore, 'cause we can make 'em ourselves!" Hopefully, one of those spells would allow me to give my friend the biggest, most grateful hug ever. "You're amazing, Summer!"

"I know." She nodded, then headed back to our hillside hideout.

Making magic.

It seemed too good to be true. No buying, no scrounging. Back to good old-fashioned self-sufficiency! I ran through everything in our inventory, every tool, weapon, and piece of armored garb. Could we choose what kind of enchantment it would be? Make it up as we went along? It was all there for the taking. And in just a few minutes, we'd take it all!

"How do we start?" I squawked as soon as the door was shut.

"Let's see . . ." Summer thumbed the pages. "First off, we need to craft an 'enchanting table,' which requires diamonds . . ."

"Check," I confirmed. "Plenty of those."

"Obsidian."

"Check." *Good thing we packed some for making Nether portals.*

"And . . ." Her eyes fell.

"What?"

A sigh, then one of her arcane swears.

"What!?"

"We need"—she could barely get the words out—"another blank book."

"Oh." I repeated her insectoid profanity. "You gotta be kidding me!"

For a moment neither one of us spoke, too upset by the letdown.

"Look," I said sadly. "If you want to . . ."

"No." Summer snapped out of her funk with a forceful, "No cow killing. We'll stick to the original plan."

"Yeah, but that was for just one book. We're talking about a whole giant leap forward."

"And back!" Summer's answer made me cock my head in confusion. "Enchanting items might be moving forward scientifically, but back morally. And just like with the first magic book, it's simply too high a price to pay."

For the second time today, I wished I could hug my pal.

"And since we're back to Plan A," she said with renewed resolve, "replenishing our trade items is the top priority."

"Another sucky but true observation," I said, glancing at my diminished inventory. We'd exhausted all our trade carrots, along with the wheat—which we also still had to pay back those hay bales to the farmer, and after making a mint off the fisherman, I was now down to only a few lumps of coal.

That last resource was the most precious because it had so many uses. "Looks like we're broke," I observed glumly, "except for the new Vesson: shopping might be fun, but you gotta spend your money wisely."

"Quite," agreed Summer, "but at least this world won't let you get into debt."

That was a really good point. Debt was a huge problem where we came from. Too many people got in too far over their heads by taking out loans they could never pay back. Even if it wasn't their fault, like they were desperate or taken for a ride by some shifty lender, it still left them in the same trap. "At least this world takes care of us in that way, like not letting us overeat or oversleep."

"And on that note"—Summer closed the door on the setting sun—"we'll need a full night's rest for tomorrow's day of mining."

"Good plan. Coal first, then we'll restock everything else."

Now, if you're thinking, "wow, those two sure did pivot quickly from their crushing disappointment," then you're right, we did. And it was totally intentional, because as painful as the enchantment dead end was, the best way to get past it was to find something productive to do. Summer understood that even more than I did, and after getting beat up emotionally—and in my case, physically—we both really needed a win.

That's why neither of us could wait to put this day behind us, and why, the next day, I hopped out of bed, scarfed down breakfast, loaded up on food and potions, and attacked the bunker's back wall like it had insulted my mother. I'd intended to mine a steady downward staircase and figured it wouldn't take too long to hit a vein of coal.

What I didn't figure on, however, was tunneling right out into daylight. "Oops," I muttered with embarrassment, "didn't know this hill was so narrow." I turned to the right, ready to start back down the other way, when Summer abruptly called, "Hang on then."

"What gives?" I asked, looking back at her.

"The land," she answered, staring past me.

I turned back to this hill's new exit and realized that I'd totally missed a completely different biome! Yeah, at first glance it appeared to be like the savanna, with trees and grass and all that, but the colors! Greener greens, like on my island. And the trees themselves were apple oaks and speckled spruces! And there were flowers! Everywhere! The standard red poppies and yellow . . . whatever they are, mixed with blues and pinks. There were tall red bushes like roses and similar sized shrubs with . . . violets? I know next to nothing about flowers, but that didn't stop me or Summer from admiring their beauty.

"Mining can wait," she declared, pushing past me into the sun. "I think a little exploration is in order."

"Oh," I breathed, inhaling the fragrances of this new valley. "It's like a buffet for your nose."

Summer didn't answer at first, finishing her long, intoxicating whiff. "I think that's why people back home love having them all about, or why I read somewhere that, a long time ago, they used to put them in their pockets to cover the smells of disease and death."

I gave her a sidelong glance. "Well, that doesn't ruin the mood at all." It didn't. Summer's guffaw only completed the idyllic scene. The only thing better than finding an awesome place is having an awesome friend to share it with. I was so lulled by Summer's musical laugh that, for a moment, I missed the other sound under it.

Bzzzz.

Hm?

As her chortling died, I cocked a flat ear to the sky.

Bzzzz.

There it was again, faint and far . . . and strangely like a power tool?

"Is someone building something?" Summer glanced back in the direction of the village. "Are we missing a new construction project?"

For all the changes this world kept throwing at us, it had yet to give us super-hearing, so I couldn't pinpoint the source of the omnidirectional noise.

"I wouldn't be surprised," I said, and was about to head back to the village, when a small, thick yellow and brown bird came floating over from behind a tree.

But it wasn't a bird.

"A bee!" declared Summer. *Of course! With all these flowers!*

"Don't get too close," I warned, as the striped, bunny-sized drone buzzed closer. "You don't want to get stung."

"Don't worry," Summer chuckled, "it's not interested in us."

True enough, the large black eyes never looked in our direction, as short, white, nearly transparent wings bobbed it up and down over the flowers. It was kinda cute, with those stubby legs and equally stubby antennae. Like the panda in the jungle, it was nice to see a new life form that wasn't automatically hostile. I would have been content to just watch it glide away, but, naturally, Summer just had to take off after it.

"What are you—"

"C'mon then." Summer hopped away giddily. "Let's find the hive!"

"Why in the Nether," I protested, "would we ever want to do that?"

Summer sang one word. "Honey!"

"Okay, yes," I said as I hurried after her, "but we've got other sweet things: apples, cookies, cakes . . ."

"I absolutely adore honey," she said, trailing the randomly zigging bug. "Which I didn't remember till this moment. Honey on toast, honey in tea, or even just a spoonful from the jar!"

I didn't argue. I could see the potential reward. If "don't ask me about the past" Summer was now willing to risk unlocking some old memories, then this could be a golden—literally honey-colored—opportunity!

We followed the bee farther down the valley, patiently pausing every time it halted to examine a new flower. "Maybe there's no hive," I said. "It doesn't have to behave exactly like the bees of our world."

"Possible . . ." agreed Summer hesitantly, but then pointed straight ahead and exclaimed, "That must be it!"

At the edge of a wooded patch, we saw a yellow striped box, nestled under the canopy of a large apple oak. We ran ahead of the buzzer for a closer look. "Bull's-eye," declared Summer, her triumphant fist pointing to a glistening, yellow slime seeping from the two entrance holes.

"Great," I said with returning concern. "Now how do we safely extract it?"

"With this!" Summer produced her empty water bottle, then held it toward one of the holes.

Careful! I prayed silently, mindful of a million consequences. I pictured the rest of the colony swarming out in a cartoonish cloud. Were their stings poisonous? Fatal? Should we run back to the cows for some milk? All these thoughts cycled through my head in the half second it took for Summer to collect her prize.

"Have a sip!" she said, offering me the golden liquid.

"Nah, that's all you," I refused, and with a cautious glance over my shoulder, added, "and let's make tracks before that bee discovers we just robbed her house."

"Sensible enough," agreed Summer as we headed farther down the valley. At what looked like a safe distance, we stopped so Summer could have a taste of the sweet treat. The bottle went up, the honey went down, and Summer hummed before suddenly freezing, silent, eyes fixed straight ahead.

Was the honey actually poisoned? Or was it unlocking sad, terrible memories?

"Summer, wha—" She cut me off with an outstretched fist. I turned to see a dark patch extended across the valley's opposite hills. We walked a little closer and stared up in awe. It was a cave, monstrous in both size and appearance. The entrance was a roundish, mouthlike shape complete with top and bottom spikes for fangs.

"Stalagmites," I said, impressed with myself for knowing the word.

"Never seen anything like that here," Summer mused and, picking up one of the broken rocky points, she observed, "Definitely stone. These vertical lines look as if they were made one layer at a time."

.   "Maybe from that," I said, pointing up to water dripping from the overhead stalactites (that's the name, right?). Some fell directly onto their opposite, while others pooled into little open squares below. I noticed that a few of the upper and lower points appeared to have joined into complete columns and, just like Summer's honey memories, this sight unlocked something I must have learned back home. The dripping water carried minerals, and over time, the minerals hardened into layers. That's how these artificial teeth formed in our world, and now here was a version of the same process in this one.

"Won't be easy going," Summer breathed, as we took in the sheer number of these natural obstacles that stretched back, out of sight, into the depths of the cave.

Just standing at the edge of this mammoth maw gave me the shivers. The entrance opened into a cavern so large that, even now, in broad daylight, its depth disappeared into darkness. At least that daylight helped us through the initial descent. Picking our way down the jagged slope, we were grateful not to waste our remaining coal on torches. That didn't stop me, however, from accidentally stepping on a spearpoint that had craftily hidden itself in a puddle.

I growled angrily, which prompted a "You all right?" from Summer. "Yeah," I said, smarting with pain and embarrassment, "just getting used to this new terrain."

"I suspect," she understatedly replied, "that this won't be the only change we encounter."

How prophetic she was. We hadn't gotten too far down before noticing a nearby rock embedded with flecks of iron. The flecks were slightly bigger than usual, though, more pronounced, and as I picked it up, only the iron, instead of the whole cube, came free. "How about that," I said to the pinkish nodule.

"How about this?" called Summer, standing over another metal impregnated rock. This wasn't iron, or gold, or anything we'd ever seen. These freckles were orange with hints of green. I was about to pick it out when a low zombie groan echoed from the darkness.

"Seems we have company," commented an unconcerned Summer. She looked up, marking the sun's position, and said just casually, "Best to stay put and let it come to us."

A simple tactic, which had served her well in the past. During those first few days in this world, cold and starving and with the barest wood and stone weapons, she'd discovered the cave entrance to her mountain—and several zombies that had come slouching out into the burning sun. This is what she was clearly planning now.

And, as the solitary ghoul stepped into the light, burst into flames, and struggled to get to us through the toothlike stones, I almost felt a twinge of sympathy.

"Poor wretch," chuckled Summer as it poofed into smoke. "Doesn't quite seem fair."

"Guuuuu . . . grrrr. . . . gaahhhh . . ." A whole melody of zombie moans, with a harmony of skeleton clicks. How big was this cavern? How many mobs were converging on us?

I reached for my night vision potion when three arrows came whistling from the cave-created midnight.

"Back up!" cried Summer. "Way up!"

We turned and ran, hopping, dodging, and wiggling up the porcupine-ish slope.

Traitors, I thought to the spikey forest, *you helped stop that first zombie, and now you're doing all you can to stop us!*

Arrows whipped the air around my ears. No room to dodge. Zigzagging was impossible. I winced as a missile struck my calf, then the small of my back. Then a perfectly placed shot nailed me right between the shoulder blades, knocking me forward into a puddle—and onto a submerged dagger.

"Almost there!" encouraged Summer, "only a little—UFF." The sound of an arrow in the back, knocking her face into a stalagmite, finished the sentence.

There was the top, just ahead. Hop, dodge, climb. One last row of stone stakes, then out onto the cool, soft grass, with nothing but flowers and freedom before me!

"C'mon!" I shouted to Summer, who, for some reason, had decided to stop right at the edge. "Let's run for the hills . . . literally."

"Won't do," she said, blocking an arrow with her shield. "We've got to make our stand here!"

I thought I knew what she was up to, but I had to talk her out of it.

"Dude," I said calmly, as an arrow thocked off my own shield.

"I get that you want payback. I get that you want revenge for having to retreat. But remember that story I told you about nearly getting killed in the caves under my island? How I was so obsessed with hurting the mobs for hurting me that I didn't see how I was hurting myself?"

"Guy." Summer's voice was a master class in patience. "This isn't revenge, it's strategy." And after a quick glance over her shield when another arrow clattered against it, she continued, "If we outrun them, they'll turn back for the cavern, and wait for us to come fight them on their terms." Another glance downward, another deflected shot. "But out here, they'll be on ours."

CHAPTER 8

I wasn't sure what she meant, especially when I saw what was chasing us. Three skeletons, six zombies, and two creepers. There didn't seem to be any spiders, though — not that we didn't already have enough to deal with. Other than the time I'd accidentally angered that pig-zombie mob in the Nether, this would be our most outnumbered fight.

"Eleven to two," I breathed, cocking my crossbow.

"Eleven to five," corrected Summer. "Don't forget our three allies: spikes, uphill terrain, aaaand . . ."

She waited for our pursuers to surge out from their protective shade.

"Sunlight!"

The horde, creepers aside, looked like they'd been hit with a flamethrower. And having to navigate both the slope and the stalagmite maze allowed more time for them to burn before reaching us.

So that's her plan, I thought, as my battle buddy commanded, "Skeletons first! Take out the long-range shooters!"

I aimed my crossbow at the closest boney, took a breath, then let fly. My shot caught the fleshless archer just as it was about to return the favor. Already burning, it puffed away instantly. I didn't gloat. There wasn't time. The second, smoldering archer was already lining up on my friend. "Summer, duck!" I shouted and fired again. Another hit, but not enough to kill. This clicker probably hadn't absorbed enough solar damage. And to make matters worse, my arrow had knocked it back into the safety of the cave's shade.

Unlike Summer, the rude word I shouted made sense. But, also unlike Summer, I couldn't take credit for the kill. Her bow twanged a second later, puffing it into a hovering femur.

"Nice," I commented, then lined up on the next most dangerous target: creepers! Somehow one of them had gotten close enough to countdown. It was blinking, vibrating! How many seconds before the boom? We shot together, our impact kicking it down the slope.

BAM!

FLASH. NOISE.

"You hurt?" I asked as the blast petered out harmlessly before reaching me.

"Tip-top," answered Summer. "But . . ." Following her pointing arm down the slope, I could see that the explosion had taken out some stakes and cleared a path for the burning zombies.

"Ruddy sapper," sneered Summer and loosed a shaft at the closest ghoul.

I cocked my crossbow and tried, in vain, to find the other creeper. Where was it? Behind the zombies? I wasted precious seconds peering through the approaching wall of flame. I could have shot one, *should* have shot one, but, as I've explained before, I was trying to conserve my arrows.

"On your right!" called Summer as another zombie shambled close enough to hit me.

The impact was negligible, but the fire . . .

I was burning! Flames licked up before my eyes. Searing, sizzling, the brain-punch memories of all those times I'd nearly been roasted alive roaring back into my brain. Ironically the expression is "freezing," but that's what I did. I froze. Just for a second, just long enough for Summer to rush over, sock me in the back, and send me stumbling forward into a quenching puddle. The flames died, my eyes cleared, and this time, thank the square heavens, I didn't freeze.

The other creeper was right in front of me, its hiss signaling only one last second before . . .

My shield absorbed the detonation as hot, ear-popping pressure washed around me. I blinked hard, felt debris fly into my pack.

I lowered my shield, frazzled, and scanned in all directions.

"I think we're clear." Summer's voice rose above the ringing in my ears. "Nothing but bones, zed-bits, and creeper wreckage." She reached into her pack and fished out a nodule of that new orange-and-green metal. "What do you reckon this is?"

"Got me," I responded, yawning and swallowing to get my ears to un-pop. "Copper?"

"Seems about right," she agreed. "Like what they make into water pipes and wire and pennies."

"You call them pennies, too?"

"Of course, and pence . . ."

"Ah, good. For a second there, I thought we might actually have one word for the same thing."

Summer laughed, bumped my shoulder with hers, then exchanged the hunk of copper for her bottle of night vision potion. "Let's see about collecting some more."

I chugalugged my own brew, and watched as it revealed the chasm before us. You could fit the whole village in here, and then some.

"What I could have done," Summer said as she slowly walked toward the edge, "if I'd stumbled across something like this instead of having to hollow out a whole mountain from scratch."

"Kinda glad you didn't," I said, coming to her side, "'cause making that mountain helped make you the person you are now, like me on my island. If I hadn't accidentally burned up all my apple oaks, I might still be living on them, and nothing else. Heck, I might still be on that island, with you holed up underground." And remembering a lesson from those early days, I finished with a solemn, "Problems force progress."

"Yes, thank you, E-mop," Summer quipped dryly, "and while I'm always grateful for your philosophical niblets"—her arms swept out to the rising walls—"I think there might have been another reason for coming down here."

Coal caches! So many of them, either alone or next to iron

and that new coppery metal. "Okay," I agreed, hefting my magic pickaxe. "Less talking, more mining."

"And let's keep an eye out for more baddies," Summer warned. I noticed she hadn't swapped her bow for a digging tool. "You pick, I'll guard." Her eyes scanned up and around us. "The problem with such a wide-open space is that they can come from any direction."

She wasn't exaggerating. Like the Nether, or the canyon under my island, we faced a 3-D danger zone. Threats could come from anywhere; back and forth, side to side, or even up and down! And the deeper we delved, the more exposed I felt. It was almost like that first night in the taiga, when I was a total mob magnet. How much time would we have before the night vision potion ran out? How much time had we already wasted chitchatting?

No time to wonder. Just get to work! Which I did, speed-picking while Summer watched and listened for threats.

Initially, all I could think about was safety. I kept waiting for a zombie moan, a skeleton arrow, or the crackle of a suicide-bombing creeper. Nothing happened, not at first. Even when we saw giant spiders skittering nearby, Summer had to remind me that they're docile in the daytime.

I started to relax, shifting all my attention to rock-breaking. Coal, iron, copper . . . lots of copper! *This stuff must be so useful,* I thought as dozens of nodules flew into both our packs. *I can't wait to start experimenting!*

Could they be electrical wire? More efficient than redstone trails? If I could fuse them right into any other blocks, instead of digging tunnels, what would that mean for house building? And what about water pipes? Like electrical wires, would they meld right into building blocks? And what if that was only the beginning? Could I build whole new machines with copper? A water pump? A windmill? And then there was money! Would ten or a hundred pennies equal one emerald? Would that stretch our buying power in the village? And what about simply selling it? One of the villagers must be looking to buy copper. And I bet it could be combined with other metals—alloys, that was the word. Like on my island, when I'd first discovered iron and thought it was brass or bronze. What was the difference? And what could you do with it? Countless possibilities, just waiting to be explored. I fantasized about finding a library book just for copper, the way I'd found three on redstone.

Soon enough, I mentally salivated, *soon as we cart this loot out of here.*

The night vision in my veins must have heard my thoughts, because it started that "nearly done" blink. Day to night, day to night, as if the potion itself were shouting, "Alert! Alert! Night blindness imminent! Prepare to panic!" Okay, maybe that last part would only be my personal alarm. It certainly wasn't for Summer.

"Just in time," she said, calmly placing a torch at our feet. "My pouches are near bursting with mined minerals and rock debris."

"Then let's call it a day," I said and turned back to the now far-off entrance.

"Pains me to have to invest more coal on torches," Summer lamented, "but at least we won't have to depend on potions in the future."

"Guess that's why they call it an investment," I commented, planting the flickering stick, "a little bit in to get a lot ou—"

"HMHMHMHM!"

That cackle. From somewhere in the darkness. A witch!

"Don't move," whispered Summer. "Stand back-to-back!" Weapons up, we moved to guard each other's rear.

"HM-MMMM!"

The sound was close, but coming from where?! And with all the changes in this world, was there a new variety we had to deal with?

"More torches," I rasped, "more light!" Using our hyper-reach, we expanded our circle of vision. "It can't sneak up on us," I said with forced confidence. "We'll totally get off a shot before it gets too close." That might have worked on open ground, but here, amid the cover of stalagmites . . .

Off to my left, three squares away . . . one of them moved! No, not one of them, something behind them. Purple eyes!

"Over there!"

My shot was blocked by a spike.

"HMHMHMHM!"

CRASH! SPLASH!

Glass and liquid, covering me!

Weakness! Limbs dangling, muscles quitting, neck drooping to support a head of lead.

With all my might I fought to cock my crossbow, but the weight felt like trying to lift an elephant from a ditch.

Pull . . . pull . . .

SNAP!

Flabby fingers letting go! Back to square one!

Pull!

"HMHMHMHM!"

Another CRASH, the splatter of poison in my face.

Sickness seethed up inside me as the noxious fluid seeped into every organ.

"Summer!" I called feebly for help, and got back a pained, "Meee . . . too!"

Both of us were hit, the splash potions acting like hand grenades.

Focusing, straining, watching the crossbow string scrape slowly into place. Too slow. Too late!

The witch was in the light now, another sickly green potion in its hands. More poison!

No time to run. No time for food or our own healing brews . . .

Here it comes!

WHP!

Summer's arrow! Weak and non-lethal, but just enough force to interrupt the witch's toss. Witchee Woo stumbled back, producing another bottle! A pink one this time, a healing potion, erasing all the damage of Summer's arrow!

"Run!" That was Summer, as we sped for the exit. At least the weakness brew didn't affect our legs. But the blacked-out ground did.

We should have planted more torches, I thought as slowing puddles and painful spikes took their toll. *We should have planned for this!*

"HM-MMM!" It was still behind us, slower, but now fully healed. Were we far enough to avoid another lob?

I heard glass crack behind us, jumped just to be sure, then

gritted my teeth for the nightmarish slog back up the spindly slope.

The smug cackle sounded right behind us, which prompted Summer to taunt, "Keep up then! We'll see you off soon enough!"

For once, timing worked in our favor. The weakness and poison wore off just about the time we reached the cave's sunlit border. I might have kept running, but as Summer turned to shoot, I wasn't going to let her have all the fun. Rejuvenated muscles jerked the crossbow spring back just as the high-hatted hater appeared from out of the gloom.

"Which way you gonna die, witch?" I called as our burning pursuer took two arrows. It fell back into the shade, produced another healing potion, but then, finally, succumbed to our second volley.

"Well, that was rather rude," Summer huffed with mock indignance. "Not even leaving us any loot."

"Unless you count the warm, fuzzy memories." My comment got a musical laugh from Summer, which went down well with a recharging snack of chocolate chip cookies.

"We've still got plenty of daylight," I said, gesturing at the noonday sun. "What say we try unloading some of this raw copper?"

Strolling happily through "flower valley," we rounded the hill, then headed straight for the busy little village.

It was a great day; the mobs were smoked, our packs were full, and both wins had banished last night's blues. Between the trading and experimenting, I was looking forward to one heck of an afternoon . . .

Then the metal giant showed up.

"Uh-oh." I gulped as the iron constable clanked into view. "Forgot I had a criminal record."

"Maybe you've been paroled?" Summer suggested. "It's a new day, second chances and all that."

"You think they're that lenient?" I asked as the red, lifeless eyes swung toward us.

"Only one way to find out." Summer strode confidently forward, leaving me behind as she said over her shoulder, "And only you can take that risk."

Why does courage always have to be a full-time job?

I swallowed hard, mentally marked my escape route, then walked shakily toward the menacing machine.

"Afternoon, Officer," I said respectfully, waiting for more blows from the long arms of the law. But those arms kept swinging casually at the automaton's hips. "Nothin' to see here." I balked as robo-fuzz ambled on by. At least they weren't punishing me forever, which made sense given that I hadn't committed a forever crime. I hadn't killed anyone or done anything that couldn't be undone. I'd taken my lumps (literally), and now I was ready to rejoin society.

Another Vesson, I thought with a huge sigh. *The punishment should fit the crime.*

"Ehh-uh!"

What was that?!

"Ehh-uh!" That sound wasn't from the robot. It was new, and horrible!

I spun, expecting to see . . . what? Some new monster? A pig-horse? A zombie-spider?

"Ehh-uh!"

They were standing next to a nearby house. Two creatures. Both brown, with long, upright necks, and short, cream-colored snouts that matched their off-white hooves.

"What in the Nether?" Summer stepped back next to me. "Are these some kind of horse-sheep hybrid?"

"I don't think so," I answered, noticing that they both seemed saddled. Not the kind we'd found before, though. These looked more like . . . well . . . maybe I'm retrofitting the memory here, but they looked more like saddle bags, the kind that carry cargo instead of people. "You think it might be in the wildlife manual?" I wondered as Summer took off for the library. A soon as she left, I noticed that the "horsheeps" weren't just saddled, they were leashed. Two long, thin, easily missable brown lines led from their multicolored saddles back around a house to . . .

"HM?"

Another villager came around the bend, but not like any I'd ever seen. This one was clad in a hooded, multicolored robe that matched the horsheep's saddles.

"Oh, hey," I said, raising my fist in welcome. "You new here?"

"HM?" it asked. Yes, asked, because I could definitely hear a questioning tone.

"My name's Guy," I answered, "if that's what you're wondering."

"HM?" Clearly it wasn't.

"Okay, no problem." I stepped to within trading range. "Here's to the universal language."

My left hand opened to reveal not two but six trade slots, and only for buying.

I could purchase blue dye, blue ice, a spruce sapling, a colorful fish in a bucket, a pinch of gunpowder, or a brown mush-room.

"Of course." I shook my head. "It all makes sense. You're a—"

"Llamas," called Summer, running back from the library. "They're llamas!"

"And this is a peddler!" I gestured to the robed visitor. "Or traveling salesman or . . ."

"Really?" Sidling up to me, she glanced at the trading slots. "Gunpowder?!"

"Oh, yeah," I said, embarrassed that I hadn't immediately realized the significance. Just like me, so caught up in the discovery of this trader that I'd glossed over what was being traded. "Be nice to eventually stock up on some more."

"Not eventually!" Summer rummaged through her inventory. "This wandering peddler may wander off at any time!"

She'd hit on something, a phrase so important in my homeland that it was practically a religious chant. "For a limited time only," I muttered, then searched my inventory for emeralds. "Musta left all my cash in the bunker."

"Me too," said Summer, then ran over to the nearest villager. "But we've still got plenty to trade."

Not from Green Shirt, though, as Summer swore a moment later. "What kind of a nitwit are you?!" She huffed at the hrrh-ing villager. "And how are you the only one here without a job?"

"Let it go," I said and strode over to Weaver. "I know you're in the wool business, but maybe you'd like some copper for . . . something?"

No sale. And I should have remembered that if selling this

new ore was possible . . . then it would only happen at the next level.

Paper! I thought, running down to the river. *Harvest sugar cane, sell its paper to the librarian, and do some level bumping at the same time to earn emeralds for gunpowder.*

The sugar cane stalks were ripening, their height already doubled, but as I collected and counted the tops, I realized it would be a much larger harvest if I replanted them for later.

But the gunpowder . . . What if that blew our chance? What if the wandering trader left before this larger crop was ready?

For a limited time only.

I was struggling with this dilemma, quick profits over long-term investment, when I was hit with a crazy and possibly brilliant idea!

What if we could have both by finding a way to make the trader stay longer? I glanced in my pack, saw that it was practically spilling over with cobblestone debris from our mining.

It won't be pretty, I thought, imagining a small hovel, *but if I could build a place to stay, like a hotel with enough room for a bed, and maybe a fenced-in area for the llamas, then the peddler might hang around a while.*

It was worth a try. And, would you believe, as I ran up the bank, cobblestone in hand, I saw Summer doing the exact same thing!

"Thought I'd build an inn," she said. "Maybe coax our traveling merchant to halt his travels for a bit."

"Totally had the same idea!" I crowed, running to help.

"Of course you did," Summer said with just the teensiest sarcasm.

"No, I did!" I insisted, finishing the cobblestone roof on our small hotel.

Summer laughed, no doubt winding me up, then made a crafting table and shears before rushing off to harvest wool for a bed.

I stayed behind to spruce things up. A door, fencepost windows, and a large enough pen for the animals. "It may not be the Ritz," I told the peddler, "but why not kick back here for a night or two?"

All I got was "HRR?" which felt a lot like, "Are you gonna buy something or not?"

"Here we go!" Summer came bouncing back with white wool.

"I'll craft the bed," I offered, noticing the late afternoon sun. "And in case it doesn't work, why don't you use the last of our daylight to trade some coal to Fisher for emeralds."

"Right then," she said as we exchanged her sheared wool cubes for my mined coal, "I'm off."

As the wool flew into my hand, I turned back to the hotel crafting table. It didn't take long, even with the picked poppies for red dye. I stained the wool, laid them over wood planks, plucked the finished bed from the ether, then set it against the opposite wall. "Not bad," I said with a nod, and was about to set down a single torch when I suddenly heard Summer's voice.

First there was an annoyed "Oi," then a surprised "Oh," then another, softer "Ohhh."

"Summer?" I asked over my shoulder. "Everything cool out there?"

"Oh my." Summer's voice was louder, and . . . embarrassed?

"Summer?" I was out the door just as I heard the next sound, a villager's "hrrh," but much higher in pitch than usual.

Summer was standing at the town center, by the well and bell, along with the crowd of villagers. That wasn't unusual. We'd seen them congregate here around this time of day. But what I saw next . . .

"Hirr!"

"Summer . . . what did you do?"

CHAPTER 9

A new villager! Smaller than the others, it looked up at the adults—because there was no denying that it was a child.

"Summer . . ." I repeated with totally faked sternness. I wasn't upset; in fact, I couldn't have been more fascinated, but to hear such intense, rare embarrassment in Summer's voice made me want to relish every torturous second. "What did you do?"

"I—I," Summer stammered. "I'd just sold Fisher some coal and was using the emeralds to buy gunpowder when I realized that I didn't have any free inventory slots . . ."

"And?" I pressed. She was so flustered. This was awesome!

"And . . . well . . . I thought, maybe I'll drop something, just temporarily, to make space for the gunpowder, which, of course, I'd collect again before it disappeared. So, I dropped all that bread we'd bought earlier and"—a quick glance at the villagers—"and then they all started snapping it up."

That must have been the "Oi" I'd heard.

"And then Farmer and that green-shirted nitwit just started looking at each other, and then the hearts rose, and Bob's your uncle . . ."

"Hirr!" the village's newest resident chimed in.

I couldn't take it anymore. I let loose a guffaw. "Well said, kid!" I couldn't stop laughing. "I don't know who Uncle Bob is, but let's hear it for Aunty Summer!"

"Har-har!" Since this world couldn't let her blush, a punch on the shoulder would have to do. "Very funny."

I was about to concur heartily, but then looked at the baby villager staring at me and said, "Maybe it isn't. Not because you're uncomfortable, that's still hilarious. But the gravity of helping to make a whole new human life, even by accident, is another *big* level up from breeding animals." I paused to take in the entirety of the village. "We might have altered the whole culture of this community."

"Or," Summer said defensively, "they might have gone and done it anyway, and I just helped hasten the process."

"You might have," I conceded, "or you might not." I took another look at the baby who was now wandering around its new home. "We've been rushing in without thinking, interacting, interfering. We don't know what long-term consequences we might be causing, whether we're doing more harm than good."

I suddenly flashed back to the memory of a TV show, of a spaceship exploring strange new worlds with its crew being darn careful never to violate its prime rule of non-interference. Now, seeing how different this village was from how we found it, I could see why that rule was written.

"I think we need to slow down," I said. "Go with our original plan before the first villager came wandering over."

"You mean an observation bubble?" asked Summer.

"Observation, yes," I said, "but without the bubble. We should still come visit, say hi, walk around the village, but not do anything. No more trading and"—I motioned to the new inn—"no more building. It's time to listen and learn."

Which we did. For several days straight. First thing in the morning we'd head into town, amble around, and take careful mental notes, which we compared, of what we observed our neighbors doing.

We learned that they started their day with a morning meander, just wandering around the village and surrounding area. Maybe they were enjoying the scenery. Maybe they were going over what they'd have to do for work that day—because that came next. With the exception of the child, and the green-shirted "nitwit," the rest of them headed straight for their specific stations. And, as I'd postulated before, they were rigidly specialized. The farmer stuck to the garden, the librarian in the library, and so on.

And most of those specialized professions, at least from our viewpoint, didn't really seem that professional. I personally watched the weaver just look at the loom every morning, for three days, without ever doing anything. Likewise, the fisherman never caught any fish. I guess you could argue that the librarian was working by just minding the library, waiting for us to check out a book.

Which we did, on minerals, and the good news was that there

was a chapter on copper! But the bad news was that there isn't much you can do with it. No electric wires, water pipes, or pennies. But there were two new inventions, and one of them practically blew our minds. Not the other one, though, which was the only one we could actually craft. It was a lightning rod, which took three copper ingots and could be placed on any surface to attract lightning in a storm.

I guess that's a big deal. Who wants to be struck by lightning? But like life jackets or seat belts, it's hard to get all jazzed about preventing a potential crisis. What we were psyched, and frustrated, about was the other invention: a spyglass.

That's right! Finally! After so many months of squinting at faraway objects, after so many situations that made us pray for a pair of binoculars, here was the next best thing! An honest-to-goodness device that let us reach out and see the world.

And that's what was so frustrating. We couldn't make it! In addition to copper, spyglasses needed something the mineral manual called an "amethyst shard." From the illustration, we guessed that it was some kind of crystal, and given that we had never come across anything close, we also guessed that it was a recent addition to this world. But discovering one would have to wait. Right then, our priority was learning as much as we could about the villagers.

And another important fact we learned was that our new little resident was just part of normal village life. Watching the farmer working—really working, not just standing around—we saw that the harvested food was later shared with the other villagers during their communal hang time.

That was their afternoon routine. As the sun started its decline, the whole population would meet at the fountain to hrrh at one another, and, in the case of the farmer, drop food for others to pick up. "Well, that's a relief," breathed Summer, as the wheat and carrots were swiped up quickly by the other residents. "I just wonder why our new little chap is still an only child?"

I watched the baby villager bouncing and hirr-ing among the adults, looking up for . . . what? Guidance? Praise? Then it stopped to take a flower from, would you believe, the lumbering iron golem! That's what another library book had taught us, that the mecha-cops were called "golems." And it had also taught us that they were potentially wished into existence by the villagers. Nice to know that they really were there to protect and serve the public. That book, or any other book in the library, had yet to tell us anything about how babies were made, though, which is why Summer and I were having this conversation.

"Maybe it's got something to do with the quantity of food," I offered. "See how little wheat Farmer's able to harvest versus how much bread you dumped on them the other day? Maybe they have to store away a tremendous amount of food before they feel comfortable enough to start a family. Don't people back home do the same thing? Ask themselves if they can support a kid before going ahead and having one?"

Summer thought about this for a moment, then added, "That might explain the beds, too." At my silence and confused stare, she continued, "Look how many villagers there are, versus the number of beds available. There wasn't room for a new resident until we set down an extra cot for the peddler."

Oh, yeah, about that.

Turns out our traveling trader didn't need a bed to stick around. Buying some gunpowder was, we think, enough of an incentive to stay. But then what about surviving the night? Good question.

We discovered the answer the day the baby was born, when, as the sun set, the kid promptly ran into the new hotel and snagged the trader's bed.

"Maybe we should build another house," I'd mused, seeing that we had a few precious moments before dark. "I know I said don't interfere, but . . ."

"Don't worry." Summer chuckled on her way to the hill bunker. "That bloke didn't make it this far without having a few tricks up those colored sleeves."

But what trick could that be?

As Summer hit the sack, I stayed up to watch the village. It wasn't easy, not from all the way up on our hill. *We gotta find one of those crystals to make a spyglass!* I thought as the stars rose above the rooftops.

There was the peddler, standing with the llamas, and, it seemed, without a care in the world.

Dude, c'mon, I thought nervously. *You gotta get to cover before . . . Whuuu?*

Gone! The peddler had vanished!

"Summer!" I shouted, not taking my eyes off the window. "Summer, wake up!"

She was out, sleeping soundly. And if this was any other situation, I would have just let her snooze away. But this was an emergency! "Sorry," I hissed, and punched the bed out from under her.

"Guy!" she barked. "What the Neth—"

"Thepeddlerisgone!" I frazzle-mouthed, then, slowing down to take a breath, I continued, "I watched it happen! One sec, right there, and the next . . ."

Summer was already past me, heading for the door. "C'mon then!" she called, clutching her bow. "In case a ruddy Zed's got 'em!"

Weapons in hand, we raced down to the village. All around us were the sounds of spawning mobs. Had one of them already finished the job? Would we find nothing more than smoke and a hovering robe?

"Where was he?" called Summer, as the rasp of spiders hissed off to my right.

"With the llamas!" I shouted over approaching groans. "That was the last place I saw him!"

The animals were still there, standing calmly as if it were the middle of the day. But the trader . . .

"I don't see him!" I shouted, whipping my head around.

"Me neither!" responded Summer, looking for the same hovering evidence I feared.

Then . . .

"HM?"

"What? Where?" I twisted and turned.

"HM?"

It was so loud, like he was right next to us.

"Oh, hang on." Summer shook her head, drawling, "Haaaang

on!" Reaching into her pack for torches, she set one down at our feet. "Mystery solved."

In the flickering light we not only saw that the llamas' leashes led to a spot of open air, but that that air was coated with dim, rising gray bubbles.

"HM?"

"Potion of Invisibility." Summer shook her head. "That's how the old dodger manages to dodge the mobs."

Turning to the transparent trader, I jokingly asked, "How come you're not selling those?" Then, I looked back to Summer and asked more seriously, "How come we never made those?"

"More trouble than they're worth," she dismissed, "given that in order to be truly invisible, you can't wear any armor or carry anything in your hands."

Yeesh! I imagined suddenly materializing, unarmed and practically naked, in the middle of a monster mob. "Thanks for the nightmare I'm sure I'll have tonight."

Summer giggled, just as an arrow flashed between us.

Skeleton!

Running back up that hill, among hisses and groans and the occasional stray arrow, I couldn't stop my racing thoughts. *So much to learn*, I thought, slamming the door behind us. I had no idea that another mind-blowing Vesson was waiting for me the very next day.

After breakfast, we headed into the village for another day of listening, learning, and, most importantly, reading. I'd planned to visit the library first, but was suddenly stopped by a villager I didn't recognize. A plain maroon shirt, white pants, and an olive headband.

"Oh, h-hey," I stammered. "Morning, uh . . ."

"This is the baby." Summer, stepping in between us, nodded approvingly at the new adult. "All grown up."

"Whu?" I looked past the new hrrh-ing villager, searching for the playful little one. "So fast?"

"Goes with the rest of the rules"—Summer shrugged—"the short days, the rapid growth of plants and animals."

"Yeah, I guess that makes sense," I conceded, then, with a tinge of sadness, said, "Kinda miss the little version, ya know? Scampering around, talking to everyone, like we were all one family."

"It takes a village to raise a child," Summer said with no more weight than if she were noticing the weather.

This wasn't the Vesson, I know I've heard it before. But the fact that she reminded me of it started a chain of events that would rock my world.

"Well," I said, stepping to within hyper-range of the newly minted adult, "now that you're grown, let's see what you've got to trade."

Nothing. Not even an open hand.

"Just our luck." Summer huffed. "This one turned out just like its nitwit parent."

"Hey," I snapped, "that's not cool. You shouldn't prejudge anyone by who their parents are. Everyone's a blank slate." Yes, that's a Vesson, but not the big one. Trust me, it's coming.

"I'm not prejudging anyone," Summer batted back, "I'm just stating what I see, another lazy git who's not contributing, and expecting the rest of us to do all the work." A glance at the green-shirted villager wandering nearby. "Just like their parent."

"Yeah, but . . ." Summer was wrong, she had to be. "You can't just blame the nitwit, or the other parent, Farmer. Didn't you just say that the whole village raised this child? Aren't we all responsible for providing the basics? Food, shelter, education?"

The last word stuck.

Education.

Something was churning, bubbling in my mind like a potion in a brewing stand.

"That's the bleeding point!" Summer threw her arms up in frustration. "The whole village has been taking care of this child. But now the child is an adult." She turned to the full-grown resident. "And you've got to take care of yourself. And if you choose not to, well that's on you and nobody else."

It sounded harsh, but at the same time, logical. Something was missing, though, something I kept struggling with. "What if it's not a choice?" I queried. "What if . . . okay, Nitwit, until I can think of a nicer name, and our new friend here, would like to have a job but, for some reason, just can't."

"Orrr . . ." Summer dramatically drew out her R, "what if they just won't? How in this world can we tell the won'ts from the can'ts?"

Won'ts and can'ts . . . That was it!

"Won't and can't!" I blurted.

"What about them?"

"No time to explain!" I said, dashing back to the bunker. "Just gotta show you."

"What," Summer hallooed after me, "*are* you on about!?"

I couldn't talk, couldn't wait. I grabbed a stack of cobblestone and tossed another to Summer. "Here," I said, then ran back out to the village.

And as soon as we reached its outskirts, I slammed the first block down. "Here!"

"Wha . . ." Summer began.

"Just help me," I said, laying the foundation for another hut. "The faster we build, the faster you'll see."

Summer didn't argue. She must have figured it was easier to go along now and call me crazy later.

We threw up the crude walls, the ceiling, holes for windows, and finally a crafting table and a storage chest.

"How's this?" she asked, placing them next to each other against the far wall.

"Great," I said, "but move the chest one block over."

"Making room for a bed?" she asked.

I shook my head, and as she made a space in between the crafting table and the storage chest, I placed four planks of wood and two ingots of iron on the former.

"Ohhhh," sang Summer, as I placed a smithing table in the gap. "Now I see what you're up to."

"Let's just hope I'm right," I said, leading her back outside. The timing couldn't have been better. Morning meander was over. The villagers were all heading off to work—all except Nitwit, who kept to their carefree stroll.

But here came the new one, just like I hoped, right past us, into the hut, and over to the new workstation.

Green sparkles rose, and a black apron suddenly appeared over the maroon shirt.

"That's how you do it!" I crowed through my signature happy dance. "That is how you tell!"

This was it, the big Vesson I've been leading up to:

The way to tell those who won't work from those who can't work is to give everyone the opportunity!

It's a powerful word, opportunity. So powerful that I think the country I'm from is actually nicknamed "The Land of Opportunity." I don't know if that's always true. But at least, it should be. Everyone should have the opportunity, the choice, to improve themselves, just like this formerly unemployed villager.

And if that Vesson wasn't enough winning for one day, we still had the extra gravy of a new trading partner.

"Interesting," Summer hummed as the brand spanking new specialist offered a stone hoe for one emerald or one emerald for fifteen coal.

"Don't need the hoe," Summer said, strategizing, "but we now have plenty of coal."

Black lumps went in, green gems came out, and in a purple-bubbled blink . . .

"Now we're cookin' with gas," I rejoiced as our latest trader offered us a bell for thirty-five emeralds or an emerald for four iron ingots.

"Iron's not a problem," I said, and forked over enough of the rectangular, silver-colored metal to get us to . . . you guessed it, the next level!

And at that level, we both took a moment to gasp.

"That what I think it is?" Summer asked rhetorically. She wasn't talking about the emerald we'd get for twenty pieces of flint. It was the other trade, the one that asked for twenty emeralds for an iron shovel.

A *glowing* iron shovel!

"Enchanted!" I breathed. "We can buy an enchanted item!"

"More iron!" rasped Summer. "Sell more iron!" But the shop was closed, our newest specialist already refusing to buy more iron for the day.

(As a side note, I should point out that the traders were open to these sales again each day, but we wouldn't learn that till later, and it certainly wouldn't have helped us now.)

"Coal!" I scrambled for the chunks we had left.

Forty-five pieces for three emeralds. Just enough to afford that magical, mystical prize.

"Look!" It tingled in my hand, sending small shivers up my arm. "What do you think it can do?"

"Well, stop mucking about," Summer barked, "and start digging!"

"Oh, right." I tore into the earth between us. And *wow*, could this thing move! It was just like the pickaxe we found in the Nether. Even better! No wear and tear! Well, a little, but the amount of dirt I was digging should have been taking a more serious toll.

"Unbelievable," I gasped, examining the barely scratched blade, "efficiency and toughness!" Then, taking care to replace all the displaced earth, I looked up at the villager with a hearty, "Thanks, Smith."

"Smith?" asked Summer. "Where did that name come from?"

"That's the job, right?" I asked. "Blacksmith, or toolsmith, some kind of smith. More accurate and respectful than just 'buddy' or 'dude.'"

"Smith." Summer rolled the word around in her mouth, like a piece of hard candy with a yet to be determined flavor. "You know"—she looked around at the other villagers—"I think I know people back home with last names like Farmer and Weaver." She paused. "Miller, Baker, Smith," she said slowly before another pause. "Do you think that's where some people got their family names from? Because the family did those jobs, it became a way to identify them?"

"I think," I said, suppressing a laugh, "that we'll make an E-mop out of you yet."

Summer giggled and shoved my shoulder. Then, looking up at the setting sun, said, "We should be getting home. We've got a lot to do tomorrow; a lot of coal and iron to replace."

I held up the shimmering shovel. "Back to mining!"

CHAPTER 10

The next morning, packed and prepared, we headed back to "Monster Mouth Cave." Just like last time, the mobs came swarming, and, just like last time, we set up a defensive sniping position at the top of the slope. Summer did most of the sniping. I was running extremely low on arrows, a reminder that, sooner rather than later, I would have to make some really tough choices.

But that choice wasn't today, and some of those arrows would have to fly for a worthy cause. I took out a couple of skeleton archers before they could spoil Summer's aim. And once, as a creeper glided too close for comfort, I shot its sizzling, exploding form right into a duo of climbing zombies. The rest of the living dead died by my sword. Whoever had once said "Blades don't need reloading" couldn't have known how grateful I was for that truth.

After a few tense, hectic minutes, we'd dispatched enough of the attackers to go on the offensive ourselves. There were still plenty of mobs waiting, including the spiders, which might be docile in daylight, but only if that daylight is shining on them. Even before quaffing our night vision drafts, we could see their glowing eyes dotting the darkness. "I guess we gotta do it now," I said, "before dusk switches them on."

"Almost doesn't seem fair," commented Summer, as the low light brew revealed our target's position, "like shooting fish in a barrel."

"Why would you wanna do that?" I asked, feeling sorry for the proverbial fish.

Summer lined up on the first wall-bound arachnid. "Gotta have something to go with your chips."

Now that the path was clear, we moved on to mining coal, iron, and, with a little luck, crystals.

We found a little bit of the first two, but not much. Despite its size, we'd done a good job previously picking this cavern clean. And when we added up the ratio of coal to iron, I realized that there wasn't much of the latter to begin with.

"You think this world's new change swapped out some of the iron for copper?" I asked Summer. "Or maybe sunk it deeper with the redstone and lapis lazuli?"

"I think we're about to find out," she answered, standing at the back of the cave. I could see that she was looking down at something, but what? My night vision had faded, and as I reached for the extra bottle, she said, "Save the second. We're going to need it where we're going."

As she placed a torch between us, I finally saw what she was talking about. The floor didn't meet the wall, but opened into a long, horizontal crevice. It would have been easy to miss, especially if you didn't know what you were looking for. The crevice descended into a low-ceilinged slope that disappeared into subterranean midnight.

Neither of us had ever encountered this kind of formation. I didn't like it, specifically the way it made me feel. I hadn't been claustrophobic until this point. Not in the Nether, or in Summer's mountain, or in any of our underground adventures. And that includes the first night on my island, buried alive with a zombie one dirt block away. It hadn't freaked me out then, but now, something about the wideness of the slope with a mirror image roof right above me . . . it almost felt like they were closing in, like any second, it could all come down with a me-splattering "THUD."

For the sake of my own ego, I'm going to believe that I could have just fought through this awful feeling. But the good news was I didn't have to. After a few unnerving minutes of climb-hopping through planted torches, Summer stopped with a sudden, "Now that's odd."

The crevice ended at a solid wall of graystone with a strange, solid black square in the middle.

"That's not obsidian," I said, getting closer to observe it in the torchlight. "Not dark enough."

Summer peered closer, nearly touching the surface with her flat face. "We've seen it before. I just can't place where."

"Basalt!" I exclaimed. "Remember? When the Nether changed, there was this whole, sub-biome of the stuff."

Summer nodded. "But what the Nether is it doing here?"

I reached for my magic pick. "Let's give it a closer look."

Knocking it out revealed more black blocks, and beyond them, the first white one.

"Another first," I commented as the pale cube fell into my hands. It wasn't diorite, or nether quartz, or the blocks of solid bone that made up those giant nether skeletons. This was slightly mottled, a rippling pattern of white and ultra-light gray, and as the torchlight hit it a certain way, the reflection looked crystalline.

"Can't be amethyst," clucked Summer. "Wrong color."

She was right about that, because while I might not have been a gemologist back home, I at least knew that the crystals we were looking for were . . .

Purple!

Right in front of me! The next block behind the white! Purple and translucent with a luster that rivaled diamonds!

"Bing-bang-boom!" I shouted through ecstatic pick swings. "Crystal city!" Lavender blocks flew into my pack, along with a bonanza of fantasy scenarios my mind had started to spin. "Who knows what else we can make out of this stuff," I called back to Summer, "on their own, or combined with other materials . . . isn't there, like, a whole superhero franchise where a guy throws a crystal into the ocean and . . ."

I stopped at the next pick. Open air. Pure darkness. And when I planted a torch through the hole . . .

"Holy . . ."

"Don't tell me," Summer snarked sarcastically, "you've found your crystal fortress."

"Ummm . . ." I picked out a hole big enough to slip through. ". . . maybe?"

A second later, we were standing in a small cave, roundish in layout, with every surface made of amethyst! And not just the blocks. Crystal shards, about the size of our shins, sprouted sporadically on the flat surfaces. And they sang! No, I'm not making this up. Walking across the glimmering floor produced a tinkling music!

"If I were a superhero," I said, spreading my arms, "this would definitely be my HQ."

"It is impressive," Summer admitted, "like a larger version of those . . ." She searched for the word in her memory. "Those round, unimpressive stones you break open to reveal a crystal center. Geodes, that's it. We're standing in a giant geode."

"And the changes just keep coming," I said, feeling like a kid in a toy store. "Copper, drippy-stone, now this!" I looked around excitedly, planting more torches in case I'd missed something. "There's gotta be more coolness. Maybe new minerals to work with. What are airplanes made out of? Aluminum? Is aluminum natural?"

"First off," said Summer, punching up a shard of dark crystal, "they're pronounced aeroplanes and aluminium, and second"— still gathering shards—"let's just take what we have, craft what we can craft, celebrate our success, then come back down here later for another go."

"Why wait for later?" I asked with open arms. "Why not make this our forward base right now?" Before she could answer, I barreled on, "We're gonna keep digging, right? And who knows what's waiting for us down there?" My eyes fell to the sparkling, purple floor. "Why not make this place livable, a place to retreat to, rest up, and, before we go any farther, make a . . ." I set down a crafting table, then, holding up an amethyst shard, crowed, "spyglass!"

"You do realize," Summer said flatly, "that in all the time you've spent yapping, you could have already made one."

"Well . . ." I started to say, but realized that no matter how burning my comeback could have been, it was still burning up craft time. So I swallowed the zinger, set up a furnace, then filled it with the coal and copper we'd collected on the way down. A few seconds later, the shiny orange ingots popped into my hands, and a second after that, they were laid on the crafting table below a single crystal shard.

"Bing-bang-boom." I nodded, brandishing the new invention. A real-life spyglass, complete with the zipping sound when you extended its range. "Whoa-ho-ho," I laughed as Summer's face filled the eyehole. "Check it out!"

Summer took the spyglass and, instead of pointing it at me, aimed back up through the tunnel we'd just come through. "Well and truly brill." She lowered the spyglass, but, with a deflated tone, added, "Too bad we won't need it down here."

"Are you nuts?" I scoffed. "With all the monster caves?" I started picking at the opposite wall. "There's gotta be more here! Just like Monster Mouth up top! And soon as we find one . . ."

My pick broke into empty air.

"Ha! See?"

She did see, walking next to me and raising the spyglass to the gap. "I would," she teased, handing it back to me, "if only this monocular had a low-light setting."

I could "see," literally and figuratively, what she meant. This new cavern I'd hit was pitch black. We couldn't see anything—no walls, no floor, not even another block for me to plant a torch on.

Summer huffed, surrendering to her own curiosity. "At this rate, we're likely to dig all the way through to the other side of this world."

"I wonder if you can do that," I pondered, as we both stared into the abyss. After a few minutes of silence, I finally said, "We'll probably have to backtrack, find a spot closer to where we came in, and dig a staircase down the side wall."

"Or." Summer produced her full pail.

"Another watervator?" I whined, knowing the answer.

"Water 'lift,'" she said, pouring the blue cube.

"Okay," I relented. "Let's at least drink our night vision . . ."

But she was already gone, riding the blue column into the black unknown.

I think I said something witty and original like "I'm going to regret this" before plunging in after her.

Holding my breath. Unable to see. This time, the walls were too far to place torches. I did try, though, looking all around with my torch-gripping hyper-reach. No luck. We were truly in a void. How long could I hold my breath? How long before I'd have to jump? And would the water below us break my fall? Were we too high? How high were we?

I looked down, hoping to see the bottom but expecting to only see more nothing, and instead saw . . . a squid? No. Not down here. And aren't squids grayish black? How could this one . . . these two . . . look so bright and shiny?

This has to be an optical illusion, I thought, *a trick of the water or . . .*

The arrow caught me in the left hip, knocking me out of the column.

Falling.

Blind.

SPLASH!

Underwater again, this time in a giant lake! And face to sharp-toothed face with a glowing squid.

"Whblrblr!" I burbled and shot for the surface. Whether this new species was as harmless as their surface cousins, or, like cave spiders, they packed a poisonous punch, I wasn't sticking around long enough to find out. I splashed up into open air, took a deep breath, and tried to find Summer.

WHP!

Another arrow struck the water next to me. A high angle, as if the archer was above me on a cliff.

Dive! Evade!

I ducked back underwater, squinted in the bluish haze to find the outline of land. There it was! Too far for one breath? I had to try. I swam hard for the beach, but made the mistake of swimming in a straight line.

Another arrow, slamming into my back, pushing me deeper, knocking the literal wind from me.

Dodge, zig, but just as I zagged away from a near miss, I felt the last of my air pop away.

Up! Breathe! I broke the surface, tried to inhale, but ended up OOOF-ing as another arrow hit the back of my head.

Down again, straight on. No spare air for dodging.

Another shot, in my shoulder. Stinging wounds, burning lungs.

The bottom! My feet touched cold, hard stone. Up and up, climbing the underwater slope. I popped into darkness again, breathed deeply, then heard, "Keep going!" behind me. Summer! When had she jumped in? I didn't ask. I thrashed up onto the bank, planted a torch, and saw that we were on a narrow strip of land hemmed in by sheer rock walls. I also saw that we weren't being shot at anymore, and voicing my thoughts, Summer said, "Blighter must be out of range, probably on the other side of the lake."

"Can skeletons swim?" I asked, trying to remember.

"Before we go looking"—I caught the glint of a potion in her hand—"let's finally recharge our night eyes."

I reached for my own potion, downing the fizzy, metal-and-carrot-tasting brew in a nose-burping gulp, and blinked as all was revealed.

"Wha-hoy . . ." It wasn't as big as the Nether, but it totally dwarfed Monster Mouth Cave. Beyond the lake was a cavern that went on and on, and just beyond the lake, we could see a humongous pillar holding up the roof—not like it needed any support, since the physics of my world rarely ever applied here. And as I raised the spyglass for a closer look, I could see that on that pillar was a skeleton . . . riding on a spider!

So THAT's why all its shots seemed wrong.

"Well, it's not the first time I've seen that horrid pairing," said Summer, no doubt wishing she could stroke her chin, "but definitely a new one in these circumstances."

"What can we do?" I asked her. "Swimming and shooting's out, and it'd take forever to try tunneling around . . ."

"What about a proper naval battle?" Summer threw down her crafting table. "I think my people were rather good at that." She whipped up a boat, placed it in the water, and turned to me with an impatient gesture toward the watercraft. "Well, come on then, our night vision's not going to last all day."

Crafting my own skiff, I could hear her humming a tune, "Some-thing something," she sang, trying to remember the words, "and something 'bout the waves . . ."

On "waves," I had my boat in the water. "New song?" I asked. "Like the one we used for my first ghast?"

"Super," she agreed, and set off to draw their fire. Just like when engaging the ghast, she sang "Run Rabbit" while I took careful aim. I won't brag—well, maybe just a little. So what if it was easier than hitting a moving ghast, and so what if my solid crossbow steadied my hand more than a straining bow. It was still a heck of a shot.

I squeezed the trigger, watched the skeleton fall out of its saddle, then paddled furiously over to where it had landed in the lake. Switching from crossbow to sword, I hacked it to bits faster than you can say, "Wow, dude, you're a really awesome skeleton slayer." Which you're totally saying, right?

"You're next!" I called up to the spider, paddling over to its pillar.

"Guy!" called Summer from behind me, her voice ringing with alarm.

"No problemo," I shouted back. "I'll just wait for it to come to me. Or, if you wanna take the shot . . ."

"No!" she cried, then said another word that sent my stomach right up into my mouth. "Waterfall!"

I looked down to the opposite bank and saw that it wasn't there! The lake didn't end at more land. It just ended!

I tried to stop, spin, paddle away!

Too late!

Over the side!

Eyes shut, bracing for impact!

"Aaaaaaaaahhhhhhhhhh!"

Then . . .

"Aaaahhh?"

I looked down, around, and realized that I wasn't falling. Don't get me wrong, I was still going down, but at the same slow pace of a Summer-built watervator.

And speaking of Summer . . .

"Guy!" her urgent, clipped voice called from the lake above. "Guy! Answer me!"

"I'm fine," I said with a laugh. "C'mon down."

The boat descended gently, across slowly dissipating water, then, to my surprise, across the stone floor.

"Well, will ya look at that," I called up to Summer. "You can paddle across the ground. Who knew?"

"Gaaaaahhhhh," came an answer from someone who was clearly not amused.

I should have seen them: spiders, skeletons, creepers, zombies, and one of those fast little baby zombies . . . riding on a chicken? If I hadn't been so distracted with the waterfall and the boat, I might have had time to do anything except what I did do. Which was, of course, freak out.

"Go back up!" I shouted to Summer. "Go back!" I was so frazzled, I actually tried to paddle across the floor and up the waterfall. An arrow whizzed past my ear, close enough to switch my brain on.

Panic drowns thought.

Out of the boat, cocking my crossbow, I turned to face the closest threat. The little zomblet was almost on me. My shot knocked it from its feathered mount. "Get outta here!" I yelled to what I assumed was an innocent hen, then cocked my crossbow for a second shot at its rider.

But before I could pull the trigger, another arrow, from above and behind me, sealed the chicken's fate.

"Summer!" She was riding the waterfall, and somehow had discovered that she could not only stick her head out to breathe, but also her bow to shoot. Arrows rained down from my guardian angel, knocking back the nearest mobs and buying precious time to strategize.

"We can't go back up!" Summer called down. "The boneys'll snipe us before we get halfway."

And no spiny slopes like Monster Mouth Cave, I thought, surveying the terrain in front of us and to the sides. But behind . . . I turned, peering through the water curtain and saw that it ran back into another, deeper cave.

"That way!" I yelled and sloshed a hasty retreat. Summer was right behind me, jumping out of the column to land safely in minicube-thick water.

We splashed, slid, then ran down a slowly descending tunnel. For a moment, I thought there was something screwy with my night vision. The stone around us seemed darker and slightly reminiscent of basalt. I figured my potion might be running out, but when Summer suggested blocking up the tunnel behind us, I knew this was a completely different material. It was definitely darker than the cobblestone we used to block the mobs. And when I tried picking out a cube from the floor, it took more effort.

"Blackrock?" I wondered. "Like that stuff we found in the Nether to make tools and a furnace?"

"Close"—Summer shook her head—"but not quite." Later, in the library, we'd discover that it was called "deepslate," but the name wasn't important right now. What concerned us was that we were now deep enough to encounter an entirely new world.

"I don't like it," I said as I wheeled in a slow circle. "Too dark. When our night vision goes, it won't reflect as much torchlight as gray stone."

"Well, let's not waste any more time then," quipped Summer. "Onward and . . . well . . . downward."

We didn't get very far. Barely a minute or so down the deepslate tunnel and our low-light vision began blinking. "Note to self," I said, reaching for a torch, "next time don't skimp on the night-sight juice." Before either of us could fix a fire stick to the wall, we both noticed a faint light ahead.

"Has to be lava," said Summer. "Too deep for anything else."

"Except a mineshaft," I suggested. "If it was molten rock, wouldn't we be feeling the heat?"

She didn't answer, a sure sign I was right.

A few more steps brought us to a turn in the tunnel, which

narrowed, straightened, and leveled off. We could see a torch, though, clear as day. And despite being a little ways away, there was no mistaking the posts and planks of a mineshaft entrance.

"Called it," I said, humming jauntily as I pushed past my partner.

Swaggering under the torchlit crossbeam, I abruptly stopped as the wooden path faded into yet another wide expanse.

I could barely discern the outlines of wooden bridges, criss-crossing one another like they'd done under my island. This time, though, they were surrounded by light-absorbing deep-slate.

"You see that?" Summer asked my back.

"Yeah." I nodded to a couple lanterns up ahead. "They got 'em on chains just like that ruined Nether keep."

Summer huffed, impatient. "No, not that." She stepped in front of me to point down. "Up ahead and a little off to the right."

I squinted hard at what looked like a large, whitish rectangle. "Can't make it out." But after raising the spyglass, the problem wasn't my eyes, but my brain. I knew what a cave spider lair looked like. I'd almost been killed by one, but that web-a-tarium had been encased in a hallway, not out on an open bridge.

"Gotta be a spawner in there," I said with a shiver. "We better stay well clear of it."

"I was thinking the opposite," Summer said cheerily.

"Are you mad?" I asked, copying her accent.

"Not at all," Summer said with a giggle. "If spider silk can make the same white wool that Weaver is willing to pay for, then we've just found a veritable 'jackpot,' as you call it."

"Yeeahhh," I responded with skeptical slowness.

"You're not scared," asked Summer, "are you?"

"Wha-me-no!" Of course I was, but that wasn't the reason for my reticence. "It doesn't seem worth the price. I mean, chopping up webs'll wear down our diamond swords. I should know. And since we haven't found any diamonds yet—"

"What about iron?" And on the last word, Summer scooted past me toward something embedded in the tunnel wall. And what a something it was. Not just the regular-flecked stones, but also a whole square of raw orange ore.

"I do believe"—Summer held for dramatic effect before spinning back toward me—"that this qualifies as a worthwhile investment."

"So it seems." I shrugged, pickaxing out the prize while she set down her crafting table and furnace. I still didn't like the idea, but it was hard to argue with her logic.

"Just two ingots for a blade," she began, throwing in a couple nodules, "plus the wood for fuel, which we get right here from the mineshaft supports—which, by the by, also gives the sword a handle. A bare pittance for all the profit we'll reap from the webs."

I tried to say something, fumbling for a term that was just beyond my conscious thoughts.

Summer must have sensed my doubt, because she plowed ahead quickly. "And don't worry about wearing down your beautiful pickaxe. We won't be picking our way down." She held up her empty pail. "Another waterlift will do just fine." The empty pail pointed farther down the tunnel. "And if I'm not mistaken, that's the sound of a running spring."

I heard it, too. Somewhere in the nearby darkness was a source of water.

"Shall we?" Summer headed for the gurgling sound.

Think, my brain whirled, *what is that term? What does it have to do with what you're getting yourself into?*

Summer was a little bit ahead of me, planting a torch where the tunnel descended into a short staircase. "What's this then?"

She wasn't reacting to the water that gushed from a hole in the wall. It was what was in the water that made both of us blink our square eyes twice.

A creature. Small, pinkish, with four legs and a tail. It was swimming, or wading, up and down the liquid blue carpet, and, at least for the moment, didn't seem to notice us at all.

"Is that a crabupine?" I wondered, and off her look added, "My nickname for silverfishes."

"Oh"—Summer nodded—"those nasty little nippers who live in stone."

I pointed to the varmint. "Is this a new, amphibious version? An aquapine?"

"If it is," Summer mused, "then it doesn't seem hostile."

"Until you take its water away."

"Right."

Summer moved cautiously, lifting her bucket to the spring's source. I raised my sword. We thought we were ready for anything.

We were wrong.

"What in the Nether . . ." Summer blurted, turning to show me that she'd not only captured the liquid, but the creature as well! "It just swam up at the very moment I was—"

"Pour it out!" I yipped, nervous to have a potentially danger-ous life form in my friend's hands. "Let's try again."

"No . . ." Summer's tone had that hint of mischievous initia-tive. "If this beastie is as nasty as its rock-born cousin, we could pour it down on the cave spiders to do our work for us."

"That's not cool," I moaned, "setting them against each other."

"It happens naturally, you know." Summer was already head-ing back up the stairs. "Like when skeletons shoot at each other."

"Yeah, but you're not causing that," I protested, "and if it isn't dangerous, you're putting it in dange—"

"Ssssp!"

It all happened so fast. Summer, a step ahead of me, came face-to-face with the small greenish arachnid.

Another hiss, a bite, and my poisoned friend staggered back beside me.

"I got this," I said, drawing my sword with a flashing swipe.

Sharp diamond connected with ruby eyes. The spider rasped, jumped back, then skittered forward for another attack. "Not today!" I spat, slashing it to a smoky end.

No time to gloat. *Seal the entrance!* If the spider had found a way up from its spawner, others would surely follow. I rushed to the edge of the bridge, placing cobblestone as fast as I could. "You okay, buddy?" I called, and got back an exasperated, "For-got to bring the infernal cow's milk!"

"Just eat something," I said, turning back to help her, "any-thing."

"Already on it," she answered, wobbling up the steps to meet me. The poison bubbles had stopped, but it would be a moment before her bread loaves sealed the wound.

"Hidden costs!" I cried, suddenly remembering the term I'd been searching for. "That's what we didn't consider!"

Not exactly a Vesson. More about managing your money than living in a village, but a lesson learned is still valuable When making an investment, always consider the hidden costs!

"Going after those webs wouldn't just cost us a couple of iron ingots," I pontificated, ignoring Summer's groan. "We'd need, like, a pond of cow's milk for spider poison, and food just to be safe, and arrows, which I can't replace, and time, a whole lotta time, which could be better spent harvesting safer wool from the sheep."

"Thank you, Professor." Summer sighed, looking slowly around the dark mineshaft. "And unless you've scheduled another lecture from the University of Guy, it might be prudent to head back to the village with what we already have."

"Fine with me," I said, a little miffed at her mocking, "but we better figure out a solid plan for getting home." I glanced at the blocked tunnel, imagining all that lay between us and the village. "There's this mineshaft, and above that is the other cavern, and above that is the underground lake, and above that . . ."

"There you go again,"—Summer chuckled—"always overthinking when there's a simple solution right here."

"Oh, really." I raised my arms, gesturing theatrically all around us. "And where would that 'simple solution' happen to be?"

Summer didn't say anything, but raised her fist to the roof.

"Oh, yeah." I lowered my arms and said slowly, "We can just tunnel out another way."

That had never been an option before, either under my island or in the Nether. This was the first time the ground above us was just regular ground. Not that there couldn't be lava pockets, like in the Nether, or water, like the underground lake, but at least it was worth a try.

"Let's get going," I announced and swung my pickaxe against the wall.

CHAPTER 11

We didn't strike lava or water. Our only real challenge was te-dium. Up and up, me in front, planting torches, then picking out a few blocks, with Summer as rear guard and torch collec-tor. On the way we hit a few mineral pockets, mostly coal and copper, with a little iron and redstone. We were pretty bored by the time we'd bored all the way to the surface.

But breaking out of that last layer of dirt and into the clear, bright sunlight, we got a pleasant surprise. The village! Right in front of us. "Must have gotten turned around," I said as Summer climbed out next to me, "which means we should probably carry a map, and maybe a clock so we don't actually break up into mob-filled night. Right, Summer? Summer?"

She was off, prancing toward the villagers with an excited "Let's go shopping!" She was holding out the water bucket, see-ing if anybody wanted to buy that weird lizard thing we'd found.

Nobody did. Not even the trader, who was, thankfully, still hanging around (you'll see why I said "thankfully" in a second).

"No takers?" Summer snorted. "Not one of you?"

"Not a shock," I chided, "given that we already knew all their buy and sell lists."

"Yes, but"—Summer gave a flustered huff—"what's the flipping point of this world letting us capture this oddity if we can't do anything with it?"

"Maybe we can't now," I consoled, "but how often have we both found something that became useful later?"

Summer huffed again, this time with acceptance. "Right then," she said to the creature in the pail, "I guess you're stuck with us for a bit longer. But you're not taking up this valuable tool." She walked over to the little pond and dumped it in with a curt "Off you go."

Okay, back up a few pages. Remember the pair of brown fish I'd bought earlier? Well, they were still there, swimming peacefully in the pond.

Until . . .

Both of us let out a shocked "Oh" for very different reasons as the cave lizard attacked the fish with the speed and lethality of a guided torpedo. I was horrified, while Summer was jazzed.

"She's a predator," my huntress friend breathed, then scooped up the floating corpses. For a moment she just looked at them, mental wheels grinding loudly enough for me to hear.

"Summer?" I said suspiciously. "What are you thinking?"

Her answer was, "Won't be a moment," before darting into the library, then bursting out a minute later with the wildlife book. "It's called an 'axolotl,'" she said, flat nose buried in the pages, "and they prey on live fish."

"Like wolves on sheep," I said, wincing at a bloody memory of that exact scenario happening in the woods near Summer's mountain.

"Precisely!" Summer slammed the book shut, then ran to the river.

"Again," I asked, "what do you have up your painted-on sleeve?"

"I'll tell you when I'm sure," she said, rushing back to the pond. I didn't move, didn't follow her, didn't ask any further questions. Even when she cried, "Yes . . . yes, it might just work!" I did move a little closer when I heard her say to the axolotl in the most tender, caring voice I'd ever heard her use with animals, "Thank you for letting us find you, little Ax, because I've got a business partnership that I think you'll positively adore."

That partnership became part of our . . . wait for it: routine! If you read the first two books, you knew that this part had to happen sometime. And if you haven't, don't sweat it. Just picture a montage, the part in a movie where things that should take a really long time whiz by in a few moments. You can even add your own personal soundtrack.

Picture me and Summer advancing Fisher with sold coal, then bumping up Smith with sold iron, then taking the combined emeralds from both interactions to grow Weaver's experience as a salesman by buying beds for our hotel. That's what we called it, although I guess the term's not technically accurate. A hotel is something you visit temporarily, while we intended this to be a permanent residence. What is the correct term? Dorm? Bunkhouse? Whatever. We were proud of it. Two floors with plenty of fencepost windows for breeze and the floors, door, and slanted roof made from that local wood the library book calls acacia. Its rust color makes a nice contrast with the gray cobblestone. And when we added multicolored beds and some paintings for decoration, it couldn't have been more ready for the coming baby boom.

That took a little more time—which is why you need a montage. In order to grow our population, we needed to grow more food. We cleared a patch of land well away from the village, and planted several rows of wheat and carrots. And while torches and water rows helped to speed up the harvest, the real star performer was the compost bin. Throw in some organic stuff, like saplings or seeds, and bing-bang-boom: you get bone meal!

Picture how fast our crops grew with that boost, especially when you add in the bone meal from slain skeletons and a few extra pinches from Summer's "fish farm." Yes, she started a fish farm; that was the business partnership she'd pitched to our new friend, Ax.

She pinpointed the exact spot in the river where fresh schools of salmon spawned, then dammed both ends and walled off the land on every side. After dumping in the snapping killer, all she had to do was watch as it slaughtered the whole school, then collect the carcasses to sell to Fisher.

I have to admit, the project was both efficient and profitable. And, yeah, sharing in those profits did make me compromise my ideals a little. What I wouldn't compromise, though, no matter what, was killing cows to make a book. But you'll see how that turns out soon enough.

For now, just continue this montage by picturing our harvested crops helping Farmer to grow, which allowed us to buy the "birthday" cake, to celebrate all the new babies. And there were so many! At one point there was a whole gang of little rascals running around the village. They were so cute, hrrh-ing at all the grownups, darting in and out of houses, and playfully jumping on the beds. Not a bad life, to be a kid. Who doesn't want to play all day without a care in the world? The catch was that they wouldn't stay kids forever, and, like it or not, those cares would come looking for them soon enough.

That's why Summer and I worked as fast as we could to provide job opportunities for their future. Like with Smith, we crafted small, one-room sheds and stocked each one with a workbench. "One more cool thing about this world," I said to Summer as we were setting down one of those bow-and-arrow tables in the final shed, "no school." I looked out at the children scampering from house to house. "When you're a kid, you just get to be a kid, then BAM"—I glanced back at the workstation— "instant job training."

"If they want it." Summer's tone was lukewarm. "There's no guarantee we haven't helped raise a whole generation of nitwits."

"Maybe one or two," I allowed, "but I gotta believe that most of them want to contribute to the community."

"We shall see," Summer sniped.

And we did.

As soon as the first little one grew up, it wandered over into

the shed where we'd placed the map table, and came out wearing a gold-rimmed lens over one eye. "What did I tell you?" I
prodded Summer as the new merchant offered to buy twenty-
four sheets of paper for an emerald or seven emeralds for a blank
map. "This one wants to be a mapmaker . . . or cartography-ist.
That's the word, right?" Summer shrugged through her own
trading. We still hadn't found a book on what exact jobs were
out there, but we figured we'd find out soon enough.

The next couple of weeks were like a job fair, with unemployed adults snapping up new careers. The blast furnace (what
I'd originally thought was just a souped-up version of the original) gave us someone who sold armor. Nothing exciting at
first—and if you ask me, a little overpriced. I mean, seven emeralds for a pair of steel pants, and nine for a chest plate? That's
highway robbery. But at least buying them would eventually
give us more merchandise.

We mistook the next workbench for another toolsmith. The
reason was we could buy an iron axe and sell coal for emeralds.
"Maybe this one's not as skilled," Summer suggested, pointing
to the patch over one eye. "Bit of a numpty, don't you think?"

I hummed skeptically. "Maybe it's not a tool, but a weapon."

"You think Numpty here is a weaponsmith?" she asked.

"Why not?" I fired back. "I killed my first spider with an axe,
and the Nether piggies down below are practically married to
them."

It was an intriguing idea, and one that really got the mental
juices flowing. "Maybe"—I paced as my brain swam through
swirling thoughts—"maybe all weapons started out as tools. You
know, like, way back in our species' beginning. You're workin'

on your farm, cutting down a tree with your trusty axe, and then here comes a wild animal or some bad guys. You have to defend yourself, and you can't afford to own both an axe and a sword, so . . ."

"I suppose we'll prove or disprove that theory as they advance," said Summer.

I didn't need proof to be proud of myself. But it was nothing compared to the new Vesson a day later. I was heading into town, passing by the shed with the circular saw, when a villager in a black apron came out to greet me. "Morning," I said, and got a hrrh-ing offer of either ten clay balls for an emerald or an emerald for ten bricks. "So you're a . . . brickmaker," I declared, not knowing yet that the correct term was mason (Summer filled me in later). "Sorry, I don't need any bricks right now, and I don't have any clay to sell you. Unlike my island's lagoon, it's pretty scarce around—"

I stopped, feeling the signs of an oncoming realization. "But you don't need any to make bricks, do you? You got the finished product right here! And as much as I can pay for." I shook my head at another strange fact of this world. *Just because the rules don't make sense to me doesn't mean they don't make sense.*

"I don't know how you do it. I don't know how any of you make your goods out of thin air. But it really gets me thinking about my own world's transportation: raw materials, finished goods, raw materials to be turned into finished goods. It's pretty amazing when you step back and look at the whole picture. Houses built from bricks that might have been made hundreds, thousands of miles away, and the clay to make those bricks might come from another thousand miles away. And not just bricks.

MAX BROOKS

Everything. Stuff moving all around the world, allowing everyone to live anywhere and not miss out on anything."

"Hrrh," interrupted the mason, to which I answered, "Yeah,
you're right, not everyone. You still gotta pay for it all, and I'm
betting a whole lotta people can't afford fancy stuff from all
around the world. But it does make me think about what I already learned about money, and specialization. I think . . . I'm
pretty sure that this web or network . . . all these boats, planes,
trucks bringing stuff all around the world lets people become
even more specialized. Because if they need something really
specific to help them with whatever their specialized job is, they
might be able to order it from anywhere on the planet. And the
more that trade network advances, the more we're able to advance our specialized skills."

My head was swimming, my mind dizzy with the discovery. I
tried to imagine our small blue and green planet, seeming
smaller and smaller as people became more and more connected. And although I tried, I still couldn't imagine what my
house back home looked like—but I bet there wasn't one thing
in it that was made, from start to finish, with just local resources.
"Amazing," I breathed, looking down at my iron shoes. But
when I looked up, Mason had ambled away. "Yeah, I know," I
called after them. "It just makes you wanna go off by yourself
and really chew on this for a while."

I, of course, couldn't restrict myself to contemplative isola-
tion. This was just too important to keep in.

"Summer!" I called, running down to the riverbank. "You
gotta hear this!"

"Funny thing," Summer interrupted. "I found Ax today,

swimming about in the village fishpond." She glanced out at her amphibious pet. "I reckoned she might be a bit of a land walker," she continued with a head nod to the stone perimeter around the fish farm, "which is why I raised the whole enclosure a block higher than the waterline." She gave another pensive stare toward Ax after inspecting the enclosure. "How did she do it?"

"Yeah yeah yeah,"—I nodded excitedly—"very interesting, but, seriously, you gotta hear this!" As I related my revelation, she just nodded politely, mm-ing with each detail, while keeping her eyes on the water. It was "fishing time," that part of the day when the salmon spawned and Ax got axing. I tried to ignore the carnage, the quick darting at the fleeing fish as Summer waded in to scoop them up. Fortunately my sermon wrapped up just as she climbed back onto the bank. "So what do you think?" I asked, wishing this square body could bend for a bow.

"Rather interesting," she said, walking over to a riverside workstation I hadn't noticed before. It was a cool setup, a crafting table, furnace, and storage chest trio set against another trio of apple oaks. "I like the idea of everything knitted together," she said, slipping one salmon in the furnace, "but what happens when the strings are cut?"

"Huh?" was all my brilliant brain could manage.

"When the network fails," Summer pressed, sliding a lump of coal under the salmon. "What happens when all these marvelous trade routes are cut for some reason and we're all suddenly left on our own?"

"Oh." I hadn't thought of that. "Well . . ."

C'mon, genius, think!

". . . we'll just have to go back to making stuff ourselves."

"Really?" she challenged, as the smell of cooking salmon wafted past us. "All of it?"

"Wha . . . n-no . . ." I stuttered, "that's impossible, but, like, maybe we could at least handle the basics. I mean . . . I'm not saying we need to know how to build a car from scratch, but maybe . . . know how to take care of it, like all our other things, and our own bodies, like, first aid. Basic stuff, you know, until the network can come back. And maybe in addition to having those skills, we should have some emergency supplies as well, like food and medicine and . . . well . . . we might not poop here, but when we finally find our way home, a top priority'll be toilet paper."

"Charming," commented Summer, then reached for the furnace. "Fancy a spot of lunch?"

I recoiled at the cooked fish. "You're not saying . . ."

"Guy!" Summer snapped, exasperated, then reached into the chest for an apple. "An added bonus of the oaks I grow for tool wood."

"Right," I said, crunching down the delicious fruit. "Sorry." And as my stomach digested a clone of the first food I'd ever had in this world, my mind digested a new Vesson:

It's great to depend on others, but always be ready to depend on yourself.

The next morning, we witnessed more job creation, and this one could not have been more of a surprise. Instead of going to the village, the village came to us. We were still in our bunker, prepping for a mining mission, when suddenly our door flew open and an unemployed villager sauntered in. "Hey, g'morning," I said happily while my partner barked a terse, "Oi! Can't you knock?"

"You know they can't," I said protectively. "And you also know this is just their morning constitutional."

"I know," Summer acquiesced, "I just don't like being surprised is all . . ." She peered out the doorway and down the hill. "Must be our hotel, extending their meandering range." She looked at the doorway. "If we replaced it with iron, and carried buttons in our belts, it'd be the closest thing to a lock and key."

"Keep yer painted shirt on," I said impatiently, then chuckled at the image. "Nothing's gonna get broken or stolen, and it's not like we don't violate their personal space every day."

Summer gave a huffing nod, then turned to the villager. "Go on then, have a gander." Her rectangular arm swept out toward the square room. "But don't even think of jumping on my bed."

The villager didn't jump—obviously grownups don't do that—and there wasn't even any gandering. Instead, our hrrhing neighbor went right over the brewing stand, looked at it for a couple seconds, then . . . PLING . . . green sparkles rose from its new purple robe!

"Whaaa?" I gasped.

"The brewing stand made them a brewer or chemist," clucked Summer. "We never figured on it being a career choice."

"But if they're a chemist, where are the chemicals?" I asked, looking to see what trades were on offer.

One emerald got us two pinches of redstone, and thirty-two scraps of zombie flesh got us an emerald. "Well, that's a letdown," I said glumly. "Not like I was expecting, oh, I don't know, magic potions."

"Keep in mind," said Summer as she opened one of our storage chests, "this is only the beginning." Out came sixty-four scraps of stinking meat. "Never thought I'd be grateful for these trophies." A few trades and growth bubbles later, Chemist offered to buy gold and sell lapis lazuli. We'd brought plenty of the former with us, both from my island and Summer's mountain, and, until now, we'd only needed a smidgen of it for various potions. How crazy that it took all this time to trade what would have been commodity number one in our world! The yellow metal transformed into green gems. Nearly enough for another level bump. "Let's buy a lapis," I suggested, "just to shake things up."

One emerald in, one hunk of blue rock out, and PLING . . .

Four rabbit feet got us one emerald, which prompted a self-critical "No time to hunt," from Summer and a "Speaking of hunting" from me. I was looking at the next trade we were being offered, and the material we'd spent months hunting for.

Glowstone. It had been the whole reason for our Nether adventures, nearly killing us and our friendship. And now here it was, as much as we could afford.

"Oh, good lord!" Summer laughed. "Where under earth were you a few months ago!"

"Well, look on the bright side," I guffawed, "literally! Now we can ditch these torches for some high-end redstone lamps."

"Why stop there?" Summer gestured to our cramped, featureless burrow. "Since we're going to be here for a bit, why not build ourselves a proper house, or, given our new urban setting, a building where each of us can have our own flat?"

"Flat what?" I asked.

Summer paused, glaring at me hard. "You winding me up?"

"Like an old-timey watch," I replied, and got that wonderful

Summer laugh. "Apartment building it is," I announced, "and if you don't mind really shaking things up"—I opened another storage chest—"how about we use all this deepslate? We've got so much of it, and if my pickaxe is telling the truth, it's just a tad stronger than cobblestone."

"But isn't it a bit dark and sinister?" Summer countered. "Like living in a Nether fortress?"

"You won't notice," I promised, "between the decorations, the windows, floors . . . you'll love it, trust me."

Summer shrugged. "If you say so, Mister Slate."

"Mister Slate," I repeated, my mind suddenly triggered by a memory. "That name."

"What about it?" asked Summer.

"Him," I said through a mental mist. "He is, or was, a great leader from our world. I can't place it . . ." I exhaled hard, blowing away the memory. "Doesn't matter. What matters is that it reminded me not to forget our mission." I looked around at everything: the bunker, the villager heading away, and the village they were heading to. "We'll build our new apartment building, build up the village, learn everything we can, but never forget that the ultimate goal is to find a way home."

To my great relief, Summer responded, "Well, let's stop dilly-dallying," and, reaching for a stack of stored black rock, she declared, "Onward and upward, Mister Slate."

Back to the montage! Picture Slate House, our block of flats on the top of the hill, twelve-by-twelve and four stories high. The ground floor was only for storage, with nothing but rows of chests, and I'm not stretching the truth when I say that we found a use for all of them!

The next floor was for work, all the appliances from our bunker, and then a few copied from the village like the cartography table and blast furnace and a new brewing stand for Chemist down in the village. This floor was, for the moment, the only one we could afford to light with redstone lamps. The next two floors had to settle for old-fashioned torches.

Those were our personal apartments, which each had a bed, chest, and some personal decorations like pictures and shelf-mounted potted flowers. Not that we had a lot of room for those because three of the four walls were solid glass windows (and two trapdoor windows on either side for breeze). The view was spectacular, almost as breathtaking as the fenced-in roof deck.

This was where we had our first "architectural row," as Summer called it, because she thought a hot tub would be great, and I thought she was truly nuts. "Remember hearing about my first house?" I reminded her, my voice pitching upward as I continued, "The creeper? What if one spawns on our roof, blows up the glass surrounding the lava?"

"Then we won't surround it with glass," argued my indomitable foil. "No creeper can blast through obsidian, which we can make at the same time we gather the lava."

"Which we've only seen back in the desert," I countered, "which is a whole day out of our life."

Summer just laughed. "Oh, Guy, you'll thank me later."

And, yeah, I would, for the first reason that a rooftop soak on a cool savanna night is awesome, and, second, for another reason I'll get into much later in this story.

What I didn't thank her for, however, was the upgraded "modcon" of another waterlift. Because our hill was next to the river, Summer insisted on crafting a drownavator at the edge of a diving board. No, you heard me, a diving board. A six-plank path that stuck out from the roof right above the small blue ribbon below. "Think about all the time we'll save," she beamed, laying the last wooden plank, "swimming up here and leaping down there."

"Yeah," I groaned. "I'll take the stairs."

"Race you!" Summer turned and took a flying leap off the edge. Up and into the morning sun, then down, down, as I winced through thumping heartbeats. Only when I heard the splash did I dare to peer toward the river. "Come on in!" called up her distant, miniature self. "It's absolutely brill!"

"I'll take the stairs," I repeated, then watched her climb out of the river and walk off to talk to Weaver. I was about to turn away when I heard her shout something unintelligible.

"What?" I asked, but I was too far away to make out her answer. And it looked like an important answer, the way she was jumping up and down, waving her arms and pointing to Weaver. But was that Weaver? Even from this distance I could make out the brown hat, but was there less white in their outfit?

I reached into my belt for the spyglass, and its magnification got me close enough to see that Summer wasn't talking to our local wool worker but to a whole new villager. Only the pants were white, along with a little piece of the brown hat. I could also see that Summer wasn't just waving, but showing me something in her hand.

Arrows!

"Get out!" I yelled, and almost dove off the diving board . . . but didn't, turning to hustle down the stairs.

"Took you long enough," Summer sniped as I came panting down the slope.

I was too winded for a witty comeback. Instead, I just wheezed, "Did I see it right? Are those—"

"Brand-new arrows." Summer held out the handful of projectiles, then nodded at the villager. "Thanks to our latest shopkeeper, Mr. Fletcher."

"Hrrh," the villager with the feather in their cap chimed in.

"That table you crafted back in the forest," Summer explained, "the one with bows and arrows on it that didn't do anything. Remember how we crafted a duplicate for one of the new work sheds?"

I gave a puffing nod.

"I think it's a fletching table," Summer continued, "if what I'm starting to remember is true about the correct term for making arrows." She waved the example at our seller. "Sixteen for an emerald. That's what they sell them for."

"Just sells them?" I asked, knowing that it was too good to be true. "They don't have to kill—"

"Chickens?" Summer cut in again. "Nether no! It's just like all the other villagers. Out of thin air." She tossed me a bundle of arrows. "Can't you see the label? 'No animals were harmed in the making of these arrows.'"

There was no label, but it didn't stop my laughter. What a lucky break! No more rationing ammo! No more wondering if I'd ever have to kill another bird. "Never thought I'd find a workable substitute," I breathed, "like on our world where people wear leather that isn't leather or eat hamburgers that aren't beef."

"Just goes to show," said Summer, "it might take a little more time, and a little more effort, but there's always a way to shop responsibly."

"Why, Summer," I said with mock shock, "did you just coin a Vesson?"

"Don't get used to it," she replied sternly, which sent me into more peals of laughter.

Fletcher gave us a "you're welcome" hrrh, then scooted back to their work shed.

"Thanks, Fletch," I called after them.

"And thank you for reminding us," Summer added.

"Reminding us?" I asked, turning back toward her. "Of what?"

"Of the original project we've both totally, utterly, stupidly forgotten to complete." Summer seemed a little cross with herself. "I suppose it's understandable, what with all the mining, and raising the new generation of villagers, and building the Slate House, and . . ."

"Summer," I cut in, "what in the cubed world are you talking about?"

She jerked her head to the river—specifically, to tall bright green crops.

"*Ohhhhh.*" Now I got it, and I felt equally foolish for forgetting. "The librarian."

Summer nodded. "The librarian."

I guess if there was a silver lining to this embarrassing cloud, it was that all the sugar cane we planted, and replanted, was now fully grown. And there was more than enough to finally get our bespectacled book-keeper to the next level. But when we did . . .

"Gordon Bleedin' Bennett!" Summer swore, as the new trade slots offered a lantern for an emerald, or what looked like one of those decorative bookshelf blocks.

"Not the end of the world," I said, trying to stay positive, "we just have to keep trying." I eyed the second item on the list before saying, "And hey, at least this bookshelf block will make a nice decoration for Slate House."

I coughed up nine emeralds (what a rip-off!), pocketed the new adornment, and headed back to our block of flats. Summer got there first, thanks to her liquid death trap. "Let's try your apartment," I suggested, trying to console her.

"Nine emeralds," she grumbled under her breath as I set the bookshelf against the nearest wall. "Next time we buy nine lanterns."

"So what do you think?" I asked, stepping back from the multicolored addition.

"Hm." Summer stared at it for a second, then pointed to the far corner. "Maybe over there?"

I started punching the bookshelf, expecting the whole thing to come right up as usual. Instead, the block vanished on the ninth or tenth blow, and in its place were three hovering . . .

"Books," Summer whispered, as I shamelessly shouted, "Books!"

What happened next could be described as a world-class flip-out. The two of us ran around the room, babbling frantically at each other.

"Backtothelibrarian—"

"Don'thaveanyemeralds—"

"Sellsomethinganythinggogogo!"

Rifling through the chests, racing back down the hill, darting from one villager to another, offering everything we had, scraping together our combined emeralds, whooping that there were just enough, then scrambling over to the librarian with the seven gems and one blank book.

Pling!

In my hand. Shining. Vibrating. The title on the cover: "Flame."

"Back to Slate House!"

Like lightning up the hill, into the workroom.

"What do we do now?" I asked, heart finally slowing as I was slapped with the reality that we didn't know.

"It's probably combined with another item," said Summer. "Try your sword!"

"No." I stopped pacing and turned to face her. "Your bow." And before she could argue, I bulldozed onward. "You remembered this, so it's gotta be your bow."

"Thank you, Guy," Summer said with the slightest vocal quiver, and stepped over to the crafting table. She placed her bow in the center square, then I placed the flame book next to it, then below it, then above it, then diagonally on all sides.

"What the . . ." I started to say.

"The anvil." Summer grabbed her bow and threw it in the anvil's right slot. I placed my book on the left. Nothing happened. "Switch!" Left to right, right to left. And then . . .

I could practically hear the big booming drums in my head as Summer lifted her now-glowing bow. "It tingles, and feels the slightest bit warm."

"We gotta try it!" I bolted for the door. "The roof! C'mon!"

We burst out into the cool evening air. "Away from the village!" I said, pointing down to the river. "Just in case it starts a fire."

"Righto!" Summer stepped out onto the diving board, aiming into the darkening blue.

WHP!

A flaming arrow! Streaking like a meteor at the head of a smoking tail, before disappearing into the river.

I was going to say something triumphantly eloquent, like "Woo" or "Yeah," but Summer quickly turned to me, excitement pitching her voice high as she said, "Your turn now! We have to enchant something."

"Not till morning." I sighed. "Librarian's asleep now."

"No matter!" Summer zipped past me for the door. "The enchanting table! Remember? We never crafted anything because we never could!"

"Oh, Summer," I yelled into the stairwell as I chased after her. "You absolutely, positively, utterly, totally *rock*!"

"Tell me something I don't know!" she called back.

Four obsidian, two diamonds, topped with a blank book.

What we set down was a red and black box with an open book hovering above it. And to make the magical part look even more magical, there were arcane letters or symbols that floated up from and dove back into the pages. Stepping closer, I saw a collection of empty slots. Three long, empty, horizontal spaces on the right, and a smaller, square opening on the left that held the exact outline of lapis lazuli.

Snatching the blue nugget from the chest, I placed it in the right slot, then held up the last blank book. But then I stopped, thought about what I was doing, and uttered a contemplative "Hm."

"What now?!" barked Summer, as if I'd just paused a movie right before the climactic end.

"Just ironic," I said, holding up the book. "We'd gone through so much to get this thing and now"—I slipped it back in my belt—"after seeing your bow, I just wanna cut out the middle-man."

"Well, for Nether's sake!" Summer was practically vibrating like a creeper. "Stop blathering and give it a go!"

I set my crossbow in the left slot, then my jaw dropped as the three right slots gave me three insanely awesome options. "Piercing," which probably meant that the arrow could do more damage, "Unbreaking," which was pretty self-explanatory, and a third that could have had a lot of meanings, "Multishot."

"I gotta try this," I said and chose the final one.

The lapis lazuli disappeared as the crossbow jumped into my hand. It was glowing, tingling.

Back to the roof!

It was nightfall by now, the full moon halfway up the starry sky. Where to aim, where to find a target?

"Sssp!"

I turned just in time to see a spider climbing up onto the deck. I reacted on instinct, raising my crossbow and pulling the trigger. But instead of an arrow, I got three! Multishot had turned my crossbow into this world's version of a shotgun!

The spider hissed, knocked right off the building to fall four stories down to the ground, where it poofed out on the grass below.

"This is a game changer!" I exclaimed, holding up my shining weapon.

Summer held up her bow to touch mine. "We've just leveled up."

"We gotta do more!" I chattered. "Enchant everything! All our tools, our armor! We can start right now!"

Summer shook her head. "No more lapis lazuli."

"No problem!" I hopped excitedly. "We'll just go wake up Chemist and buy more."

"With what?" Summer countered. "We don't have any emeralds."

"Not yet!" I sang, dancing around in a circle. "We wait till morning, go trade with the villagers, pocket some greenies, bing-bang-boom . . ."

"Or we could just go mining tomorrow," suggested my partner, "which wouldn't only give us more minerals to trade, but also the chance to dig for lapis."

"Yeah, right," I snorted playfully. "You're just achin' to try out that bow!"

"Well . . ." Summer sounded sheepish as she said, "maybe a little." We both laughed, continuing to celebrate under the starry sky. Dancing and singing, and shooting the occasional (and in my case, guilt-free replaceable) arrows into the river. It was a wonderful night, the best since this adventure started.

And neither of us could imagine that the good times were about to come crashing down.

CHAPTER 12

I don't believe in omens, which is when people believe something happens to warn you that something bad is coming. It's a primitive superstition, and I've never thought they were real. But maybe I should have believed in them after waking up that morning to the newly weird weather of this world. It was a gray day, the first one I'd seen since stepping from the jungle out into the desert. And like that hard, fast line that separated the jungle downpour from the overcast desert, the same phenomenon only let the clouds open up over Flower Valley. I could even smell the difference from here, as the extra moisture carried all the pleasing scents in right through my ventilation windows. I inhaled deeply, savoring the flavored air, then thought I saw distant figures.

They were small, dark, and just at the edge of Flower Valley's mist curtain. People? Villagers? Couldn't be. Flower Valley, even the closer part, was still outside the range of the villagers' morning walks. I reached for my spyglass, but realized it was still in the storage chest. By the time I retrieved it, the specks had vanished. A moment later, they also vanished from my thoughts as the apartment door opened.

"Morning, Guy," chimed Summer, offering me some bread. "Fancy some brekkers?"

"Thanks," I said, and chomped the loaf while she noshed on some cooked fish.

"Look how much it's changed," said Summer, gesturing to the village beneath us. "The new houses, workshops, and the trading post . . ." She was referring to our latest creation, a small, one-room shack with wall-to-wall storage chests that held trade-able items. It was a great addition to the village, and not just because it cut down on trips back and forth to Slate House. Having our own place of business alongside all the other sheds gave us a real sense of ownership. We weren't just strangers anymore, outsiders. We belonged. "We really have helped build a proper town," Summer said with pride.

"Not bad for a couple of immigrants," I added, "or guest workers, or whatever the closest term is."

"Doesn't matter," said Summer, "it's a good point about new people mixing in, fresh ideas, boundless energy."

"Yeah," I agreed, accepting an offered cookie. "I think that's really important where I come from. Immigrants making us stronger."

Another Vesson: immigrants make a village stronger.

After crunching on her own biscuit, Summer said, "Shall we be off then?"

She was talking about today's plan for mining.

"Sounds good," I answered, reaching for my armor. "You want to brew the potions while I harvest food?"

Summer answered with a fist bump, and a cautious, "But, given our gold reserves, I'll have to be judicious with the choices." She was referring to one of the key ingredients and, if you've never brewed anything in this world before, know that gold is necessary to gild melon slices for healers, and carrots for night-sight. We should have thought about this before selling off the bulk of our dawn-colored metal to Chemist, but now . . .

When shopping, always have a budget!

"Brew what you can." I waved dismissively, heading toward the door. "I'm sure we'll mine plenty more down below."

Hopping down the hill, I couldn't have been in higher spirits. The anticipation of mined loot had my mind whirring, and, as I approached our farm, I noticed that the half that lay on the greener, Flower Valley side was set to burst with mature crops.

More than we'll need, I thought, punching up pack-loads of wheat and carrots. *And I can sell some of this stuff to Farmer right now.*

Heading into the village, I didn't see our agricultural expert. *Probably wandering,* I reasoned. *It is time for their morning stroll.* I headed for Slate House, packed up all the other stuff I'd need, then told Summer I was going back for a quick cash crop sale.

"Don't be too long," she called after me. "Baddies will spawn underground just like on the surface."

"Back in a flash," I reassured her and bounced back down the hill. By now it was the middle of the day, and there was no reason not to see Farmer deep in the crop rows. But the garden was empty, and for the first time, I got an uneasy feeling.

"Hey, Farmer," I called, going from shed to shed. "Where are you? Anyone seen Farmer? Farmer?" This was irrational, I know. It's not like the villagers could answer me. But while my thoughts weren't yet drowned by panic, let's just say they were paddling through some emotionally choppy water.

"Guy!" An annoyed Summer came striding up behind me. "Why are you lollygagging about? We should have been off ages ago."

"I can't find Farmer," I said, glancing at the garden, "and this is work time."

"Except for Nitwit," Summer snorted.

"That's not the point," I sniped, in no mood to joke. "I can't find Farmer anywhere. Something's wrong. I know it. I feel the same way I did after our fight, when I came back to the mountain and you hadn't come home."

Summer thought about that, then validated my concern with her scanning eyes. "Much as I'd like to dismiss your anxiety," she admitted, "it does sound like a missing person situation." She glanced at one of the golems, because having more villagers had somehow spawned more of them. "And since none of these coppers have been promoted to inspectors"—she switched out her pickaxe for her bow—"the inspecting falls to us."

We searched for the rest of the day; all around the village, on the other side of the river, over in Flower Valley, even in our old hillside bunker, which was now a mushroom farm. There was no trace of Farmer, not that we'd know what a "trace" would look like.

At the end of the day, we did find something that came closest to a clue. It was a hole in the middle of the savanna where the sheep and cows grazed. "We must have passed this a dozen times," I said, realizing that the two-block rise had shielded it from view, "and it's the only likely place Farmer could be."

"Agreed," said Summer. "Probably wandered in this morning, took a wrong turn, and got lost down there in the dark. These villagers don't exactly seem like the sharpest tools in the storage chest."

I would have said something in their defense, but looked up to see the setting sun. "If we head back to Slate House and stock up on all the stuff we'd gathered for mining . . ."

She was already starting down.

"Hold up," I called, "at least pass me a Night Vision Potion."

"Don't have any on me," she answered, striding into the gloom.

"Oh, good," I said sarcastically. "Anything else we should have but don't? Extra arrows? Coal for torches?"

"Stop whimpering," she chided, planting a torch on the wall. "You barely had anything when you came back to the Nether for me."

"Yeah"—I quivered at the memory—"and we barely made it out by the skin of our square teeth."

"Sorry," chirped Summer, "didn't hear that, too busy acting instead of quaking."

You know what, fine! I mentally puffed. *You rush in blindly and take the first arrow, see if I care.*

A moment later, I cared, and felt horribly guilty for even thinking such a thought. Because an arrow whistled out of the darkness and right into my friend's stomach.

She growled in pained anger as I jumped in front of her with my shield raised and a chant of "Sorrysorrysorry!"

"About what?" she asked as another arrow thocked off my protective board.

"N-nothing," I stammered, "just—"

"Well, get clear then and stop spoiling my shot."

I shifted sideways as one of her flaming arrows came ear-heatingly close.

"What are you shooting at?" I asked. "You can't see anything!"

"I will in a moment," Summer boasted as the arrow hit . . . what . . . the stone floor? A back wall? I couldn't tell, because the flame wasn't lighting anything other than itself. Was she hoping it would act like a mobile torch?

"See!" I scolded and blocked another incoming projectile with my shield. "Flaming arrows don't . . ."

I shut up as the distant beacon . . . blinked? That's the only word I can think of because it went dark for just a fraction of a second, blocked by an object passing in front of it.

The skeleton! So that was her plan. Every time the bonehead CLACKED between us and a flickering arrow, Summer had a chance to clock its direction and speed.

"Whoa!" I breathed as she nocked another arrow to her string.

"I'll take that as an apology," she said and loosed a shaft right on target. The skeleton lit up like it'd been hit with a flame-thrower.

"Nice shot!" I crowed as the bonefire danced in distress.

"Care to have a go?" Summer asked politely.

"Genius and generous." I raised my crossbow. The shotgun blast of arrows not only extinguished the fire, but the un-life of the skeleton as well. "Consider us truly upgraded," I said, ambling over to the hovering arrows and leg bone.

"And it does tend to save on torches"—Summer planted a flickering stake—"which we'll need to use sparingly."

And we did, heading down the twisty-turny tunnel that, thankfully, stayed pretty much at the same level. We still had enough torches to see, but not enough to see well. We had to plant them so far apart that it was almost as bad as the Nether.

And speaking of the Nether . . .

"Feel warmer?" Summer asked after a few minutes.

"Definitely." I stopped, cocking my head to listen. "And there's nearby bubbling."

"Lava." Summer halted beside me, ear to the air. "A lot of it."

The tunnel curved slightly, and both of us thought we could see a faint glow up ahead. "Gotta be a molten lake," I said, "and if it's anything like the one under my island, we might be approaching a canyon."

Summer gave an affirmative hum and slowed to a cautious creep.

"Huuugggghhh." We both froze.

"Zombie," I said, crossbow held at the ready.

"Yes, but . . ." Summer held up a cubed fist.

There it was again. "Huuuuggghhh."

"It doesn't sound right," she whispered. "Lower? Deeper?"

I nodded, looking in front and behind us. It wasn't a baby zombie, or one of those husky desert types, or even one of the gurgling drowned versions. This was clearly a new member of the ghoul family, but where was it?

We could hear footsteps now, getting louder, closer. "Infernal acoustics," Summer whisper-grumbled, "can't tell where it's bloody coming from."

"Probably up ahead," I said, pointing to the glow. Weapons ready, eyes peeled, we stepped as softly as we could down the tunnel. A minute or so later, we were standing on a cliff. Just like my island, it was an underground canyon above a roiling lava lake.

"Huuuuggggghhhh."

Where was it? A tunnel next to us, or on the other side? A land bridge we'd missed?

"Huuuuuggggghhhh."

Above us? Another opening?

"Huuuugggghhhh!"

"Guy! Look out!"

I turned too slowly. A dead face in mine. Tattered clothes, green skin. Arms raised to strike. And . . . a hat. A straw hat!

"Farm—" was all I could say before a flaming arrow knocked my undead friend off the cliff.

I looked down just in time to see Farmer's burning form disappear beneath the glimmering sheen of red.

"I'm sorry," breathed Summer, her voice choking in remorse.

"It all happened so fast! I thought if you were touched, or bit, you might get zombified like Farmer!"

"You did the right thing," I said with what I hoped was comforting assuredness. "Just"—another glance at the lava—"how? How did Farmer get zombified?"

"Maybe getting touched by a regular zombie?" Summer theorized. "It only hurts us, but maybe villagers turn into right rotters."

"If that's the case"—I looked up, past layers of rock and dirt, to the village above our heads—"how did Farmer manage to get attacked by a zombie? They're all indoors before dark, and the golems are always on patrol."

"It could be"—Summer paused, clearly trying to shake off what she'd just had to do—"bad luck? Farmer getting caught out after sundown and running into an odd zed head at the exact moment none of the golems are nearby."

"We gotta find out," I said, confusion hardening into determination. "Tonight—no, tonight's almost over. Tomorrow night, we'll stay up, like when we studied the merchant. We'll keep watch until we see how the villagers are in danger."

We stayed up the next night, standing at the corner windows of my apartment. Spyglasses in hand, we watched, we waited—and nothing happened. The villagers all went to bed, the peddler drank another of his seemingly inexhaustible invisibility potions, and the golems kept up their constant vigil. As expected, mobs spawned close to the village. And, as expected, the golems whomped them. There was nothing out of the ordinary. Nothing to tell us why or how Farmer had met such a horrible fate.

"Maybe it was a freak accident," Summer suggested. "A one-in-a-million chance of the poor blighter taking the wrong turn and ending up in that horrid cave."

"Maybe," I conceded, "but let's not give up so fast. If something like that happened all the time, we'd have known about it a lot sooner." Dawn was breaking, making me yawn. "I'm not saying it's so uncommon to make it a freak accident, but maybe it's uncommon enough to warrant a few more nights on watch."

Summer agreed, and the next night we resumed our posts at the window. This time something did happen. The bat creatures were back.

"Been a while," I said, as they dove and weaved in front of our windows. "I was beginning to think that they were only native to the jungle."

"Perhaps it's got something to do with sleep," yawned Summer. "I think this is the first time since the jungle that we've been awake for three nights straight. Perhaps they can sense our fatigue, smell it like a shark smells blood."

Do sharks smell blood? My stomach gurgled at the thought. "Whatever brought them back," I said, "I don't think they're what we're after." At that moment, one of the green-eyed shriekers dove within a half cube of the glass. "See how they're only interested in us? They haven't gone anywhere near the village."

Summer held up her bow. "Maybe it's time for a bit of target practice."

"Save your arrows"—I held up a cautioning cubed fist—"and the wear and tear on your bow."

"Well, I've got to do something," Summer hissed with exasperation. "I'm tired and bored and going positively mad."

"Maybe we should take tomorrow night off," I suggested. "I know it's a risk if we miss something, but"—I waved at our airborne foe—"it might banish them for a few more nights, and it'll at least give us a much-needed rest. And as far as the boredom goes"—my voice rose with childish excitement—"you've got me to talk to!"

Summer answered with a low, emotionless, "Brill."

We slept the next night and resumed our watch the following evening. It felt good to chase away our sleepiness and the night fliers. The boredom was constant, though, and, as it always did in times like this, the lack of an immediate task set my mind to wandering.

"You ever think about the history of these villagers?" I asked.

"No, but clearly you do," came Summer's acidic reply.

"I'm just wondering," I continued, "if they were the same people who built all the big structures, like the temples and mineshafts."

Summer chuckled without humor. "Not bloody likely." She waved down at the villagers, who were all breaking up to find a place to sleep. "Look at them. Content, unambitious."

"What's wrong with that?" I asked in their defense. "If they want a balanced life of work, wandering, and hangin' with their buds by the fountain, who are we to judge them?"

"I'm not judging them, Guy," said Summer in her own defense. "I certainly don't think everyone has to be as driven as me."

"Especially 'Nitwit'?" I teased.

"That's different," she said with an emphatic head shake. "Working just hard enough to take care of yourself is fine, but taking from others so you don't have to work at all"—her arm drew an imaginary line on the floor—"is simply not fair to everybody else."

She pivoted back to the window. "But that's not the point of what I was getting at." Her eyes fixed on the village. "I wasn't criticizing, just observing. And from what I've observed of our neighbors, they haven't done anything new since we've gotten here, even with the growing population. They don't seem to want anything more than what they have."

"No," I allowed, "but maybe their ancestors did. Isn't that a thing on our world? Some people go through these energetic phases where they build and invent and create these huge civilizations. Then, after a while, they slip back, slow down, choose a simpler, less stressful life?"

"Unless it's not their choice." Summer's tone darkened as her eyes scanned the horizon. "Weren't some of those great builders on our world conquered by other chaps who liked what they saw and chose to march in and take it?" She looked down at the village. "That may be the case here. A long time ago. This village, and maybe others like it, might be all that's left of someone else's rampage."

"Who else?" I asked, as icy worry worked up my spine.

"Who knows." Summer shook her head. "Either they're long gone, or we haven't yet . . ." She stopped, pressed her face against the glass. "Look there!"

I turned, raising my spyglass. I didn't have to ask what she was pointing at. The zoomed-in picture was enough. One of the villagers, Fletcher, was coming out of a house and into the darkened village.

"What the—"

"C'mon!" Summer cut me off, running for the exit.

We took off for the stairwell, but as I turned to go down, she yelled, "No time!"

She was right. This was an emergency. Up and onto the roof deck, then over to the diving board without pause. She jumped. I followed.

Falling! Fast!

Ohwhatifwemissthewater?! I thought, a second before splashing into the chilly river.

As my feet touched the muddy bottom, I pushed back up for the surface. Spluttering next to Summer, we swam with all our might for dry land. "I saw Fletcher and Mason go into the same house." She panted up the bank. "One of the old houses, with only one bed!"

That might have been what happened to our friend. Instead of wandering into the hole, Farmer might have lost the race for a bed, wandered outside to find another house, and accidentally run into . . .

"Ghuuuuuh!"

We raced into the village—and into instant combat. A zombie was chasing Fletcher, while all the golems were either bashing other spawning mobs or patrolling too far away to notice the ruckus. "Hang on, Fletch!" I called, diamond sword flashing in the moonlight. I dashed in between the ghoul and its prey, slashed at its green, gargling face, and didn't stop until only smoke and meat were left.

"You're okay, buddy!" I said, turning to see Fletcher had almost made it to the safety of the hotel. But there was another zombie coming from around the corner. "Get outta there!" I hollered, running as fast as I could. Not as fast as a flaming arrow, which Summer sent into the ghoul's chest. "Nice shot!" I complimented, then rushed in to finish the job.

Bad idea! As the burning zombie reached out to punch me, I was suddenly engulfed in fire. Heat. Pain. I swung through flickering blindness, feeling the impact of my blade. The zombie groaned its last just as my skin stopped sizzling.

"Drink!" Summer was in front of me now, holding up a potion. I gulped deeply, feeling its magic healing.

"Fletch!" I coughed, scanning frantically for the villager.

"Is all right." Summer opened the hotel door. "In here."

We entered to see Fletcher in one of the beds, sleeping soundly as if nothing had happened. "Well, that's it then," said a relieved Summer. "At least we know what happened to Farmer."

"Yeah, but"—I was the opposite of relieved—"how do we stop it from happening again?"

"We can't." Summer still didn't sound the least bit concerned. "They have their golems, and most of the time they do a right good job."

"But they didn't tonight," I argued, "or else we wouldn't be here!"

"But we can't be here every night," Summer reasoned, "and we won't be here forever." Summer couldn't have been cooler or more logical. "We can't be the world's policemen, always rushing in to save the day." She motioned to the sleeping villagers. "Look, Guy, I feel for these people. I really do. But as you keep reminding me, the point of staying here is to learn all we can to, hopefully, find our way home." Her arms rose in a wide, resigned, full-body shrug. "We can't keep involving ourselves in their problems."

"No, but"—heart beating, brain cloudy—"as long as we stay here, we are involved! We built these houses, grew extra food for extra people, gave them jobs, helped them advance their skills." I pointed to her shining bow. "And it's not like we haven't benefited from those advancements. At least for the moment, we're as much a part of this community as everyone else, which means helping to"—I held up my sword—"provide for the common defense."

CHAPTER 13

I'm not sure where the words came from. I just know that they matter. Back on my world, maybe in that part I called "home," they mattered so much that they shaped the way we lived. If we were going to benefit from one another in the good times, we had to protect one another in the bad times.

"Provide for the common defense," I repeated, as much to myself as to Summer.

She didn't respond. Not right away. Instead, she looked at the villagers for a second, took a deep breath, then said, "Yes, I suppose you're right. As long as we're here, we need to help keep everyone safe. The question is"—she paused again, looking out the window to the collection of buildings—"how best to help. We can't keep watch every night, even in shifts. We'd never get anything done."

"I got it," I declared proudly, as an idea popped into my head.

"We lock them in. Every night when they go to bed, we just barricade the doors with earth or wood, or whatever keeps them inside."

"Are you mental?" Summer asked incredulously.

"What?" I answered with equal incredulity. "What's the problem?"

"I can think of several!" She scoffed, holding up her cubed fist as if she could tally things on her perma-clenched fingers. "Like taking too much time to block every door, as well as it being a temporary plaster before we eventually move on. And neither is half as bad as the fact that we'd be trap—"

"A wall!" I cut her off. "That's it, oh, yeah, that's totally it!" I took a step back, awed by my own genius. "Just like we talked about with the abandoned desert village! Remember? We'll use all the cobblestone and mining debris we've got left to build a wall around the perimeter, then light the interior with spawn-cancelling torches. It'll be a self-contained fortress that gives the villagers everything they need."

"Except their freedom."

Freedom.

Summer's word felt like a bucket of cold water. It was another important word from my other life. I wasn't sure why, though, and before I could try to remember, Summer continued speaking. "A fortress without the freedom to leave is also a prison. Remember, these chaps like to wander, and we'd be taking that away from them. And if, sometime in the future, they change enough to want to wander away for good, we'll be taking that away, too."

Okay, she was making sense, but I knew I was right, and I wasn't going to let her win.

"Yeah, no, freedom," I mush-mouthed, "it's important, but, you know, so is safety. I mean, you can't be free if you're dead or zombified." I struggled for the next point, and the logic to back it up. "There's gotta be, like, a compromise, right? A line somewhere between freedom and safety."

"I couldn't agree more," conceded Summer, and for a moment, I thought I had her, but then she sucker punched me with, "But who gets to decide where that line is? You? Me?" She glanced at the villagers. "Them? We're talking about their lives, their freedom and safety, but they're not a part of the discussion. Don't they get a vote?"

Vote.

Another word, another sledgehammer pounding at the back of my mind. The freedom to vote, to decide your own fate, that was the bedrock of civilization, at least where I came from. And from what Summer said next, where she came from, too. "Look, Guy, I know your heart's in the right place. I know you care about these people and only want what's best for them, but setting yourself up as their king, even a good king, is a very bad idea."

King? I hadn't thought about it that way. But if it meant protecting the villagers . . .

"Why is a good king a bad idea?" I challenged. "If it gets stuff done, and if the king knows what to do? If I know how to protect the villagers better than they know how to protect themselves . . . like . . . remember that story I told you about my island, when the creeper blew up my house and the animals kept walking toward the lava . . ."

"These aren't animals!" Summer shouted, so forcefully it

made me jump. "They're human beings! Maybe not exactly like us, but they still deserve the same rights we have, including the right to decide how they live their lives, even if those decisions are wrong."

I thought I saw an opening, that she might be proving my argument. But just before my awesomely crafted response left my flat lips, she one-two'd me. "And let's say *you* make the wrong decision. Say you're their king and you have all the power. You're not perfect; no one is. Even if you genuinely want to do what's right for them, you could still innocently muck it all up. But there'd be no one to stop you, no one to argue. If you're the only vote, and that vote's the wrong vote, you could end up getting them killed. That's why a king, even a good king, is a bad idea."

I was wavering, wrestling with unlocked, hazy memories. "I think . . ." It was right there, just beyond my conscious mind. "I think . . . back where I'm from, that's why we got rid of our king. Kicked him out, or something."

Summer nodded, sifting through the sand of her own memories. "I think we still have one—a king, I mean—but I don't think he has any power anymore. I think his whole family are . . . well . . . rather like characters in an amusement park; wearing fancy costumes and waving for pictures and whatnot. I think that's all we let them do nowadays."

"I guess that makes sense." I sighed. "And I guess it also makes sense about letting the villagers have a vote."

Wow, this was complicated, everything we were learning about communities. Big choices, big consequences.

"Okay, so let's say everyone gets a vote," I started hesitantly. "How does that even happen? If we don't speak the language, and since there doesn't seem to be any way to learn it, then how do we give them the chance to vote?"

Summer didn't hesitate. "With their feet."

"Say what?" I'd heard that expression before, but had no idea what it meant.

"Simple," she said, "we build the wall . . ."

"See! Told ya I was ri—"

"Buuuuut," she continued, slamming the door on my gloating, "we add doors. That way the villagers can go out anytime they want during the day, and close them up tight at night."

"But what if they forget to close one?" I asked. "Or they forget to come in at night?"

"Then that's their choice."

I'll be honest, I wasn't totally convinced. But since I didn't have a better idea, I figured I'd go along for now.

So, we got to work, but it didn't happen like we planned.

Jogging back to the Slate House, we began cataloging our inventory of materials.

"Not nearly enough," I said, counting our meager supply of cobblestone. "Between all those new houses and work sheds, there's no way to wall off the entire village."

"Maybe we won't have to." Summer walked over to the corner window. "Maybe we only need to connect each outer house." I narrowed my eyes, trying to imagine her layout. It wouldn't be as neat, and we'd still need a whole lot of blocks, but using the outlying buildings as barriers would go a long way to stretching our resources.

"It's worth a shot," I said as the sky lightened in the east.

It wasn't an easy job, even with every mined block we had.

Filling in the gaps between the outer buildings allowed us to enclose the entire village. It wasn't as neat as a square or rectangle. From the air, it must have looked like a giant, sideways "T." But, if you were standing at the eastern head of the T, the wider, jutting corners allowed you to see right down the north or south wall. I thought I'd seen a similar design in ships from our world. The big ones, I mean, where the command centers, or "bridges," have sides that stick far enough out for the captain to look down the entire length of the vessel. The design made sense, both for them, and us.

"Better for sniping"—Summer nodded—"especially when we finish raising the wall to its proper height."

"Yeeeahhh," I breathed, surveying the completed, one-block-high foundation, "about that." Connecting the houses might have allowed us to complete the wall lengthwise, but height was another matter. "Looks like it's back to mining," I said, glowering at the pathetic barrier. "Shouldn't take too long to pick out enough rocks."

"Or." Summer stepped over one section to punch up the dirt in front of it. "What about a trench? At least as a temporary measure? The next time we go mining, we can gather proper stone or deepslate, but, for the moment, a one-block-deep trench wouldn't only raise the wall by default, but the added dirt could also be a new layer."

"And we've got the tool to do it!" I agreed, hoisting the enchanted shovel. What should have taken half a day was accomplished in only a few minutes! And just in time, too, because the last dirt cube popped into position right as the sun dipped below the horizon.

"Perfect timing," I observed. Racing the darkness, and the monsters it would bring, we planted light sticks in every nook and cranny. On the houses, against the walls, and, finally, on every patch of darkened ground.

"We're definitely going to have to go mining after this," griped Summer, "because I'm almost completely out of coal."

"Me too," I chimed in from across the village, "but look at all we've done."

An island of safety, all walled in and noonday bright.

And this is just the start, I thought, imagining what improvements we could make. *We'll definitely have to replace the dirt with the cobblestone, and maybe a ledge to walk along its length. Should we put in watch towers? One on each side? That would give us a secure view of the land around . . .*

"Ghuuuu."

I froze, sword out. "Summer?"

"I heard it," she called, "maybe outside the wall?"

Pow!

A rotting fist clocked me in the back of the head. I fell forward, oofing out a surprised breath, then spun to face a mask of mottled green.

"Where did you come from?" I asked as my flashing blade sliced the ghoul away. The responding "Ghuuu" sounded suspiciously like "Wouldn't you like to know?" And as I chopped it to chunks, I said to Summer, "It must have come in one of the doors."

"That's impossible," she argued as another zombie groan echoed through the night.

"It's the only way!" I insisted. "Maybe the latest change allows them to open doors like Nether piglins!"

"But we haven't installed the doors yet!"

Oh, right.

Another "Ghuuuu!" rang in our ears followed by a quicker, softer "Ghu!" I knew that sound. I'd first heard it under my island when a zombie had practically dropped on me from a cliff.

"Guy!" Summer was battling this new ghoul, bashing it with her shield as she reached for her netherite axe.

"I think I know!" I declared, running over to help. "I think I know where they're coming from."

"That sound." Summer was way ahead of me. Stepping through a cloud of dead zombie smoke, she raised her eyes on the wall. "We must have missed something. A low rise or hummock next to the wall! They must be using it to climb over."

"Has to be!" I agreed, and slapped together a crude dirt staircase. Together we rushed onto the narrow wall.

"You go one way," Summer yelled, running down its length, "I'll go the other!"

I took off in the opposite direction, trying to balance speed with, well, balance! One misstep and I'd go tumbling into mob land. I could barely make out the trench that ringed the wall, which, now that I thought about it, meant that the zombies couldn't have used a rise to climb over. But then how were they getting inside? I could see a few out in the darkened pasture, along with glowing spider eyes, and the faintest hint of camouflaged creepers.

Did a creeper blow a hole in the wall? No, I would have heard the blast. And besides, didn't you have to be right next to them to trip the fuse? The answer to my question came the barest second later as I trotted right above a creeper that didn't blow.

Of course, I sneered confidently, *the wall's too high for our mere presence to set them off. But then how did the zombies . . .*

A skeleton's arrow stabbed into my shoulder, knocking me off the wall, into the village, and into the pummeling arms of another zombie.

"Again?!" I whined at the fist in my face. I raised my shield, blocked another blow, then gave back what I'd been getting.

The zombie smoked away just as Summer called out from the wall, "That's how!" I looked up to see her pointing at the nearest house's roof. "They're still dark!"

We had missed something: We'd neglected to light the rooftops!

"On it!" I shouted, racing to build more dirt stairs. It wasn't easy, or safe, because climbing onto all those roofs made us targets for skeleton snipers. Most of the time I could anticipate the WHP of incoming arrows, but at least twice, they swatted me to the ground. The last time was the worst, because it was off the two-story hotel.

"Argh!" I grunted from the leg-bone-fracturing impact. "We gotta work together!" I shouted to Summer. "One stands guard while the other lights up each roof."

"No time!" she shouted back, then reached for her bow as a zombie spawned atop Mason's unlit shed. Her arrow flew, the ghoul blazed, and I finished it off with a sword stroke.

I was just about to reclimb the dirt steps to the hotel when a spider's hiss pulled me away. Legs, eyes, climbing over the wall! "We got problems!" I yelled, slicing the arachnid back. *What do we do now? If the wall doesn't work against spiders . . .*

"No, we don't!" Summer ended the fight with another flaming arrow. "Only zombies go after villagers!"

"Really?" I asked, charging up the hotel steps. "How do you know?"

"Haven't you been paying attention?" Summer snapped.

I guess I hadn't. When the zombie had gone after Fletcher the night before, I'd been too focused to notice that all the other mobs were only interested in us.

"I guess we don't have to worry," I said, placing the last torch.

"Not anymore," said Summer, proudly picking off the last stray ghoul.

Climbing down from our rooftop perches, we spent the last nighttime minutes just standing by the fountain, waiting for more attacks that never came.

"We did it," Summer declared as the sun rose—and with it, the villagers. "Or rather, we will, once we fit all the doors."

"I've been thinking about that," I said, setting down a crafting table. "About villagers forgetting to close the doors."

After knocking out a hole in the wall, then filling it with an orange, slatted, acacia wood door, I then went back to the crafting table and whipped up a thin horizontal square. "Pressure plates, see?" I boasted, setting it at the foot of the door. "Just like back in your mountain to keep the cold air out."

After a night of combat, Summer was clearly in no mood to argue. All I got was a curt "If you must," before she walked away.

It didn't bother me. Success was the best compliment. So, while she completed the east, west, and south doors, I followed up with handy-dandy pressure plates.

"Can't wait to see how they work tonight," I mused, but got a yawning, "Tomorrow night," from Summer. "We don't want our insomnia to lure in more batty battlers."

"Tomorrow night it is," I said, and headed back to the Slate House for breakfast.

The rest of the day was spent mining for minerals, and rocks to reinforce the wall. We didn't find much: a little iron and coal, too much cooper, and, deeper down, some redstone and long-missed lapis lazuli.

At this point, you might be thinking: "Hey, if they just found the stuff to enchant all their other stuff, why didn't they do it?" And if we hadn't spent two hectic nights without sleep, we might have agreed with you. But since those nights had practically turned our brains to mushroom stew, we hit the sheets the moment we got back.

The next morning brought clarity, but also focus on the job at hand. We spent that whole day using our mined rocks to re-place the dirt in the wall, then stayed up the next night for me to show off the mental masterpiece of my pressure plates.

That's when things got crazy.

We weren't just sitting around that night celebrating my ge-nius. There was a lot to do. We'd not only fixed the wall (replac-ing ditch-dug dirt with cobblestone), we also added another improvement. Ever see an old castle with those peggish barriers on top of walls that make them look like half a zipper? That's what I was doing: laying a block every other space on our perimeter wall, figuring that they'd be great to hide behind in case of more skeleton arrows.

I must have been about nine-tenths of the way through when I heard a door open and shut. I looked up from my work, scanned the village, but couldn't see anything out of place. It wasn't a villager going from house to house, and Summer was busy working on a distant section of the wall. There was no movement other than the golems lumbering on patrol. I shrugged and went back to zippering the wall when I heard it again a few moments later, and this time, it was followed by a zombie's groan.

What the . . . I started to think, then heard another moan followed by a series of angry zombie grunts. Was a ghoul fighting someone out there? And where was that second moan coming from?

I pivoted, reaching for my precocked crossbow, and got both my answers at once. Right next to the wall's north door, there was a golem. I turned just in time to see the red-flashing meat bag fly backward from the two-fisted blow, and as the steel guard clunked forward for another punch, I watched it step on the pressure plate, open the door, and let another ghoul lurch through. "Su . . ." I started to say, but a flaming arrow told me she'd seen it, too.

"I know," she yelled from the opposite wall, "the patrolling coppers are setting off your plates!"

Oh, so now they were "my" plates, I thought, swapping out crossbow for axe. "I'll take care of them!" I called, rushing for the wall. "You just take care of the ghoul!" I swung down hard, aiming for the thin ground square, but accidentally hitting the golem right next to it.

"Oh, I'm so sor—" I started to say before mechanized fists grabbed me.

Crushed, battered, flying!

Up and over the wall, into the mob-filled night. The CRACK of my own bones mixed with the groans, hisses, and CLICKETY-CLACKS of incoming beasties.

"Run!" cried Summer amid a storm of flaming arrows. "I'll cover you! Get to Slate House!"

I limped as fast as I could, with pursuing mobs racing my hyper-healing. A creeper loomed up in front of me. I shot it with my crossbow, raised my shield, and felt the explosion knock me back into a spider. Fangs scraped armor as I switched from cross-bow to sword. A swipe. A rasp. I retreated as a flaming arrow turned it into a bonfire.

"Keep running!" Summer hollered from the wall, and my hyper-healing let me do just that. I bounded for the slope, but looked up to see a reaching zombie.

"Keep—" Summer started.

"I heard ya!" I shouted, and dodged the downward blows. I hopped, skipped, and jumped up the rest of the hill, focusing on the light of the building. I was almost at the door when a creeper glided around the corner.

Back up! Lead it away! I couldn't afford to let it burst next to Slate House. I retreated a few steps, then I laid in with a tactic I'd perfected under my island. It's called a "sizzle fizzle," and it consists of striking once, backing up to let the creeper's fuse burn, then striking again once the sizzling stops. If done repeat-edly and correctly, it'll not only kill the bomber, but add a pinch of gunpowder to the pile. This is what happened that night: strike, back, strike, back, strike, powder!

And just as the explosive booty popped into my pack, I looked out to see Summer riding her waterlift up to our home's diving board. Racing to the stairs, we met in the middle of the roof deck.

"You all right?" she asked.

"I will be," I answered, but realized that as the physical wounds melted away, the emotional wound still smarted. "That was so messed up!" I growled, looking back down at the village. "I tried to tell the golem it was an accident, but it didn't listen! They never listen, just like last time!" I was seething now, getting angrier the more I talked. "It's not cool! Not fair! Back home, there'd be a chance to hear my side! There'd be a court and jury and lawyers! But here . . ."

"You don't have a voice," finished Summer.

"Exactly!" I fumed.

"So the creators of this video game are making all the decisions."

"Right!"

"Even though they have the best intentions, they might have made a mistake with the golems."

"Right!"

"But their mistake hurts you."

"Ri . . . oh."

"Right." Summer glanced down to the town. "Now you know how they feel."

"I guess I do," I admitted sheepishly, "and now I see how important freedom is."

"Including the freedom to leave," continued Summer. "You might not like everything about their criminal justice system, the same way I don't approve Nitwit's idle scrounging, but that's simply the price of living here, and we can either choose to accept that price or vote with our feet and jog on."

Her words felt like golem punches. Hard and powerful with the steel of truth.

"Everyone should have that choice." She sighed. "Everyone should have that freedom."

I returned her sigh. I got it now. "You're right, Summer . . . mostly."

"Mostly?"

"That whole part about being in a video game. So not true."

"Well, you also have the freedom to be wrong."

We shared a laugh, then stayed up to watch the sunrise. "Something's still bothering me," I said as the first warm rays lit the village. "Why didn't the bell ring? If it's an alarm, why didn't the zombies going after Mason trigger it?"

"Either they didn't have time to ring it," suggested Summer, "or, like we've said, there's another threat out there that we haven't seen yet."

"And hopefully never will," I said, wishing I'd never brought it up.

"No point dwelling on it now." Summer headed for the door, saying, "We've got a full day of mining ahead of us, and one last task to perform before that."

To perform that last task, we headed down the hill and over to an open piece of land next to the village garden. We set down a cube of earth, planted a handful of wheat seeds, then surrounded the cube with white diorite fencing. We lit the four corners with torches and placed a signpost on the section of fence that would oversee the growing wheat. On the sign was written one word. "Farmer."

"Not much of a memorial," said Summer, "but at least it's something."

I looked over at the villagers, all going about their day as if nothing had changed. "Nobody seems to be in mourning," I said with a touch of resentment. "No grief, no recognition. It's like they don't care."

"Not showing doesn't mean not caring," countered Summer. "Different cultures grieve in different ways, don't they? Like your lesson about respecting different beliefs." She looked at me with open arms. "Some cultures are taught to express everything they feel exactly when they feel it. While others"—her eyes fell—"are taught to hold it in tight."

Was she talking about her culture? Or just herself? Or both?

I turned back to the little marker and bowed my head. "Should we say something?"

"How about just a moment of silence."

I nodded, closed my eyes, and spoke a few words in my head.

Farmer, I don't know if you can hear me. I don't know if this world . . . or any world . . . lets your soul live on past your body. But if that's true, then I just wanted to say thank you for being the first to welcome us into your community. Thank you for being such a good neighbor, friend, and teacher. You will definitely be missed, but you'll never be forgotten.

I opened my eyes right into the upward-looking face of a new baby villager. "Oh, hey, little one," I said, taken aback. "Didn't know you were here."

"Maybe someone's come to pay their respects," suggested Summer.

"Wouldn't that be nice," I said, as the little face turned to the memorial with a "Hrrh."

"Well said," said Summer, nodding, and the two of us repeated a solemn "Hrrh."

CHAPTER 14

Now that we'd secured the village, or, at least, made it as secure as it could be without taking their freedom away, it was time to get back to mining. But before we could do that . . . "How 'bout we try enchanting more gear?" I asked on the way back from Farmer's memorial.

"Super," Summer chirped, "and now we have the lapis lazuli to make it happen!"

The previous day's explorations had yielded just enough blue nuggets to magic-ify everything, from our helmets down to our boots. Starting with the former, we were given the choice of "Protection," which Summer took, and another, stranger option called "Respiration."

"We should probably choose different powers," I suggested, "to get the full range of what works." I donned the glowing Respirator helmet, but couldn't see, feel, or breathe any differently than normal. "Maybe it just helps make the Nether smell better."

Moving on to our chest plates, Summer chose the obvious "Blast Protection," and for her trousers she chose "Fire Protection." *All pretty self-explanatory*, I thought as my own chest plate was given the option of "Projectile Protection." The question mark came back, however, when my pants were marked with the potential spell of "Thorns."

"Not sure I like the sound of that," I winced, imagining if the thorns were on the inside. "But here goes nothin'."

There weren't any on the inside, or out, from the looks of them. "Guess we'll know soon enough," I said as we took off our boots. The three options I got didn't exactly inspire a happy dance. "Depth Strider" sounded like something for the ocean, and "Soul Speed" either helped over soul sand or just made them really stylish. Since neither seemed helpful for the upcoming mission, I chose the boring but useful "Unbreaking."

Summer also struck out with "Soul Speed" and "Depth Strider," but got a potentially cool bump with "Frost Walker."

"That can't be the same as Fire Protection," I wondered, "can it?"

"Perhaps it's for walking on lava?" she countered.

"You really want to test that theory?" I asked, with raised *count me out* fists.

"Not at the moment." Summer put on the glimmering boots. "But these are the only options."

"We can always keep enchanting," I proposed. "Go find Chemist to trade for more lapis."

"We could"—Summer hesitated—"but, if this makes any sense, I feel like I'm missing more than just bluestone."

"Yeah," I agreed. "I think I know what you're talking about." All that enchanting had left us feeling a little *off*. I'm not sure how to describe it, because I'd never felt anything like it before. Not hungry. Not tired. Rather like something in our spirit that we didn't even know was there was feeling noticeably drained. "Maybe enchanting takes something out of us, some kind of 'mojo,' for lack of a better word, and maybe a solid, successful adventure will get that mojo back."

Summer nodded. "Off we go!"

Armed with food, arrows, crafting wood, potions, and now a whole suit of enchanted armor, we marched back down the hill and out to the hole that had swallowed Farmer.

At first, it didn't look like we'd need all our fancy new spells. Retreading the tunnels that had led us to Farmer, we didn't see or hear any mobs. But when we reached the passageway ending at the lava canyon, there was no mistaking the CLACK of bones.

"Behind us," I warned, then turned to see two approaching skeletons. "Just like last time." I held up my shield, giving her the cover to shoot.

"On your right," she called as I dodged left to avoid her flaming arrow. As the first skeleton burst into flames, I blocked an incoming shot from the second. "On your left," she called, and I zigged in the opposite direction.

"No prob—" I began, but was interrupted by a sudden "Ghugh!"

I turned again, back toward the canyon, just in time to see an approaching zombie. It reached out and punched me, but then seemed to recoil in pain.

"Your trousers!" Summer exclaimed. "The thorn spell!"

She had to be right. Although neither of us could see anything, the ghoul must have impaled itself on invisible, magical needles. "Thanks, pants," I said with a sword swipe that sent the zombie tumbling over the cliff and into the lava below.

"Still gives me a twinge," Summer said with a downward gaze, "thinking about poor old Farmer."

"At least we made sure that'll never happen again," I said, reaching for a bucket of water. After pouring it on the edge, we paused to watch the slow-moving column work its way to the bottom. "Even in this world," I joked, "we still gotta wait for the elevator."

"You do." Summer started walking away from me, down the cliff, and well away from the new watervator to the obsidian bottom. "I'm going to field test these Frost Walker boots.

"NO!" I cried as she stepped off the edge. I watched her fall, hit the molten rock, then disappear beneath its flames!

"Summer!" Now I was jumping, not into the lava, but onto the water-covered obsidian. "Summer!"

Where was she?! I couldn't see her anywhere.

Ohmygodohmygodohmygod!

"Right here!" Her head, poking above the surface and moving toward me, was burning!

I ran to the lava's edge, reaching for her helplessly! If only this world would just let me take her hand!

"Stand back!" She laughed, casually swimming toward the bank. "I'm fine!"

Still flickering like a torch, she climbed up onto the black stone and trotted over to the quenching waterfall.

"Sum . . ." I breathed, grateful that, unlike my world, the terror of the last few moments hadn't forced me to change my painted-on pants.

"Well, these boots certainly won't let you walk on lava," she commented nonchalantly, "and the trousers' protection is barely worth mentioning."

"Wha—? Bu—? How?" I stammered, as she held up an empty bottle.

"Fire Protection," she chirped. "Downed it the moment I sank and realized the boots didn't help. I may be rash, but I'm not stupid."

"Suuuummmmmerrrrr," I growled, wondering if her potion would last long enough for me to push her back in. I didn't, of course, but oh, did I want to. "Do *not* do that again!"

I turned away from her, breathed deeply, and tried to slow my pounding square heart.

"I'm sorry, Guy." Summer sounded serious now. "I should have warned you."

"It's all right," I said, remembering my own rule about friends forgiving each other. "But let's make sure we won't regret using up that potion." Since my eyes were on her now empty bottle, Summer took the hint and poured out her own water bucket. The boiling rock vanished, cloaking the canyon in darkness.

"Better conserve our torches," said Summer, reaching for her first night vision brew. "We'll plant just a few to mark the way back."

It was a solid strategy, especially since we'd each packed three potions. I chugged mine, squinted at something ahead and de-clared, "The end of the canyon opens up. See?"

"That it does," said Summer, placing a starter torch. We made for the opening, walking down into another, mundane tunnel. I say mundane because we didn't find anything for a while. No minerals. No monsters. Just a curving, winding pas-sage that took up half a dozen torch markers before something remotely interesting happened.

"You smell it?" I asked, slowing my step.

"What?" Summer came to a full stop beside me.

"I don't know," I said, taking a longer sniff. "Like . . . grass? Trees?"

Summer inhaled deeply. "Yes," she agreed. "Some kind of vegetation." She closed her eyes, spread her arms. "And there's a dampness in the air."

I felt it too now. Not warmer—at least, not the steamy, lava-waterfall kind. This was room temperature, or, I guess, tunnel temperature.

Senses heightened, we kept going, and noticed the scent in-creasing with each step. "I'm definitely picking up vegetation," I said, "grass, and . . . moss? And flowers, but different from the valley up top, and something new, some kind of plant that smells . . ."

"Fruity," Summer said.

"Yeah." I nodded just as my night vision potion started blink-ing.

"Not yet!" Summer raised her fist to stop me from drinking my second potion. "See how the tunnel curves ahead? See how it's just that much brighter?"

I wasn't sure. Hard to tell with the potion's omni-glare. But as it faded out, I could see that she was right. There was definitely some kind of luminescence. And maybe it would explain the plants.

We turned a corner and suddenly stopped, with my "whoa" matching her "cor." It was another of those new mondo caverns, but way weirder than the others.

The floor was a patchwork of puddles mixed with what looked like grass. And the puddles themselves were a mix of open water and giant lily pads. Trees grew everywhere, but none like we'd ever seen. They were small, bushy, and covered in pink flowers.

Everything was lit by these long, hanging vines dotted with yellow, glowing berries. "Think they're edible?" asked Summer, stepping up to the closest vine.

"Maybe we should save the taste-test for later," I said. "You never know if they're poisonous."

"I've got milk," she said, picking a luminous berry.

"Which might not work," I parried, "and even if it does, shouldn't we save the cow-tidote for possible cave spiders?"

Summer considered this, holding the glow-globe mere mini-cubes from her mouth. "I suppose you're right."

"Ahhh," I crooned, closing my eyes and rocking to silent music, "just to hear you admit that is worth the new discovery." I opened my eyes just in time to dodge a shoulder punch, and continued, "And even if these bright-berries aren't edible, they might be incredibly useful."

I picked a bunch of my own, then carried them back inside the tunnel. "Let's see if I'm right about something else." A pair of berries vanished as I tried sticking them to the ceiling, turning into a half-cube shrub that clung to the naked stone. "Now for part two." I took the leg bone salvaged from one of the skeletons, turned it into three pinches of bone meal, then tossed it up to the shrub.

"Bing-bang-boom," I declared, as two new glowing fruits appeared. "I don't know how long it'll take to grow on its own, and if we'll always need fertilizer to jumpstart it, but looks like we've now found ourselves a renewable source of light!"

"As you would say," Summer said in a horrible imitation of my accent, "this is a game-changer."

"Oh, indeed," I replied with a perfect impression of her, "now let's 'pop' on down and see what else we can discover."

Renewable. The word kept orbiting my mind. It wasn't the first time I'd thought about the differences between this world's gifts that kept giving (like growing carrots) and the gifts that only gave once (like mined gold). Right now it didn't seem urgent, and yes, spoiler alert, it's gonna be paramount later on. But for the moment, I was just mulling it over, like everyone does with our far-off to-do lists, when my foot squished on what I'd thought had been just plain old gray stone.

Clay! Right under our feet, in what had to be hundreds of cubes. "Mason's gonna love this!" I said, getting out my magic shovel.

"Let's conserve our inventory space," advised Summer, "until we know what else we might find down here."

A splashing sound pulled our eyes out to the darkness. *Looks like something found us.* We stood silently for a moment, listening, looking. Nothing moved in the patchy glow-fruit light. But another splash confirmed that we weren't alone.

I didn't know what to expect; killer lily pads, poison shooting from the dwarf flower trees, a monster made entirely of clay. The last time we'd been in such a radically different biome was down in the Nether, which had introduced us to hoglins and piglins. Shield in one hand, cocked crossbow in the other, I followed Summer across lily pad–laden pools.

It was slow going. Move, stop, listen, scan. The most frustrating part was the shadowed areas that lacked glow vines. "This won't do." Summer reached for the night vision potion in her pack. "At least we can give the whole cave a decent look-see."

We gulped a second potion, then strode forward at a quicker pace. "Ain't this something," I marveled, "and I don't see any threats around us."

"Me neither," agreed Summer, "but it doesn't mean they aren't about."

Another splash.

"Speaking of . . ." I swept my crossbow in a 360-degree arc. Again, nothing.

Summer pointed farther down the canyon, against the wall, to a spot that would have been too shaded to see without night vision. "I think I spotted something." She took off with lowered bow, and, to my greater surprise, raised pail. I was about to ask what the deal was, when I saw that she'd stopped at a large pond containing a gold axolotl.

"Just what I'd hoped for!" she chirped. "With two, I can breed a whole family! According to the wildlife guide, feeding two axolotls tropical fish will persuade them to, well . . . make a third. And doesn't our wandering trader sell tropical fish?"

"Possible," I said, wincing at the idea of buying living things just to be eaten, "but what will you do with more axolotls?"

"Make more fish farms!" Summer said in a condescending tone. "By damming every section of cod-spawning river, we can triple, quadruple, infinite-uple what we sell to Fisher."

I didn't argue, just warned her to be careful. "We don't know what else is in that pond."

"Oh, codswallop." Summer laughed, scooping the amphibian up in her bucket. "I'm sure we're perfectly safe."

"First"—I held up a fist—"there's no way 'codswallop' can be a real word, and second, let's just make sure that the pond is—"

BAM!

The creeper detonated right behind me. Dazed, wounded, flying through the air, I must have catapulted over Summer and landed right in the middle of the pond. Cold, pain. My eyes opened to see dim blue water above. And there was Summer . . . walking on the water? No. A trick of my blasted brain. Had to be.

I shot for the surface, but cracked my head on . . . ice!

The pond was frozen! How? I looked for another spot, an open space just at the cavern's wall. I swam for it, with Summer running above me. Before she got to within a few squares, the water froze over.

Her boots! That's what Frost Walker meant. It let you walk on water—but now it wouldn't let me out!

Trapped!

I burbled for Summer to move away. Pick in hand, I chopped

out a chunk of ice, just to have her accidentally freeze it again! I looked everywhere, trying to find another way out. There was a tunnel, under the cavern's wall, but it was flooded and possibly led nowhere. The only escape was up, but how?!

A horrible game, me darting from one open space to another just to have Summer close it up. I could see she didn't mean to, frantically waving her arms, shouting something I couldn't understand. I could see her own pickaxe was out, trying to help, jumping with frustration, not realizing that, somehow, she was making everything worse.

Move! I mentally shouted. *Get out the way before I run out of* . . .

Air?

Shouldn't I be out by now? How long could I hold my breath? I stopped swimming, started to sink, and tried my darndest to remember all those times I'd nearly drowned. None of them came close to this duration. Don't get me wrong, my lungs were still losing oxygen. But the rate was a whole lot slower. So much so that I could actually feel myself calming down! As my feet touched the muddy bottom, I looked at Summer and waved for her to get off the ice. She stared at me for a second, yelled some muffled question, but eventually got the message.

Okay, I thought, reaching again for my pickaxe, *still not running out of air.* And as I searched, slowly and patiently for the best place to crack my way out, the ice above me started to disappear. *If that don't beat all,* I thought, shooting for the surface.

"Dude!" I gasped to Summer. "You're not gonna believe this."

"I'm so stupid," she spat, standing on the bank with her shimmering footwear in hand. "I just realized it's these dreadful boots."

"Turned out to be a blessing in disguise!" I said with a bubbly bounce, "or else I wouldn't have discovered how long I could stay down there!" I looked at my armor: the boots, pants, and chest plate. "Something on me extends my air supply."

"Must be the helmet"—Summer pointed to my head—"you know, 'Respiration.'"

"Oh, yeah." This is how folks must feel when they're looking for glasses right on the end of their nose. "Thanks." Then, regaining my enthusiasm, I said, "This opens a whole new world for us—exploring, even mining, underwater!" I motioned over my shoulder to the pond. "And I can start with this submerged tunnel right here."

"Right," agreed Summer, "and while you're playing Fish Man, I'll dig up as much clay as we can carry."

"Be careful," I said, then modified it with, "Not just yourself, but the land." Summer gave me a quizzical pause. "I'm just saying that this is such a unique ecosystem that we shouldn't be in a rush to pillage all its riches." Thoughts of renewable and non-renewable resources were going through my head. And as I tried to explain myself, the thoughts tasted like apples. "Back on my island," I explained, "I learned that I had to take care of my environment if it was going to take care of me. So"—I drew an imaginary line down the middle of the cavern—"I divided the island, half for me, half for itself."

"Sensible policy," Summer agreed, "but two conditions." She held out a fist. "If I could borrow that super-shovel of yours."

"You got it." I tossed her the enchanted tool.

"And if you don't mind," she continued, "remember to check in every so often so I don't worry about you."

"You know it," I said, and turned back to the water. At that moment my night vision potion began to blink, so I downed the third and final one. "I'll be back before it wears off."

I stepped beneath the surface, and, for a second, had to fight a well-ingrained urge to panic.

I'm all right, I told myself. *This helmet's working just fine.*

The fear subsided, replaced by calm, and then . . . What's that feeling you get when you're totally happy in the moment? Utopia? No, that's a place. U-somethia. That's how I was feeling, and why wouldn't I? This magic helmet was conquering my first and worst nightmare. It was even better than the time I'd taken that fireproof potion in lava, because now I'd have the time to enjoy it.

And it was really enjoyable! Other than the slightest chill, the water itself felt kind of comforting, the slight pressure on my body, like a weighted blanket, matched with a lighter step like walking on the moon. Isn't there a song about that? Didn't three dudes a long time ago write about taking giant steps and hoping your leg doesn't break? I wasn't worried about that, but running out of air was another matter.

Keep it up, I thought to the helmet, sure that I had plenty of time left. *I should really go back, do a proper experiment with time, count how many seconds I can hold my breath, with and without the helmet.* Logical, practical thoughts followed me as I continued to bounce happily down the submerged tunnel.

A few seconds later I stopped at an underwater canyon, and

looking up and across, I could see the opening of another tunnel. *This is what flying must feel like,* I thought as I swam dreamily up to the opposite entrance. *When I get back to my world, it may be time to take up scuba diving.*

I landed gently, bounced forward, and saw a welcome sight imbedded farther down the passage. Iron! At least one shiny flecked square. I bounded over and started mining. My magic pick helped to speed things up because that initial comforting pressure slowed my swing, impeding my efficiency a bit. I didn't really notice, though, as I picked out the first foot-level cube, then the cube behind that, then, in order to see if there was one behind that, the stone block in front of my face. That was when I became aware of a slight suction pulling me into the hole. I looked down to see that my lower, three-deep indentation showed a thin top layer of air.

Of course, I realized, remembering the funny physics of water. *It always runs out after a few squares.*

Right then, the nuisance of slowed movement turned lethal as the last bubble of air in my lungs popped out.

CRACK! The first jolt of pain wracked my body.

Drowning! Again!

Instinctively I bolted for the surface . . . and smashed my head on the hard stone above! Up was out, and I'd never make it back to the pond.

CRACK! Another jolt. Barely seconds left!

Dig! Dig for more air! Dig faster! Dig for your life!

I hammered my pick against the rock as CRACK after agonizing CRACK broke my body.

Dig! Dig!

A block fell away—not enough!

DIG!

More stone, more space, carried forward by rushing water. And then I was breathing again! Real oxygen in my lungs! Coughing, hacking, yelling.

"Duuuuumb!" What an idiotic mistake. So careless! "Gotta watch the time!" I retched before downing a healing potion. "Next time I count. Every second! No distraction! I gotta keep track of—"

"Guuuuugh!" The wet, stinking fist smashed me in the back. Face hitting the cold stone, I turned to see the bloated, green-blue face of a drowned zombie! It punched again, but gasped at the pain of my unseen Thorns. "That's twice! Now let's end this together." Reaching for my sword, I struck the oncoming corpse. I almost felt sorry for it, trapped between my blade and the rushing water. Swing, slash, stab!

As the zombie disappeared, I coughed on its dead smoke. I don't know how long I stayed there, pinned against the wall by the oncoming tide, taking deep breaths to settle my nerves. What I should have been doing was beating the hastiest of hasty retreats back to the surface of the pond.

Why? Because remember when I was just scolding myself about keeping track of the time? Well, that should have also applied to the night vision potion, because just as I was about to head back out, it died.

CHAPTER 15

"Now?" I said, then yelled again, "*Now?!*"

I was blind. How would I find my way home?

Even though I knew to turn left out into the tunnel, there was no way I could ever find the other tunnel's entrance. Trying might get me even more lost in the darkness, or killed if I couldn't find my way back to this air pocket. The nightmare flashed across my mind, groping in the pitch-black for the elusive opening in the cliff wall. Missing it, over and over again. Turning back, missing the other tunnel. All while the precious air ran out of my magic helmet. There wouldn't be time to dig another air pocket. I'd die alone in the darkness!

I couldn't go back! But what was forward?

Up! I turned and began to tunnel a staircase to the surface. Not a perfect solution, I knew, but at least I'd escape. I'd break out onto open ground, find the original entrance we'd come down, run back to Summer, and explain that I couldn't have checked in because . . .

Water! Above me! Another underground lake! I was washed back down the stairs, pinned between this new flow and the one rushing in from the tunnel. Stuck, out of ideas. Summer! She would worry, then come looking for me, then possibly get hurt! And it would all be my fault! I screamed, loudly, angrily, and with no one to hear me.

And in that brief silence of inhaling my next breath, I heard another voice.

Moooo.

Not real, just in my mind, but from the part I'd been building up since first landing on my island. The storage chest of lessons that lit my darkest moments. There it was now, taking on the image of my old cow pal Moo.

Panic drowns thought, she reminded me, *you know that. And you know that this situation is the same as it ever was.*

"You're right," I told myself. "I always get in a jam and wig out like there's no tomorrow. But what can I do to make sure there is one?"

First, said Moo's memory, *calm down. You got any dirt?*

I did! And I knew exactly what she was talking about. More than once, just sniffing a cube of earth had grounded my nerves. It did again. I took in a few deep, relaxing whiffs.

"Now what?"

Moo's image hovered in the dark before me. *The Way of the Cube.*

"Right!" I sighed, imagining I was back on my island, talking to my trusty sidekick. "Plan: I gotta figure out a way to get outta here. Prepare: I need light! Both in here and, somehow, out there." I picked out a block next to me and stuck a torch inside the indentation. In its comforting flicker, I could now see what I was dealing with.

"Prioritize: I can't think straight with all this water!" I looked up and blocked the overhead stairway with a couple of stone cubes. But instead of doing the same with the tunnel entrance, I decided to try an experiment. Hollowing out a section of wall next to me, I laid down a crafting table, then crafted a trio of doors. I wasn't sure if this would work, placing one at the entrance, especially with these slated acacia models. But as soon as I set it at the opening, the water immediately drained away. And not only that, when I opened it again, the water stayed out. Weird, right? Standing right next to a wall of water, I found I could actually walk outside, into the wet, then walk back through the doorway, into the dry cavern, like it had an invisible force field.

"Brill," I chirped in Summer's accent, then spent another minute widening my safe-dry space. "Now let's try the next one. Practice: I'll add light to water."

I stood at the end of the "force field" and used my hyper-reach to place a torch on the tunnel floor. It flickered for a second, in a bubble of its own air, then disappeared back into midnight.

"Patience," I said, keeping my anxiety in check. "You always knew Plan A might not work." For Plan B, I tried placing glow-fruit in the same place. It wouldn't stick to the ground, and when I tried to place it on the ceiling, it only held for a second before utterly disintegrating.

"Perseverance," I breathed. "I just gotta figure out a Plan C." Another inhale of earth got me stable enough to start cataloging sources of light. A redstone lamp would be perfect, except that I didn't have the materials. I also didn't have any lava, and there was that pesky little problem of it turning into obsidian when it met water. Flint and steel was at least worth a shot. I could smelt those iron ingots now and spend the wait time digging for some gravel. But as I threw the raw ore—along with a precious lump of coal—into a crafted furnace, I started thinking of another idea.

Lanterns. Could their housing keep them watertight?

I placed one of the new ingots on the crafting table, then used the nuggets to surround a torch. And just like with the earlier torch, I placed the encased flame out into the water-filled tunnel floor. It held! It lit!

"Awwww yeeeeeaaah!" I crooned and, jumping for joy, hit my head again on the shallow roof. I didn't care. This moment was un-spoilable! *Thanks, Moo.*

Calculating how much iron I had, I concluded that there'd never be enough to light the whole way back. "No problem," I said confidently. "I'll just pick them up behind me as I go, and now that I know to keep an eye on my air"—I looked at the two remaining doors in my pack—"I can make emergency air pockets as I go."

I'll be back in no time! I thought, stepping out of the doorway. But as I punched up the first lantern, something to the right caught my eye. A light? A faint glow? It hadn't been there before. I would have seen it. Why now?

Keeping an eye on my air, and the torchlight shining through the emergency base's doorway, I took a few tentative steps down the hallway. The glow grew brighter as I approached the opening of another canyon. I looked up, paused to be sure of what I was seeing, and uttered a big, bubbly, "Whoa!"

Sometime later, I burst back through the pond and cried, "Summer! Summer, you gotta see this! Summer?"

"Where the bloody Nether have you been?!"

I looked up and behind me to see my frazzled friend at the entrance of a new tunnel. "I've just started to dig after you!"

"Sorry, complications!" I said with arms raised in contrition. "Got too far, ran outta air, and . . . you gotta see this!"

"See what?" Summer ran down a ledge she'd carved to meet me at the edge of the pond. "What could possibly be worth the fright you just gave me?"

I could have responded snarkily with, "Oh, like when you did a lava dive without warning me?" But I decided to be mature and look forward instead of back. "Just follow me," I said, tossing her my respirator helmet. "You're really gonna 'dig' this . . . so to speak."

"Wha—"

"Don't worry about me breathing," I pre-answered her obvious question. "I got it all worked out."

To her credit, she showed great restraint, refrained from further questions and/or angry comments, and put on the helmet.

I ducked into the blue again, and bounced over to my first "light bubble." This was much simpler than lanterns, which I'd discovered after running out. Hitting my head, twice, on the tunnel's ceiling had given me the idea to experiment with picking out the rock over my head. And, as I suspected, the hole was filled with air! That's why all the "light bubbles" on this side of the underwater canyon were nothing more than torchlit two-by-two holes in the roof.

Popping up into the bubble, I inhaled deeply while treading water. I was about to look down to see if Summer was following me when her head rose next to mine. "Brill solution," she admitted, then, edging a minicube closer, uttered a surprised, "Ow!"

"Oh, sorry!" I yipped, peeling off my pokey pants. "Guess my Thorns can't tell friend from foe."

Summer let it go, and instead asked, "How many more of these do we have?"

"Just stay on my tail," I said soberly. "It's gonna be a marathon."

We bounce-bobbed up to three more of these makeshift way stations before reaching the edge of the canyon. I took a deep breath, sank below the trapped air, then focused on the lantern across the way. It was a little scary, I won't lie. Even though I'd practiced it without the helmet, just having it in hand made it a whole different story than now.

You got this, I told myself, *you know what you're doing.*

Fortunately, I did, making it to the opposite side and into my other "breath base" of a door on the tunnel floor. Just the door. Nothing else. All I'd had to do was set one down and its square space filled with air! Since it could only fit one of us, I called to the patient Summer, "We're almost there."

We bounced to the second lantern-adjacent door, then past my temporary base, and finally to the last lit door at the end of the hall. Summer didn't need my instruction to look up. It was obvious what was above our heads. The surface! Bright and clear, with a distant, square sun overhead. That's why I'd missed it before. It had been night when I first entered this tunnel. Now, as the noonday sun beckoned, we shot toward it like a pair of torpedoes.

We burst up into warm, wet air, surrounded on all sides by thick, tall greenery. "Another jungle!" exclaimed Summer.

"Not another one," I said, pointing to a spot of gray among the green. "Look familiar?" It was the temple, far but visible, as was the giant tree we'd tried to sleep in on that ill-fated night.

"The lake must be somewhere up there," I said, climbing onto dry . . . drier . . . land. "And it must be fed by this river we've swam up into."

"And if this is the same river that ends at the village," Summer replied as she swam up next to me and started crafting a boat, "then we might get home well before dark."

"If we'd only brought a map," I said, placing my boat next to hers, "like we kept saying we would."

"So much to keep track of," Summer lamented, climbing into her own boat. "Details make the difference."

For a while, we paddled in silence, just taking in the beautiful scenery. I'd forgotten how pretty the birds were, and the occasional ocelot. And we even saw another panda, rolling and playing in a bamboo grove. "Nice to be taking this southern route," I said as we passed under the vines of a tall tree, "just in case we missed something the first time." I had no idea how right I was.

We passed out of the jungle, and into the blazing sun of the desert. "Didn't miss this," grumbled Summer with a quickly parching throat. By mutual decision, we halted to refill our empty potion bottles with water, but as I raised a bottle to my mouth, I stopped at the sight of a color that seemed out of place. Between the blue above and tan below, there was a definite patch of deep black.

"What's that?" I asked, reaching for my spyglass. Squinting through a sweat-ringed eye, I thought I saw the top of a structure rising above some distant dunes. "Is that a temple?"

Summer reached for her own spyglass. "Too far to tell, even with these." We resumed paddling but at a slow, cautious pace. Whatever it was, we couldn't afford to approach with our guard down.

We parked the boats at the next river bend and hiked up the baking sand until we could see the entire structure. It was a tower. A ground level of cobblestone rose up to a second, narrower, open story of dark wood support beams and lighter birch floors. Those same light floorboards made up the wider third story, which sat under a final roof of dark wood. I guess there was nothing ominous about these features, except for the banners that hung from the end of the partially fenced-in third floor; they were gray faces, with angry narrowed eyes.

"Have you ever seen anything like this?" I asked Summer.

"Never," she responded from behind her spyglass. "And given how unfriendly the locals look, I think we should keep our distance."

Through my own spyglass, I could see humanoid beings milling around the ground floor. At first, they looked like villagers wearing dark clothes and carrying crossbows. The spyglass's magnification also showed me that their skin was gray, just like a witch's. "Not friendly at all," Summer stated firmly.

"Maybe we shouldn't assume that," I countered, trying to see the other side. "I mean, they're armed, but so are we. And the gray skin . . . isn't it, like, the worst of the worst to judge people by skin color?"

"I'm not going on any of that," responded Summer flatly. "I'm going on who they've taken prisoner."

Prisoner? I swung my spyglass around to match hers. At first I saw two people, tied to stakes, with their arms behind their backs. But as I looked closer, I realized that they weren't people at all, but mannequins made of wheat blocks, fenceposts, and carved pumpkin heads. "Those aren't prisoners." I chuckled. "I think they're, what, archery targets?"

"Not them," Summer hissed impatiently, "to the right!"

I rotated slightly, to focus on what could only be a fencepost jail cell that imprisoned an iron golem.

"That golem has to be held against its will," said Summer, "and since golems are goodies, it's logical to assume that its jailers are baddies."

Never assume anything, I thought, but between the aggressive banners and the imprisoned golem, the evidence was stacking up like items in an inventory slot. "Do you think that these, I don't know, 'barbarians' or 'pillagers,' might be the reason that our villagers are the way they are now?"

Summer responded without taking her eye from the spyglass. "You're referring to our convo about why nations fall?"

"How people might choose a simpler life," I recalled, "unless it's not their choice." I focused my lens on one of the threatening banners. "What if these guys here are the reason our villagers were in the shape they were in when we met them? Maybe they were conquered, beaten down from a thriving civilization into a small band of survivors just hanging on. They may even be relatives of the abandoned village we found in the desert. In fact"— I shook my head at the realization—"that might be what their bell is for! Why they've never rung it, and why they lost their minds when I did!"

"If you're right"—Summer swapped her spyglass for her bow—"then we can't afford to let it happen again. We'll hit the tower from two sides. I'll draw their attention with a flaming arrow barrage while you rush in and—"

"Whoa there," I cut in. "Hold the phone! I'm not saying I was right about the whole pillager conquering thing."

"But what if you are?" Summer held up her weapon, glaring at me impatiently.

"But what if I'm not?" I suddenly regretted opening my big fat mouth. "And even if I am, we can't just attack them because we're afraid that they *might* attack us!"

"Oh, stop whingeing! You're just worried we won't win, which we will, of course, with our new weapons and armor and the element of surprise."

"That's not the point"—I raised two emphatic fists—"but now that you bring it up, there's no guarantee that we will win. We've got a whole village to worry about now, and if we start something with these dudes and they follow us back . . ."

"But we have the wall now," Summer reasoned.

"But we don't know if it'll stop them!" I counter-reasoned. "We don't know anything about what we're up against, what they're capable of, what kind of risk we're putting our people in."

"All the more reason to eliminate the risk now," Summer pressed, "in a, what's the term, 'preemptive strike' to pre-protect the villagers."

"But the villagers don't get a vote."

"Ye . . ." Summer must have had a comeback locked and loaded, but the whole vote argument made sure she never fired. "I . . . I suppose you're right. We can't very well start a war that affects everybody unless everybody gets to vote on that war." The bow lowered to her belt as her eyes rose to mine. "But what do we do about these baddies and their 'Dark Tower'?"

"Nothing," I said, fist swatting in their direction. "Leave them alone. We don't need anything from this area, and the villagers don't range out this far. Let's just get while the gettin's good."

Slowly and quietly, we slinked back down the dune and into our waiting boats. I was glad I'd won this argument and dodged what could have been a great catastrophe. Still, as we paddled away, I couldn't shake an uneasy feeling that I was forgetting something important. Seeing those warriors had unearthed a recent memory, or, at least, it had scraped away the first layer. The memory was still buried. I couldn't figure out what it was. I might have eventually gotten there if the land didn't suddenly change from desert to savanna.

"Getting close now," I sighed through cooling air. A minute later the tall gray peg teeth of the wall rose from the horizon. And a minute after that, we were back. Bursting through the south door, we saw the whole village gathered for their afternoon kibbitz.

"Hey, everybody!" I waved happily. "You'll never guess where we've been!"

As luck would have it, the closest villager was the child we'd met at Farmer's memorial, all grown up, and wearing a brimmed straw hat. "Hey, Farmer! Or Farmer Junior, or Junior. You wouldn't believe the adventure we just had." My tone sobered with the next sentence. "And the danger we just found. So tell your friends not to wander too far into the desert, and if you see a Dark Tower—"

"Can we dispense with the chin wagging," clucked Summer, "and get down to some serious commerce?"

"Hrrh," responded Junior, which I took for "I like chin wagging."

"Yeah, me too, but she's got a point. There's plenty of time to catch up later."

Striding over to Mason, Summer presented her copious amount of clay. As I predicted, we overloaded on so much of the stuff that the store closed halfway through our transaction. "At least we got to the next level," I said optimistically.

"Too bad there's nothing we have," commented Summer, "or want." The next trade offers were to buy twenty intact gray stones for an emerald, or sell four chiseled stones for the same price.

"Not a problem," I said, "we can sell the rest tomorrow when the store reopens. Right now, let's see who else wants a promotion."

"Chemist!" Summer called through the crowd. "Fancy a trade?" As the purple-robed villager stepped forward, Summer exchanged the bulk of our emeralds for a smaller, but very precious, glowstone. "Now we can get back to properly lighting Slate House."

"And then some." I gestured to the purple bubbles rising from Chemist. "Looks like someone just leveled up."

Chemist's new business acumen created an offer like nothing we'd ever encountered. We could earn an emerald by selling four green, oval-esque things that were labeled "scute." And for five emeralds, we could buy something called an "Ender pearl."

"I've heard of that," I said, wishing I could scratch my head, "back in the wildlife manual on my island."

"Well, maybe this one has the same passage," Summer suggested, leading me over to the library.

We hit the books, specifically one book, and the first part I read in the wildlife manual told me all I needed to know about the first trade.

"Scutes are dropped by growing sea turtles . . ." I read aloud. "There are turtles out there?! When did that happen?"

"Keep reading," Summer pressed.

"Right." I dove back into the text. "Harvested scutes can either be crafted into turtle shells to brew the 'Potion of the Turtle Master' or, when combined with other scutes, into armor."

"All very interesting," Summer said with a scowl, "but utterly useless now."

I sighed in agreement, then went back to searching for my original goal. "Enderman," I said, reading the caption under a picture of those tall, purple-eyed beings. "Endermen can be seen placing . . . yada yada yada . . . don't look them in the eyes . . . read this back on the island . . . got it! When killed, Endermen drop Ender pearls, which . . . oh my . . ."

"What?"

"Oh . . . my . . . square . . . gods," I whispered.

Had this passage been in the other manual back on my is-land? Had I missed it? Yes, I might have been more focused on the part about why Endermen are so dangerous, and yes, I admit I can be a selective and impatient reader, but could my journey—my life after leaving the island, even!—have been completely different if I hadn't skipped the words right in front of me?

"Summer," I croaked through hammering heartbeats. "This is our way home."

CHAPTER 16

Holding up the book, I read, "When combined with blaze powder, Ender pearls can be used to point the way to strongholds." Pausing for effect, I recited, "These strongholds contain portals that, once activated, open a doorway to the End."

"Oh," Summer said cryptically, "I suppose."

"Whaddaya mean, 'suppose'?" I blurted, letting my enthusiasm take over. "This is it! This is what we've been looking for!"

"Yes"—she nodded rapidly—"yes, it may be." Her tone seemed fake, forced, like she was trying too hard to seem positive.

"Wha?" I couldn't understand. It was worse than trying to talk to a villager. "Dude, what is wrong with you?"

"Nothing!" she snapped angrily, then quickly melted into a quivering, "I just . . . just . . ."

Her voice. Fear?

Uh-oh.

Was this the old fear again? Was it the reason she'd been so insistent on trudging through the desert instead of stopping to find a way home? I'd never forgot that moment, and had cataloged it in the same mental file that held the memory of her saying goodbye to the mountain, as well as our nearly friendship-ending fight about moving on.

"Summer," I said delicately, "I know the idea of going home is scary but . . ."

"No!" Summer waved my words away. "It's not that. I'm not scared of my old life anymore." She paused, took a big wet sniff, then said, "I'm just scared of life . . . without . . ."—her voice cracked on the last word—"you."

I tried to say something, I'm not sure what, but she held up her arms for silence. "When you were gone, lost in that tunnel, and I was all alone again. That feeling. It's why I tried to hide from you the first time we met. Not just because I thought you might drag me back to who I used to be, but also because I'd grown into someone who didn't need anyone. But now . . ."

She tried to talk, but couldn't. Neither could I.

Remember earlier in this story when we'd first paddled down the river, and I told you that something was bothering me but I'd tell you later what that something was? Well, later is now, and that something was the fear of separation. I'd also wondered, and worried, a lot, about waking up in our world, but not knowing where, or even who, my best friend was.

The loss. The pain.

I'd felt it after our first fight, when I thought I'd have to continue alone, and like all deep wounds, it had left a permanent scar. Sharing your life with someone, getting used to them, depending on them, then losing them is like losing a piece of yourself. I now understood why so many people spent their whole lives trying to avoid that pain.

Not making friends, or starting a family, or connecting to anything meaningful because of the fear that that connection might go away. You can't lose what you don't have. And now we had something that would hurt worse than lava if it suddenly disappeared.

"We don't know our real names," she squeaked, "or what we look like, or where we live except that it's already in different countries." Her cracking voice rose an octave on the next question. "What if we end up on opposite ends of the planet?"

What should I say? That she had a point, and I was just as scared as she was? No. Not this time. She'd always been so strong for me. Now it was my turn.

Friends take care of each other.

"If that's the case," I said, casually shrugging my square shoulders, "then I'll just find you again."

"Again?"

"Sure," I huffed, false bravado hardening into genuine resolve. "I found you the first time, when I didn't even know I was looking for you. Imagine how easy it's going to be next time."

Summer gave a small, half-whimpering chuckle. "Oh, Guy."

"C'mon, buddy." I pressed my shoulder to hers. "Let's get started getting home."

From what the book told us, this new project was going to take a lot of time and materials. Activating an End Portal required twelve eyes of Ender, and each Ender eye took (along with a pinch of blaze powder) four Ender pearls to even make in the first place. Oy.

And that wasn't the half of it!

Finding a portal meant tossing an eye in the air, where it "pointed the way." However, since the path petered out at a certain point, you'd have to keep throwing the eye, and since it would eventually break and need some backup spares . . .

Bottom line, buying enough pearls would cost us a grand total of eighty emeralds.

"Eighty?" I wooFed after we'd finished our calculations. "That's like saving for a car, or a house, or . . . or something really expensive, like college."

Summer sighed hard through her nose. "Then we better be judicious on how we spend our most precious resource."

She was talking about time, and at first we spent it essentially burying Mason in clay. Our initial haul wasn't enough for the next level, but that would change with the second trip to what I was now calling "Lush Cave." We didn't go back down the river (no sense provoking the Dark Tower) and the original land route gave us a chance to mine for other treasures. We found plenty of coal and iron, and when it came to the subterranean swamp, I'm proud to say that we only took the clay on our side. But I'm even prouder to say that, once finished, we also did what we could to repair the land. We filled every hole, replenished every pool, and planted enough grass and lily pads to make it look reasonably natural. No reason you can't give back a little bit to the land that gave up so much, right?

It took Mason a couple of days to buy our total haul, which also bumped them to the next level. "Bit of a snooze, if you ask me," said Summer, turning her flat nose up at the new trading offers of diorite and andesite.

"Not the point," I said, holding up thirty-six emeralds. "We're already more than a third of the way there!"

"A bit more mining will improve that," Summer said.

This prompted a hesitant, "Yeah . . ." from me. "I've been thinking a lot about that, especially since we took all the clay from our side. I just think, well, we've always believed that there might be more castaways out there, and that they might end up following in our footsteps, right?"

Summer nodded, silently encouraging me to go on.

"I just think it'd be really uncool if we just stripped this land bare and left them with nothing. I mean, imagine how we'd feel if we were the ones who showed up later and this whole place was picked clean."

Summer considered this for a moment, then said, "I'm guessing you have a solution."

"Actually, you gave me one," I said, gesturing to the river, "with your fish farm. I might not be the biggest fan of killing, as you know, but I do appreciate the method behind your farm, harvesting a resource that will never run out. We should be thinking that way about everything."

I reached into my pack, pulling out the newly mined coal and iron. "Don't get me wrong, we'll still sell this stuff, but future mining should be for survival, not profit. That can come from the 'renewable resources,' like your fish, our garden, and"—I swept my arm at a section of wall; more specifically, to a plot of open land beyond the wall—"I've been thinking of a 'tree farm,' like the three tool-wood oaks you've got growing at your riverside workstation, but, like, on an industrial scale, so we can use wood for fuel instead of coal, and sell the sticks to Fletch for more emeralds."

Summer looked at the wall, no doubt imagining my ambitious plans. "It won't be as fast, or easy . . . but, like you said, it would be pretty bad form to leave nothing for the next travelers."

"Renewable it is!" I said. "Let's focus on the gifts that keep giving."

Summer was right about the slow-going-ness of our new economy. Her fish only spawned about once a day, and the garden could only grow its cash crops so fast. Trees grew even slower, especially the kind I planted. Apple oaks seemed best for a couple of reasons. Unlike acacias, they not only dropped extra food, but their straight up-and-down structure allowed me to plant them right next to each other in a row.

I started slow, chopping down one oak in Flower Valley, then replanted three harvested saplings. The fourth, by the way, went right back to replacing the original tree.

I threw a pinch of bone meal from Summer's fish farm on the first sapling, and it promptly shot up into a tall, bountiful tree. "Awesome," I said, chopping down this first yield. Replanting another half dozen saplings, I headed back to the village with new apples, sticks, wood fuel, and the confidence that this plan would work.

"Hey, Fletch," I said, catching the feather-capped villager on the way to work, "you up for a load of sticks?" Thirty-two for one emerald.

"Small steps forward," declared Summer, holding up the gem she'd just earned from Fisher.

"It'll be a giant leap," I said, displaying the wooden logs, "once we start smelting that iron."

If you would have asked me to predict Summer's next words, I would have pegged them somewhere between "Onward then," and, "Well, let's stop mucking about and get on with it." I wouldn't have bet on her pausing with a contemplative "Hm."

I was about to ask what she was pondering, then noticed her eyes fixing on Mason. "Just having a think," she said, watching our black-aproned neighbor, "about Mason's new advancement of offering emeralds for uncobbled graystone." She took another beat, then continued, "If I gathered a bucket of lava from down below"—she glanced at the ground—"then poured it over water"—she glanced at a section of fish-free river—"couldn't I consistently harvest renewable cobblestone to be re-fused in the wood-burning furnace?"

"Nice!" I nodded at her ingenuity. "And if we used stone-tipped tools instead of our fancy, rare models, the only asset we'd really be spending is time."

"Then let's be off!" Summer declared, heading for the wall door closest to Slate House.

"You take this one," I said, noticing Weaver. "I just remembered another renewable resource."

Wool. It was one of the first trades we'd made. And somehow we'd forgotten it in the rush to expand the village. Now, after checking in with Weaver to reaffirm that white and black wool were still in demand, I headed straight for our garden. *Been a long time*, I thought, picking six stalks of ripe wheat, *a long time since I bred animals. And, at least this time, it won't be for their meat.*

I made for the field where the few sheep were grazing. Two white, one black. "Hey, flock," I called. "Sorry I've taken my eye off the wool ball." After feeding the two white ones to make a new, fuzzy, cute lamb, I put down a crafting table, then a storage chest to store the wool. "Gonna be some time before I get enough to trade," I said while whipping up some shears. Four white cubes went into the box, along with a couple of black ones. "You're gonna take even longer," I said to the now-naked dark sheep, "because if I try to breed you with a white one, I'll just get gray wool that Weaver doesn't want."

"Moo," mooed one of the nearby cows.

"Yeah, that's true," I answered. "I can use some of the squid ink from Summer's fish farm to dye white wool, but there still isn't that much of it. Unless . . ."

I looked down at the black sheep, then over at the cow. "You think it would work?" I asked, a scheme forming in my head.

"Moo," she responded, clearly saying, "What do you have to lose?"

"Nothing but time," I responded with a glance at the garden and tree farm, "which seems to be all I've got now."

I headed back to Slate House and caught Summer, stone pickaxe in hand, digging at the foot of the hill. "Welcome to my new stone quarry," she explained, "and if it doesn't work, I'll just seal it up and forget the whole affair."

"I got something much crazier cookin'," I said, heading up the hill.

"Care to share?" she asked after me.

"Only if it works." I chuckled, then, a minute later, came down with a dollop of squid ink. I was grateful that Summer had disappeared into her new stone pit. The more I thought about it, the dumber this plan sounded.

Maybe we're just being too idealistic, I thought, striding across the field, *all these high-minded ideals about leaving something for the people who come after us. Maybe we should just leave them the problems, take what we want, move on, and stop worrying about what might happen tomorrow.*

The cows must have sensed my flagging resolve, because one of them threw me an encouraging "Moo!"

"We'll see." I sighed, stepping half-heartedly up to the white lamb. "Here goes nothing."

But instead of nothing happening, I watched the little cloud-colored animal suddenly turn black as flint. "Aw, yeah," I cawed to the cow. "Problems force progress." And the progress paid off handsomely!

Barely a week later, our garden and Summer's fish farm had given me enough wheat and squid dye to raise another six black sheep. "I promise," I said to them on the morning of the seventh day, "no more growing the family. I don't want to overcrowd your grazing field. Plus"—I looked over at the tall tops of the tree farm—"I think we're getting pretty close to wrapping things up."

Heading over to the line of now mature oaks, I reached for a crude but renewable stone axe. Like Summer's quarry, I couldn't afford to damage our valuable tools. It might take a little longer, especially because, by now, the line stretched for a full two dozen oaks, but, also by now, I'd gotten pretty good at crafting an efficient method of timber cutting. I'd chop up the first two trees like a staircase, which gave me enough hyper-reach to get to the tallest logs. Once I reached the end, I'd go back down the line and clear the remaining two-log-high stumps. This would probably take me the whole day, and at least as many stone axes, but I didn't mind. I'd brought the spare tools, as well as a head full of daydreams.

Everything's falling into place, I thought, chopping up into my top path. *The garden's crops aren't just getting emeralds from the new farmer, they're also helping with leveling up Junior.* In honor of this new achievement, I reached into my belt for one of Junior's cookies. "Mmmm," I moaned. *Perfect snack for a perfect workday.*

Resuming my chopping, I thought, *this wood'll give us plenty of fuel to fuse our cobblestones into sellable rock, as well as stacks of sticks to sell to Fletch.* Summer's "stone farm" had yielded both selling rock and building materials for two new fisheries. Luckily, she'd managed to find another couple salmon spawn sites that were safely away from the Dark Tower. Placing the new axolotl in one and its child in the next were enough to keep her, and Fisher, pretty busy.

"I don't have any more time to mine stones," she said one night over dinner. "Every morning it's fish-fish-fish."

"You can see why people back home can have trouble growing their businesses," I said, thinking about all the ventures I was juggling. "Eventually you get to a point where you either hire more workers, or you just keep things where they are."

"I suppose that would make even more trouble," Summer had said between bites, "figuring out what's a fair wage versus how fast you want to grow."

"Business is a complicated business," I mused. "Good thing we're only in the business of getting home."

And it looked like we were almost there. As my hands continued chopping, my mind began ticking off how far we'd come. Fish, wheat, wool, stone, and sticks, all those little trickles flowing together in a river of emeralds. Last night, our accumulated gem stock stood at sixty-eight—no, seventy-two! I still had four in my pack, yesterday's trade that I'd forgotten to deposit into the chest. Would today get us to eighty? And if that was the case, how soon before we'd be moving on?

How fitting, I thought, as more apple oak wood flew into my pack. *This is right where I started, back on my island, chopping down trees just like this, and destroying them all because I didn't know what I was doing. Now look at them. Look at how much I've learned, how much I've been through. The island, the mountain, and now the village. And, who knows, by this time tomorrow, I might be stepping through a portal on my way ho—*

"Harr!"

The voice was close, and it didn't sound quite right. It was deeper than a normal villager's, gruffer. Angrier?

"Harr!!"

I looked side to side, trying to peer through the thick foliage. Nothing moved beyond the curtain of cubed leaves.

"Harr!!!"

Whoever it was had to either be ahead of or behind me, and since the path forward was solid wood, I turned to go back down the chopped-out tunnel. Just before the steps, a smell hit me. It wasn't zombie stink. More like human bodies that hadn't bathed in a really, really long time, and since that kind of BO didn't come from villagers or me and Summer . . .

Please be wrong, I hoped against hope, *please be wrong about what's waiting at the bottom of the stairs.*

I wasn't wrong.

Stepping down onto solid ground, I found myself eye to crossed green eye with one of the gray raiders. Five of them, actually; all carrying crossbows, with one of those angry-faced banners sticking up from the fifth's back. In a flash of memory, I knew I'd seen this group before. That overcast morning when I'd first discovered Farmer was missing. Those faraway figures at the edge of the mist. It had been a party from the Dark Tower. That was the nagging memory I'd had when we first met them! And now they were back. But why?

"Uh, hey, guys," I said, trying to sound very friendly and very not scared, "nice to . . . meet you?"

They didn't react, just glared.

"I don't want any trouble, okay?" I slowly slipped the axe into my belt, saying, "See, no weapon. No danger." I then held up both arms. *If there was ever a time for this world to let me unclench my fists!* "I'm not a threat. I just wanna live my life and let you live yours. Cool?"

Again, no movement, no reaction other than a hostile-sounding "Harr!" Their breath, even from this distance, smelled like they'd never brushed their teeth.

"Ummm, okay." With the care of someone defusing a bomb, I started moving a hand back into my belt. "Maybe you don't understand my words but"—I reached for the emeralds, careful to try to look as calm as possible—"we can be friends, or, at least, not enemies." I held out the verdant jewels. "Let's make a trade, okay? Let's make peace." One step. That's all it took.

The arrow THUNKed into my armored shoulder, knocking me back, throwing my mind into the most painful lesson I'd ever learned.

No matter how hard you try to avoid conflict, sometimes some people are just looking for a fight.

"You dirty . . ." I swore, the start of a stream of rude words. I won't repeat them, mainly because I don't remember them. I also don't remember how my sword and shield got into my hands. I was just so furious, like when people say that they "saw red." What I saw was gray, the nearest gray face taking a slice of diamond blade.

"Harr!" rumbled the barbarian, as I slashed them back with several more strokes.

"This is what you want?!" I shouted. "This is why you came all the way here?!" Another slice, a puff of smoke, and a hovering, battered crossbow flew into my pack.

There was no time to celebrate, as three more crossbow bolts struck my chest. "Bring it on!" I roared and rushed at my next target.

This time I was smart, getting in a few good strikes before stopping to deflect. I had enough experience with crossbows (on both ends, I might add) to know how long they took to reload. That experience, along with the creak of the weapon's string pulling taut, was more than enough warning. Two arrows bounced harmlessly off my shield, while a third found its mark in my hip.

"You'll see," I hissed, smoking the second raider. "You'll get your turn."

I scooted sideways, trying to position them into a narrower formation. Hopefully, I could trick the rear ones to accidentally shoot their friends in the back.

Score!

The closest one to me flashed red as their buddy hit them in the small of their back. Unlike skeletons, though, they didn't turn to fight each other. "Dang, you're disciplined," I snorted, "but maybe I can at least get you with a bone-bounce."

Edging closer to the back-shot raider, I tried to angle my shield for a ricochet. "Here goes," I hissed at the creak of a loading crossbow.

Whp! Thk!

I lowered my shield just enough to see the projectile bounce back!

. . . and plop harmless at the raider's feet.

"Can't win 'em all," I huffed, then felt my heart skip at the distant sound of "Hrrh."

The villagers! I was too close! What time was it? Were they all safe at work behind the wall? Was it still morning-meander-o'clock?

Lead the attackers away! Keep them after you!

I retreated back into the field, praying that these monsters didn't kill animals for sport. As the next barrage battered my shield, I realized that it couldn't protect me forever. I could see it starting to give, splintering among pinprick holes. How many more hits could it take?

Stay calm. Stay focused. Stick with the tactic that's working.

Back and forth, strike and block. I hacked the third raider down then turned to its closest accomplice. This one had the back banner. It loomed above me, those exaggerated eyes glaring down.

"Harr!" its owner sneered as I shielded myself from its shot.

"You think you scare me?" I sneered right back. "After all I've been through?" Block, strike. "Zombie, spiders, creepers, skeletons?" Strike, block. "Starvation, poison, lava?" I took the next hit; I didn't care. Strike, strike! "You think after snow and desert and every nightmare in the Nether that your rinky-dink little flag's gonna shake me?!"

The final swipe, and a now shrunken banner dropped to the smoky ground. "Yeah!" I yelled. "Think agai . . ."

The banner leaped into my pack, and suddenly, a strange sensation gripped me.

It was an ominous feeling, a sickening dread that shivered up my spine. I know this sounds crazy, especially if this has never happened to you, but there's no other way to describe it except feeling cursed.

"Harr!" Another arrow, piercing my exposed right forearm. The last raider!

I turned, shield up, ready to finish the battle. But as the crossbow aimed in my direction, its owner suddenly burst into flames.

"Summer!" As the barbarian poofed away, I could see my friend running toward me.

"Guy!" she shouted. "Are you all right?" I must have looked terrible with all those arrows sticking out of me.

"I don't know what happened," I said, shaking from the

adrenaline of the fight. "One minute I was just chopping wood and the next, there they were, and they wouldn't listen to me, and they wouldn't trade, they just . . ."

"It's over," Summer soothed. "You saw off the lot, and now you need to rest and—"

Her words were cut short by a new sound, the distant blare of a horn. And right behind it was another sound, one that we both knew and dreaded: the bell!

"This isn't over." Summer glanced nervously around us. "More baddies must be on the way."

"C'mon!" I breathed. "Back to the village!"

We ran through the south door, and into absolute chaos. The whole population was in hysterics, rushing around, sweat dripping from their faces, yelling "Hrrh" to themselves and each other.

"Don't panic!" I shouted reflexively. "Just get in your houses and shut your doors." I'm surprised I didn't say something equally useless like "Move in an orderly fashion." I knew I wasn't doing any good, but I was also trying to calm myself. "We're safe in here!" I insisted, standing up on the fountain. "Everything's gonna be fine."

And then, amidst the frantic hrrh's came a lower, deeper, "Harr!"

"They must be just outside the wall," said Summer—and just as she finished speaking, I saw a shape move between the spaces in the door.

"Look!" I pointed as another raider, then another, walked past the acacia slats. As we ran over for a closer look, a fourth figure stopped right on the other side. "We gotta block it up!" I yelped, reaching for the logs in my belt. "If they can open the doors like hoglins . . ."

"I don't think so." Summer shook her head as she peered between the door slats. "Or else they would have done it by now."

"Harr!" agreed the frustrated attacker, glaring at us through the thin orange stripes.

"Maybe they can't get in," I said, "but we can't get at them!" I could feel my heart pounding, my breath racing. "What do we do? What do we do?!"

"First," Summer said calmly, "have a snack. You need it."

She was right. My wounds ached, my stomach growled. "Where do you think this second group came from?" I asked between bites of cookie. "Were they already on their way? Or already here, on the other side of the village?"

Summer shrugged. "They must have called in reinforcements somehow. By telepathy or a crystal ball in the Dark Tower."

"Or," I sighed, as the food and hyper-healing allowed me to focus on the last, invisible wound, "it could be my curse."

On Summer's confused head tilt, I continued, "Their leader . . . I picked up its banner. It must be marked, like a homing beacon." I turned back to the eyes locked on me through the door. "If that's the case, I gotta ditch it. Get it as far away from the village as possible." I pointed to the opposite door. "If I slip out there, it'll give me a head start. I can cross the river and . . ."

"And put yourself in more danger?" Summer scoffed. "Certainly not." She gave a slight chuckle. "I'm not denying that this face flag may have hexed you in some way, but we can deal with that after we see them off." She motioned to the nearest staircase. "And we'll do that by sniping them from the wall."

"Right," I agreed as we darted for the stone steps. Lowering the mini-drawbridge, we bounded onto the walkway. "I can't see them," I said, straining to peer between the gaps in our peg-teeth obstacles.

"This way," Summer called ahead of me. "Another leader." What she meant was that this group, like the last one, had a member with another banner, and the top of that banner poked high enough above the others to give us an idea where they were.

One problem, though. They were right up against the wall; so close that, from right above, we couldn't see a thing. We could hear them, though, stomping and harr-ing furiously below.

"If we only had some lava," I pined, "we could just dump a bucket on them from above."

"Not necessary," said Summer, eyes scanning the length of the wall. "I think I've got a more practical plan."

"Shoot," I said.

"Exactly," she returned, and took off down the walkway with a shout of "Stay there" over her shoulder. And then I saw it, and was grateful for the uneven layout of the wall. Because it was shaped like a T, and because the head of that T stuck out from the rest of the wall, Summer could perch herself right on the northeast corner and shoot straight at the raiders below me. Amid pained hargs, she ordered, "Ready your crossbow." A second later, I saw why. Her shots had gotten the assailants' attention. And now three burning bodies (the fourth must have died by now) were all heading in her direction. Fortunately, my crossbow was already cocked. I aimed carefully, just ahead of them, and squeezed the trigger. One shot, three hits.

Nice goin', Magic Multishot Crossbow!

Two raiders died instantly; the last one made it a few more steps. Another sun-sparking hit from Summer, and that, as I've heard it said, was that.

"We did it!" I shouted, on my way to the steps. "It's over!"

We dashed out the door, and over to all that remained. Among the beaten-up crossbows, I noted a hovering emerald. "So, they do value these," I said, scooping up the jewel, "but they chose violence and thievery over peaceful trade."

"Proves we can sleep with a clear conscience," said Summer as she reached for the second, hovering banner.

"Leave it," I said, then realized that my cursed feeling hadn't left. I was about to tell Summer when we heard the blast of another horn.

CHAPTER 17

"More?" Numb-faced with shock, I dashed back inside the wall. "There're even more of them?!"

"This isn't a raid," huffed Summer, racing back for the wall, "it's an honest-to-goodness war."

War. There's nothing honest or good about it. But here it was, like it or not. How big would it get? How long would it last?

There's gotta be a way to end this, I thought, racing Summer to the wall facing the new threat. *It started so fast, so easily. Shouldn't there be a fast, easy way to stop it?*

Summer reached the walkway ahead of me. First with the naked eye, then with her spyglass, she scanned the horizon toward the desert. "Clear!" As I climbed up next to her, she repeated, softly, "Clear?"

She couldn't have missed them. Not Summer. And we'd

both clearly heard the horn. On a hunch, I raised my own spy-glass in the opposite direction and cried, "Flower Valley!"

There were five this time; three crossbow archers, a banner leader, and another, slightly different member. I could make out a grayish coat, dark turquoise pants, and as they approached the wall, something appeared in its hands. An axe?

"Looks like they're adapting," I observed, "which makes them smart as well as strong."

"Cover!" shouted Summer as an approaching raider raised their crossbow. We jumped out of sight, pressing ourselves against the wall's protective pegs. "Why did they come from the valley?" I wondered, peeking out for a countershot. "They must have known that we'd be watching in the direction of the Dark Tower."

Summer was silent for a moment. "Could be," she began, "unless . . ."

Her words halted at the ominous creak of an opening door. *Got to be the villagers*, I thought . . . hoped . . . *They just won't stay put!* But instead of seeing one of them run from house to house, we watched all the nearby golems converge on a spot of wall under us. The southern door!

"They're in!" Summer aimed her bow as one of the crossbow archers darted out from underneath our walkway.

Without thinking, I jumped down to see that new raider, holding an axe and running after . . .

"Junior! Look out!" I couldn't use my crossbow. The multi-shot might hit a friendly. The barbarian closed, axe raised to Junior's head. *No!* My mind flashed to the first Farmer. *Not another villager! Not again!* Legs pumping, arm switching from bow to sword, I run-hopped the last few squares and sliced my diamond blade down the would-be killer's back.

Axeman flashed red, growled a furious "Phogh!" then pivoted from Junior to me. The blow was strong, painful. I hadn't been hit like that since sparring with Nether piglin brutes. I oofed, reeled back, then gave as good as I got. Blow for blow. Sword and axe.

"Why are you doing this!?" I asked through labored strikes. "Why do you keep attacking?" My answer was a nauseating breath cloud of "Hargh!"

"Block the doors!" hollered Summer, as another sword swipe axed the axeman. "Don't let any more in!" Tossing her half my chopped tree trunks, we split up to seal the entrances. Logs stacked with eight quick pops and two very long sighs.

"Right then," huffed Summer, heading back for the staircase. "Let's take our positions again. You hold them whilst I . . ."

"Wait a sec," I exhaled, "I've been thinking."

"Now?" Summer quipped with exasperation.

Holding up a *hear me out* fist, I explained, "Every time we wipe out a raider squad, they just come back stronger."

"So . . ." Summer spun a *wrap it up* arm.

"So, let's hold off on killing the ones that are left," I said, reaching the wall's catwalk behind her. "Just long enough to try to figure out what's goin' on, why they keep coming, and what we can do to break the cycle!"

Summer paused to hum pensively, then admitted, "Good thought. But where do you propose we find all this war-winning knowledge?"

"Where else?" I asked, pointing to the library. "There might be something we've overlooked. And, if not, the break we take might allow our besiegers to just get bored and move on."

That didn't happen. Our besiegers didn't move on from boredom. Not only did they stick around, but, as we read long into the night, their angry grunts only mixed with the groans, hisses, and clacks of spawned mobs. Worse still, all of them seemed to get along, as if the other monsters were all saying, "Oh, hey, 'bout time you guys showed up. Maybe you can finally finish the job of wiping this village off the map."

It all might have been worth it if we could have found some new knowledge about our enemy. But we didn't, and it wasn't for lack of trying! Any schoolteacher—heck, any college professor!—would have been proud of how deeply we read, how meticulously we pored over every possible detail. And we would have settled for any scrap of helpful data: where they come from, why they attack, why they *keep* attacking, and how to, finally, end their war of aggression.

The only useful tidbit was how to cure a zombified villager. "You hit one with a 'splash potion,'" I read aloud, "which must mean throwing a bottle, then feed it a golden apple."

"Would have been helpful ages ago," Summer said sadly, "back when poor old Farmer topped it."

"We still couldn't have done anything," I said, feeling her twinge of guilt. "There wasn't a chance."

"I suppose you're right." She sighed with clinging remorse.

"Try not to think about the past," I said, opening another book. "We've got too much right in front of us." I was trying to be positive, to take a symbolic "page" from Summer's mental book of marching on. It didn't last long. After plowing through the unread volumes, we went back to the previously perused ones. There had to be some buried details in there somewhere. Something we missed because we hadn't been looking for it.

"Of course!" I spat angrily, as dawn broke over my last, closed manual. "Of course this library wouldn't have what we need. Nobody ever invests enough money into libraries! Why is that? Why don't people value their libraries the same way they do, I don't know, fancy cars or clothes or TV shows that distract them from life's problems, which they might be solving, by the way, if they put enough money into libraries?!"

"If you're quite finished," Summer said, presenting another book, "you might be happy to know that this night hasn't been an entire waste."

She held up the section on golems.

"Back when I first showed you this book," she said, "I completely missed the part on how to make more of them!" She showed me the pages that explained how placing four solid iron blocks in a T-shape with a carved pumpkin on top could spontaneously create the clanking crusher.

"Too bad we don't have nearly enough iron," I grumbled bitterly.

"Not for new recruits," Summer countered, "but more than enough to repair the veterans." She couldn't have been more right about that. Even before tangling with the raiders, peacetime wear and tear made many of them look close to collapse. And if it was peacetime, we would have just let them vanish and respawn. But now, we needed everyone in top fighting shape.

After gathering some ingots from the trading post, I approached the most battered, battle-scarred golem of the group.

"Guess this makes us combat medics," I said, and held out the bars. It only took one ingot to turn the last-leg robot into a model as good as new. "Now you're ready to mash something," I said proudly, then, in response to the chorus of harrs from outside the wall, added "'cause if this isn't the last raiding party, there's gonna be a lot more to mash."

"I've been having a think on that," said Summer, striding up next to me. "Not about this being the last of the baddies, but about giving us more ways to fight."

She led me back to the trading post, specifically to the crafting table, where she placed some of the logs I'd given her. "Last night gave me the chance to ponder this whole business of war, and how my country went about it." The logs changed into planks. "Remember at the underground lake, when I first recalled how people did a lot of scrapping about on the seas? Well, I still can't recall much, but I think some of those battles were in tall sailing ships." The planks were laid in two rows of three. "And, if I'm not too barmy from lack of sleep, those great sailing ships used these!"

Triumphantly, she held up a stack of trapdoors.

"Totally lost me," I admitted. *How did ships use trapdoors?*

"Oh, Guy," she laughed, then led me back outside.

Walking over to a bare section of wall, she replaced her handful of trapdoors with a pickaxe. "Stand back," she said warily, "don't want to catch a stray arrow." Still clueless as to the plan, I did know enough to get safely out of the way. Summer picked out a block of cobblestone, then filled the gap with a trapdoor window. "Here I am!" she shouted, flipping down the flat wood square. "Come and get me!"

And as she raised her bow, I got it. "A gunport!" I'd seen them before, either in movies, or, I think, a ride at an amusement park. I remember the sides of a ship opening to fire cannons, then closing them back up to reload!

"If the enemy's adapting, why can't we?" she chirped, straining at her bowstring. She didn't have long to wait. As soon as a pair of crossed eyes darkened the opening, she loosed a shot and slammed the trapdoor. "We'll just let them simmer till the flames lick out, then start the whole process all over again."

"Brill," I said, and went off to make more gunports. Even if they weren't well suited for my multishot, non-burning crossbow, the Vesson behind them was priceless.

Adaptation is a key element in war. New weapons, new ways of using them. I guess that's true for my world as well, and I guess that's kinda sad. All that money and brain power spent on hurting people instead of helping them. But what's the alternative? Not adapt and risk getting wiped out, like these pillagers were trying to do to the villagers? I wish I had the right answer. I hope I'll learn what it is someday. But that day, what I learned was that adaptation was a race between both sides.

And this fact was driven home later that day, when we prepared to take out the last surviving raider. This bitter-ender (Summer's word) was the leader, bopping their banner around the entire perimeter. "Coming around to you," I reported from my position on the walkway.

"Righto." Across from me at a ninety-degree angle, I watched one of the gunports open. When Bitter-Ender got halfway between us, we both opened fire. The leader burned, turned, took another hit, then smoked into a hovering flag.

Please, I hoped and prayed to whatever higher power might hear me, *please let this be the last of them.*

But hopes and prayers don't end wars.

"Bahbuhbahbahbuhbaaaaaaaaah!" Another horn blew, announcing another wave!

We answered with combined curses and the full 360-degree sweep of our spyglasses.

They came across the field this time, thankfully ignoring the animals. "I can make out another axeman," I said, "along with . . . Is that a witch?"

"No mistaking it," confirmed Summer, "but what in the steaming Nether is that?"

I squinted through my eyepiece at a whole new, jaw-clenching monstrosity. The body was cow-shaped but when it thundered past the real thing, I could see it was easily twice the size. Mottled brown hide, straight horns as big as my fist, iron plates on me-high legs, a saddle chained to its back, and dark green, barbarian crossed eyes.

"Looks like some kind of monster bull," I gulped through churning guts.

Summer drew her bow. "Then let's see how many steaks it'll yield!" Her aim was perfect. The bounding bull burst into flames. "And again," she said, loosing another shaft. "And again?"

The juggernaut took four more hits, three from her and one from me, before it reached the wall without dying! "Like tennis balls at a blooming tank!" Summer rasped angrily.

"And too dangerous to keep trying!" I said as crossbow arrows whipped past my face.

"Gunports!" said Summer, as we leaped from the walkway to

ground level. I landed softly, turned to the closest oak panel, and saw its small holes darkened by a black mass.

"Here!" I called, dropping the barrier and raising my crossbow. "Gotcha!" I fired at the approaching eyes.

I must have been too close to the window because, somehow, the demon buffalo hit me with the kind of bone-crushing force that would have shamed a Nether boar.

"Oy!" I fell back, the wind knocked out of me. "Stay away from the walls," I wheezed, then realized we might have a new problem on our hands. The creature hit so hard that its energy passed through solid objects! What did that mean for the buildings? Some of them made up part of the wall!

Still smarting from blunt force trauma, I ran from house to house. "Don't go near the walls!" I shouted through a rainstorm of villager sweat. "That new thing out there can batter you right through the . . ."

"Hahahahah!" The witch cackled somewhere out there, followed by a wildly inappropriate word from Summer.

"What?" I asked, running out to meet her. "What's wrong?"

"Ruddy witch," she grumbled, "threw a blasted healing potion on the battering bull." I didn't repeat her unmentionable word, but I sure felt like it. All our damage gone, all our effort rolled back to zero. "Looks like they got their own combat medic," I said, cocking my crossbow, "which gives us Target Number One."

Summer nodded in agreement, then looked down at her painted-on belt. "I'm out of arrows!"

"Here." I reached into my belt. "Take some of mine."

As the tossed stack flew into her pack, she took a few steps back from the gunport. "They'll belong to the witch in no time!" Using the safety of her hyper-reach, she opened the trapdoor to scan for the troublesome cackler. I tried the same tactic, but found myself facing another crossbow archer.

"Harr!" they growled as I blocked their first shot with my shield.

"Will ya get outta the way?" I whined. "And stop being such a well-trained professional soldier!"

Strangely enough, they didn't listen. And as we traded frustrating shots, Summer wasn't doing any better. "Bleeding bull keeps getting in the way!" she snarled through grinding teeth.

"Try another angle," I suggested, "back on the wall!"

She ran for the staircase, up to a position that should have allowed her to shoot over the biological bulldozer. I watched her loose a few shafts, then stop at the sound of breaking glass. "Another healing potion," she yelled, "and its range is healing everybody!"

"Hold on!" I said, slamming my gunport shut. "If I can get a better angle, we can coordinate our shots!"

At that moment, I heard more glass breaking, this time high on the wall—right where Summer was supposed to be. She must have seen the potion coming and had enough time to skedaddle. "Careful when you open the port!" she called on the run. "Witchy's lobbing at us now!"

"Any chance they might be healers?" I joked, then went back to checking the ports. Squinting through the holes, I clocked archers, the leader, and the roving bull.

"Hurry up!" called Summer, scooting and shooting along the wall. "I'm low on ammo again!"

"Doin' the best I can," I griped back, then thought I saw a hint of purple. "Got 'er!" I called. "Just keep shooting! Keep them distracted!"

I cocked my crossbow with the last arrow, opened the gunport, took aim—and saw an incoming potion! I tried to dodge. I almost made it, but, like a real grenade, the impact was too wide.

"Iiiiii'm hiiiiiiiiit," I slurred, annoyed but grateful that it was only a slowness splash. Lead legs, concrete arms. I tried to close the panel, but took another arrow in the stomach.

"Get clear!" Summer jumped down next to me, slamming the trapdoor shut. "We need to reload anyway."

"Ffflletch!" I gurbled, molasses-walking after her. I thought I remembered seeing Fletcher in the hotel, and made a beeline—well, snail-line—for it, as Summer ran like a rabbit for the trading post.

I was right about the hotel. Fletch was sweat-bopping up and down the first floor. "Buuuuddy," I tried to say, feeling like my tongue had just taken one of those numbing shots from the dentist, "weeee neeeed aaarrrows." Before I could slouch within hyper-reach, Fletch scrabbled up to the hotel's second floor. Maybe the slowness of my rude word sounded funny, but at that moment, the last thing I felt like doing was laughing. At least my brain was still quick, and it told me to park myself right at the bottom of the stairs. They had to come down sometime soon, and there'd be no place else to go but through me.

And it turned out to be a good call, because, as Fletch came frantically hrrh-hrrh-hrrh-ing back down the stairs, I held out the emeralds from my pack. The villager stopped, calmed down, and opened their mobile store.

Three gems got me forty-eight arrows, and when Summer showed up a second later, the serious re-arming began. "Don't close the shop yet!" she cried as emeralds and arrows flew between them. It didn't take long, though, Fletch backed up amid rising pink bubbles. Without intending to, we'd reached another level, and were offered either an enchanted "Unbreaking" crossbow, or . . . the chance to enchant five of our arrows!

We weren't sure what the exact enchantment was. Fletch didn't say—just gave a "Hrrh!" to our questioning glances—but after completing the purchase and reading the tiny little label on each shaft . . .

Okay, there's a word, but I'm not sure what it is. Karma? Shatner-Freud? I don't know. But it most definitely applied here, because the enchantment for these new arrows was, drumroll, "Slowness!"

"Awwww yeeeeaaaaah!" I mush-mouthed, and tried a sloth version of my happy dance. It wasn't just the magic shafts, or the copious amounts of conventional munitions. It was also the brand new Vesson that came with them: when a community is threatened, everyone can make a difference. Not just the fighters, like me, Summer, and the golems, but civilian villagers, like Fletcher and Librarian, who were doing their part to support us. This must be what it was like back on our world, or at least it should be. People served and sacrificed any way they could so that when their entire community was attacked, the entire community responded. I thought I remembered images of past conflicts, of a woman with her hair tied up, flexing her biceps. I could even remember the slogan above her: "We can do it!"

We.

I'd like to say my feeling of pride in us all coming together was what drove me from a slog to a jog, but in reality, it was probably just the Slowness potion wearing off. "Good timing," said Summer, noticing the increased spring in my step, "because I think I know the best way to utilize our new arsenal."

I was about to ask for details, but she turned for the staircase and said, "No time to explain, just get yourself close to the wall. Not so close as to be rammed by the bio-tank, but close enough to draw them all to you." She ran up to the catwalk, but stayed well away from the attackers. "When you open the gunport, fire a regular shot to get their attention. Save your slowpokes for when I say." She drew her bow. "Also, when I say, be prepared to back up."

Had she forgotten about potion grenades? And how staying so close to the wall would just invite another?

I started to argue this point, but she cut me off. "Trust me."

I did.

Friends trust each other.

I crept as close to the wall as I could and, sweating under my armor, I dropped the gunport and raised my crossbow. The conventional shot tagged one archer and brought the rest toward me.

"Raise your shield," ordered Summer. "Don't run until I tell you."

She knows what she's doing, I thought as flint-tipped missiles bonked off my fracturing board.

"Just remind me," came her voice from on high, "witches usually follow slow potions up with poison ones, right?"

"Um, maybe?" I yipped, as an arrow missed my shield and landed in my foot instead.

"Can't be helped," she chirped lightly.

Please know what you're doing.

"Closer," I heard her whisper. "Closer . . ." Then, to me, "Run!"

I jumped back and to the side, as the sound of broken glass filled my ears. "You did it!" cried Summer. "Have a gander!" Hoofing it up to the walkway, I peered over the edge to see green bubbles—poison bubbles—rising from every member of the group. That had been Summer's plan! Use me as bait, then bunch them in for accidental friendly fire.

"Doh!" I taunted down to the witch. "You totally nailed your own guys!"

"Haha!" she cackled, lifting another pink bottle.

"Healer!" cried Summer, raising her bow to shoot. The flaming arrow tagged the witch square in the face, banishing the potion, and slowing her chances to grab another. "Hit 'em!" Summer commanded. "Hit 'em all!"

I responded with a tri-shot of slowpoke arrows, nailing two archers and their leader. "Keep shooting!" said Summer, slamming the witch until she finally puffed away. I ducked back to avoid an incoming arrow, reloaded, and triple-hit the group again. I almost felt sorry for them; shot, poisoned, and now burning as Summer tagged each one. Poof-poof-poof. The archers went first, then the leader, then, finally, the giant monster succumbed to our united barrage.

"Just one left," sang Summer. "Ol' Axeman's scrunched up against the wall." Jumping down from the walkway, she began opening all the gunports. "Come out, come out, wherever you are."

"Hold your fire," I said, "for now."

Summer looked up at me, her voice raising in confusion. "You're not suggesting we have another grand rest-research-strategy session, are you?"

I shook my head. "We don't need it. I think I've figured out how to end the war."

CHAPTER 18

"If the banner," I said, holding up that first captured flag, "is acting like a homing beacon for more raiders, then why not plant it far away?" I gestured to a spot beyond the wall. "Across the south field. Far enough that, if it works, they'll just mill around without threatening the village. And maybe," I said with a shrug, "we can even wall them in forever."

"I suppose it's worth a try," Summer answered skeptically, "but we've got to time it just right." She glanced at one of the north wall gunports, to a hole in the oakwood that showed the barest hint of Axeman pacing outside. "Don't go far enough that I can't see you with the spyglass, and then once you plant the flag, I'll pop the chopping chap."

"Got it," I said with a nod. "Then I'll be outta there before their buddies show up."

"Right." Summer readied herself at the eastern, log-blocked door.

"Right," I echoed, positioning myself at the south.

"Here we go." Summer chopped away the wood, opened the door, took a half step out, and shouted, "Over here, Stinky!"

"Phaw!" growled the axeman and, judging from the movement through the gunports, we could see they were on their way.

I chopped up the logs in front of the southern door, then ran out as fast as I could.

"You're doing great," Summer called, followed by the WHP of an arrow. "He'll never catch you." I looked back to see my pursuer falling back. My head start, plus the last of Summer's slow-enchanted shots, ensured a clean getaway. "Stinky" must have known that, too, because, soon enough, they turned back for the village. I kept going across the uneven, rusty-green ground.

"Keep clear of me," I called to the cows and sheep. "It's gonna get dicey around here." I spied a rise just ahead, free of animals and trees. Climbing to the top, I waved at Summer, then smacked the flag into the earth.

This doesn't feel right, I thought, as the cursed sensation remained. "Summer, don't!" I yelled, running back with waving arms. "Don't shoot 'im!" Too late. She'd obviously been watching me through her spyglass, then lowered it as soon as the banner stood up. I saw the flicker of an arrow, then the flames of its target. I was a quarter of the way back to the village when the axeman smoked out.

"Bahbuhbahbahbaaaah!"

Another horn, another wave.

I stopped, stupidly, to look back at the ominous banner. I couldn't help but hope that I was right earlier, that I'd see the new raiders rally around it like bugs to a light bulb.

That didn't happen. They didn't appear.

"What the . . ." I asked myself aloud. "Where are . . ."

"Run!" came Summer's distant cry. "Ruuuuuuun!"

As I turned back, my eyes swept across Flower Valley. So many of them! Several axemen were mixed in among the archers, along with at least three witches. They were totally ignoring the banner, instead charging right for the village—and me!

I ran, thighs cramping, lungs burning, brain pulsing with this new, brutal Vesson: it's a lot harder to stop a war than to start one.

"You're almost there!" screamed Summer behind a stream of arrows. "The door!" I could see it in front of me, light through the slats showing how she'd removed the barrier. Twenty paces. Ten.

SLAM!

The battle bull hit me so hard I felt like a crash test dummy. I flew sideways, away from the village. Landing on cracked ankles, I turned back for the door and saw that the whole squad now stood between me and salvation. "Around the side!" Summer shouted. "The east door!"

Panting, wincing through hyper-healing pain. An arrow in my back. A second in my calf. I zigged, jumped, heard shattering glass behind me. Potion grenade! Missed! The witch cackled as its partner lobbed another.

I jumped again, zagged, and dodged another splash. Too

many witches, one stopping to throw while the others kept up the chase. If they hit me with poison, or even another round of slowness, I was done for! Another arrow lanced the back of my neck.

Too much damage!

I rounded the corner wall, saw the door was open . . . then, behind it . . . more raiders! A few had splintered off from the main group, heading for the door that Summer had left open for me!

Cornered, trapped!

"The river!" Summer's voice from the wall. "Your helmet!"

Respiration! Hope! I turned and speed-staggered for blue salvation. I leaped off the raised bank, splashed down. Cold. Welcome. I dove deep among the bubbling arrow trails!

Another splash, far above me. I looked up to see a dark mass. The buffalo, swimming toward me. But it couldn't dive! None of them could! They just paddled chaotically above me like unarmed ships over an escaping submarine!

But could I escape? The fish farm dams blocked me in both directions! Trapped again, and now with a chance of drowning! I let go a bubbling swear, then regretted it a second later. The axolotl, Goldie! She was swimming toward the closest archer and . . . biting it!

"Thank you," I gurgled, grateful tears mixing with the sweet river water. But gratitude wasn't enough. I had to help my amphibian ally. The dams, my pickaxe! Thoughts clearing, I reached for my magic rock breaker, and slowly, patiently began chipping away at one of the walls. Four stones later, Ax came swimming through to help her mate. "Look out," I bubbled as the bobbing bull drew closer. I paddled to the surface, hoping to use my crossbow, but took two arrows to the face. The archers on the bank were about to wade in after me.

"Get out of there!" called Summer, still shooting from the wall. "You're pulling them all in!" I knew what she meant; the longer I stayed, the more raiders I attracted, and while the brave axolotls were doing their best to help, they'd never survive a prolonged fight.

I dove again, planning to, hopefully, swim out the hole into Ax's fish farm. That's when I saw it! The dark opening at the bottom of the river. I'd initially missed it before, looking in every direction but toward the village. A submerged cave! Maybe even a tunnel! *And if this is how Ax had gotten from the river to the village pond* . . . I thought hopefully, *maybe I can, too!*

I dove into the darkness and saw dim light far ahead. The pond? I swam with as much speed as the water would let me. I didn't think about my air supply, or how many times my head hit the rocky ceiling. Forward. Forward. Then up into the light. Splashing into bright, warm air. The village, all around me!

"Harr!" A barbarian's face in mine, an axe crashing down on my head. The splinter group! The ones that got inside! Even as I dodged the second blow, I could see two other raiders being bashed by a couple of golems. Where was Summer? Still on the wall, looking for me? "Hargh!" snarled my enemy, raising their weapon for another chop.

"Hold that—*oof* . . . thought!" I grunted as the blow caught me halfway out of the water. I couldn't afford to fight yet. I had to seal the door.

I scrambled for the door, with grunts and swipes at my back.

Ignoring the pain, I stretched my invisible hyper-reach, oak trunks in hand, barely seconds from blocking the door.

Another "Harr!" hit the air, but this time, in front of me! Just before I could plonk down a log, the acacia slatted panel swung open to reveal a crossbow archer. "Back!" I barked, using the logs to punch the raider away. As it raised its weapon to shoot, I slammed the door and started stacking logs. The last one fixed just as my first attacker struck again. I winced at the axe wound in my lower back, spun, raised my shield, then sliced and diced them into the next dimension.

"There you are!" Summer, leaping down from the walkway, was running toward me. "But how on—"

"The pond," I panted, "it's got a tunnel from the river."

Summer's eyes, and bow, flicked to the water, as if she half expected the rest of the attackers to come up after me. "At least they can't swim under water."

"No kidding!" I said as relief washed over me. Then as the wave suddenly rolled back, "The axolotls!?"

"Safe and sound." Summer nodded calmly, holding up a comforting cubed hand. "Wriggled to Ax's farm as soon as you vanished." Her eyes darted to the wall. "And thankfully, the baddies didn't follow them."

"At least that's something." I sighed deeply.

"Something," Summer repeated with a tinge of disappointment. "I'm just sorry your plan didn't work." And, as if laughing at our failure, a chorus of "Harrs" drifted over the wall. "Looks like we'll have to try something else."

"We will," I said, turning to the wall, or rather, to something far beyond it, "and I know now what it is." I had a sinking feeling, much worse than any curse. It was the same stomach pain I'd had when we'd nearly ended our friendship in the Nether. That unfair fear of accepting a necessary truth. "I think you were right," I said, trying to keep my voice even, "that day when we first discovered them. I think they won't stop until we go on the attack." I turned back to face her, my voice heavy with the weight of my next words. "Their home base has to be neutralized. I have to destroy the Dark Tower."

"We," Summer corrected. "We have to destroy it."

"No." I shook my head, burping up a bubble of nervous acid. "I have to go alone."

"Rubbish." My unshakeable buddy laughed. "We'll be much more effective if we're together."

"But we'll be leaving the village undefended," I said flatly. "And if I'm wrong, if wiping out the tower doesn't end the war, then someone needs to be here to fend off the next wave."

"Yes, but . . . but . . ." Summer stammered, frantically assembling her argument, "if you're right, then the one who stays will have the wall and golems for backup. Whoever goes after the tower goes it alone." She hesitated a second, no doubt worried that her next point would hurt my feelings. "I should be the one to go . . . because . . . well . . . I'm the better fighter."

"You're right," I agreed, to her surprise, "which is exactly why you need to stay. If I'm overpowered out there, I can always run back to the village. But if that happens here, if the next wave is more than I can handle, then this"—I swept my arm across the houses—"everything we're fighting for dies."

"No, no." Summer shook her head vigorously. "That's utterly ridiculous."

"Summer," I said softly.

"You have absolutely no idea what you're—"

"Summer." Louder, stronger. "You know I'm right."

Silence. A deep, wet sniff.

"Fine then, go be a bloody hero! But you're not just dashing off this instant with no plan or preparation or a proper kit, understand?"

"Understood."

"And," she barreled on, with a waving fist, "we're going full on with, what do you call it, the Congress of the Cube!"

I didn't correct her, just listened as she rattled off a very intricate, genius plan. I won't repeat it now. I don't want to spoil the surprise. I'll just say that she'd been thinking about it for a while, probably since we'd first seen the Dark Tower. Maybe she had been a soldier in that other life, a general or something. Because when she wrapped up with "Any questions?" I honestly had nothing to add. "Excellent." She nodded stiffly. "Now, loan me your helmet."

For a heartbeat, I thought she might be using it to run, or swim, off and attack the tower by herself, but as I trustingly handed over the respirator, she added, "Just long enough for a supply run to Slate House."

"Thanks," I said, jogging up to the wall. "I'll cover you."

I didn't have to. After reappearing in the river, she stayed safely submerged all the way to her aqualift. Even then the besiegers didn't notice. I watched her rise up to our apartment building's roof before I turned back to the village for my part in "kitting out." First stop was the trading post, where I used extra wood and iron to repair my shield. *Hopefully Summer remem-*

bers to bring extra diamonds for my armor, I thought, dropping both my crossbow and the barbarian spare on the anvil. As they fused into one pristine weapon, I muttered, "Spoils of war," then headed out for more supplies.

Next up was Fletcher, who loaded me up on arrows—both regular and enchanted. Then came Junior's food, which, after all the damage I'd taken, was sorely needed. Bought some bread and carrots, chomped them down ravenously, and as my hyper healing finished the job, tried to buy some more. "Hey-oh," I exclaimed, "whatchoo got now?" Apparently my last trade had advanced the farmer into selling two new, suspicious products. And I literally mean "suspicious" because the two steaming bowls didn't exactly look like Summer's rabbit stew.

"Maybe now's not the best time," I said, but reconsidered quickly when remembering all the good things that had come from experimentation. "I guess there's nothing wrong with curiosity," I continued, reciting one of my earliest island lessons, "as long as it's careful curiosity." The careful part came from the milk. Running back to the trading post, I snagged a couple buckets, then resumed my trepidatious transaction. "Ya know," I told Junior, handing over the jewels, "I probably should take milk with me on this mission, too, just in case they've got a poison-throwing witch."

"Hrrh," replied the nervous Farmer, which probably meant, "Dude, given that we're kind of in a war right now, maybe we could limit the extra chitchat?"

"Right." I nodded and slurped the first hot, creamy stew. It tasted like mushrooms and carrots with just a hint of bubbles. I might not have noticed any effect, but, since the sun was just going down, I saw the room suddenly lighten. "Hey!" I blurted with happy surprise. "Cream of Night Vision!" It didn't last long, about three or so seconds. "Better than nothing," I said, "given how low we are on the regular stuff." I then lifted the other bowl to my lips.

Yuck. This one tasted terrible and made my muscles feel like quitting. Weakness. "Ugh," I groaned. "You could have warned me." I reached for the milk, but the bucket felt as heavy as a tanker truck. Before I could even get the cow's gift to my lips, the effects mercifully wore off. "No offense," I said to Junior, "but you might want to change out your product line."

The farmer responded with a "Hrrh," which I took for, "Wasn't a total loss now, was it?"

"You're right," I said, and bought another bowl of night sight stew. And to my happy surprise, pinkish bubbles told me Junior had just advanced again. "Holy moley!" I crowed, as the images of golden carrots and melons appeared. "All this time, right here!" I splurged with the rest of the emeralds, grabbed the shining produce, then ran to the trading post for some empty potion bottles I'd been too lazy to cart back to Slate House.

"Chemist!" I called, sprinting over to the brewing shack, "you home?" Since the occupant wasn't there—probably off cowering with some other terrified citizens—I got right to work preparing potions. First, melons to healers, then carrots to night sight. I wish the latter could have been longer, but I couldn't spare the redstone. Again, no spoilers, but I wasn't sure how much crimson dust would be needed for the mission. It was a hard choice, but hey, three minutes of low-light vision beat the three seconds I'd get from the stew. *Thanks for doing your part, Junior.*

I couldn't wait to tell Summer, and as I bounded back outside, I saw I didn't have long to wait. She was just emerging from the pond, some glistening bottles in her hand. "Been busy brewing," she said, and presented the shimmering gifts.

"Me too!" I said happily, but then asked, "Healers and night sights?"

"Two speeders," she answered, handing me a pair of potions, "to and from the tower."

"Thanks," I said, and handed her the slowpoke arrows, "and just in case the potion doesn't get me outta here fast enough . . ."

"Excellent idea." We continued our exchange when she handed me another bottle. "This one's invisibility. Just like we saw with the wandering trader." The next two potions were dawn-colored, and easily recognizable. "The last of the fireproofs," she said, "as we're now officially out of magma cream."

"You keep one," I insisted. "My mission won't last long enough to use both."

Summer nodded, then tossed me a brew of some new cotton candy–colored fluid. "Remember those bat creatures we scrapped with in the jungle?" she asked. "Well, the other night, when we were combing through the library for war tips, I read in the wildlife book that they're called phantoms, and the bit of membrane I gathered can be used to brew a Potion of Feather Falling."

"Sweet! I assume feather falling means jumping from high places without the splatter."

"Which is why you should only use it if absolutely necessary," Summer cautioned.

"Well, I don't have anything half as cool as these," I said, but handed her three of my fresh-brewed potions. "But how lucky are we that Junior's next level gives us gold carrots and melon?"

"Smashing," she said, taking my gifts, and passing over "The Package." That was her understated term for everything I'd need to destroy the tower. Again, I won't spoil the surprise, but I will say that the whole setup was so complicated and took so much explaining that by the time I was fully ready, the sun had sunk into late afternoon.

"Good thing you've got the two speeders," Summer said reassuringly. "It'll help dodging all the night mobs on the way home."

"Yeah." I nodded, my growing anxiety tingeing my voice slightly as I said, "I was just thinking that." The mission was dangerous enough in the daytime. But now, with spawning mobs on top of attacking barbarians, my stomach was churning, my jaw clenching, and the skin of my face going so numb, it felt like I was wearing a mask.

"Right then," she said, handing me her axe, "don't forget this. Saves more time than your regular model." She reached for something else in her pack. "Speaking of time," she said, and out came a clock for each of us. "We'll need to synchronize our actions." It was just like in the movies, that scene where soldiers are about to head off on a (hopefully) death-defying mission.

"I reckon by the time you reach the tower and get done with all the early steps of the plan, it'll probably be somewhere in the middle of the afternoon." Her eyes flicked to the clock's slowly spinning disc. "When the final dot of blue day vanishes, I'll turn the last of these raiders to smoke while you . . . well . . . you know what you have to do."

"I know," I said, keeping the clock in my left hand. That sinking feeling was back, along with a scratchy throat and upset stomach. "I guess I should be going."

Summer nodded. "I guess so." I could tell she was trying to hide her emotions, too, as she gave a little throat-clearing cough before saying, "Good luck." And as she turned for the wall, I cursed this world, again, for not letting us shake hands.

Chest thumping, mouth desert-dry. *Okay then,* I thought, and walked slowly toward the pond.

"Guy," she called. I stopped and looked up. I guess I was expecting some heart-wrenching speech like, "I just want you to know how much you inspire me. I know you'll win the day. You're the strongest, toughest, bravest person in this world or any other."

But that's not what she said.

"Almost forgot to give you these." She tossed down my thorned pokey-pants. "Hope you don't mind me going into your room without permission."

"No problem," I said, slipping on the enchanted armor. "Thanks."

"Off you go."

I ducked under the water.

It was the cold that made me shiver, not fear. At least, that's what I told myself, bouncing along the bottom of the dark tunnel. Heading out into the river, I looked up to see a raider-free surface. *They must all be back at the wall,* I thought, as the axolotls swam down to meet me, *and at least our aquatic friends are out of danger.* At that moment Goldie swam so close to my face that her soft, slimy hide brushed my cheek. "If that's a goodbye kiss," I bubbled on the way to the bank, "I'll take it."

I broke the surface to the sound of a distant "Harr!"

Too close. They saw me. At least half the horde turned for the river.

"Get moving!" hollered Summer, as slow-enchanted arrows slammed my pursuers.

I splashed out of the water, fumbling in my belt for the speed potion. There. In my hand, almost to my mouth . . . No, wait. That's a healer!

A crossbow arrow streaked past my face. They were in the water now, slowed by it and Summer's shots.

Back into my pack . . . invisibility . . . feather falling . . . why were there so many . . . there! I hoisted the blue bottle, gulped down the sugary brew. Swiftness! Speed! I bolted away, across the desert, with an ancient war cry from my world.

"Meep! Meep!"

CHAPTER 19

I raced east, glancing occasionally to the river on my right. I didn't want to follow it exactly, as the twists and turns would slow me down. I didn't want to stray too far from it, either, and risk getting lost in the desert. How much farther? How much speed was left? So much to keep track of, but details make the difference. Would they be ready for me? Would they have posted sentries? Or an alarm bell like the village, ready to ring?

Ahead! The dark, roundish mass. That had to be the domed top rising just above the distant dunes. I came to a hard stop, looked right and left for some raised ground, then crept as carefully as I could to the top of a nearby sand hill. Through my spyglass I could see that they weren't expecting me. No extra guards, no new fortifications. It's like they were so sure of their success that the concept of an attack had never entered their square heads.

Any relief I might have felt at their slipshod security was cancelled by the fact there seemed to be just as many as before. How can they keep sending out raiding parties and still have this many dudes at home? Was there a spawner somewhere inside the tower? Something I couldn't see from out here? I would have liked to keep watching a while longer, but the clock in my left hand, as well as the setting sun, reminded me of our tight schedule.

"First, I need to see everything," I said, downing the night vision elixir, "and now I need not to be seen." I gulped the invisibility potion, wincing at the pukey, carrion-carrot combo. I didn't feel any different, and when I looked down, I didn't look any different, either. "Oh, right. Now for the clothes," I said, and stripped off my armored boots. It was so weird, that first moment of seeing nothing where my feet should be. If I hadn't been in such a rush, I probably would have stared a lot longer. But the ticking clock didn't care about my curiosity. So, without pausing, I packed away the rest of my armor, then my shield, then made a quick mental check to confirm that there was nothing left but my painted suit. I was clear, literally.

With a Summer-esque "Tallyho," I headed for the tower. But my bravado suddenly evaporated when I realized that we hadn't tested invisibility on raiders! If it didn't work the same as with mobs . . .

This is why Practice is critical to the Way of the Cube!

I held my breath, just in case they could hear me, and kept my distance, just in case they could smell me. I could certainly smell them; desert heat did wonders for caked-on sweat. There were four of them ahead, all patrolling in random patterns. I felt like a character in an old video game, a frog trying to cross the street. One hit and lights out. Same with me.

"Harr!" A barbarian was approaching, and we were practically on a collision course.

I widened the distance, slowly and carefully. What if it sensed me? Fight? Flight? My fist fell to the weapons on my belt, my eyes flicked for an escape route.

"Harr!" The barbarian closed, crossbow raised, then trotted right on by.

The potion worked! I really was invisible! And I couldn't announce it with my usual "Aw yeah" or "That's what I'm talkin' about!"

Summer'll get a kick out of this, I thought with a silent smile. *Finally found a way to shut me up.*

Through softly crunching footsteps, I glided forward to my first goal: the wooden post jail cell that held an iron golem. I glanced back at the raider that had just passed, saw that they were still moving away, then scanned the rest of the area to confirm that none of their buddies were close. I couldn't have asked for a better time. It was now or never.

Wait! came a voice in my head. *You don't have to do this. You can still turn back. They don't know you're here. They won't see you leave. You can run all the way back to the village. Get behind that nice, high wall. Go back to playing defense until you come up with a better plan. A safer plan.*

For just a moment, my hand froze at my belt. But then came another voice.

Moooo.

"You're right," I said aloud, raising Summer's super axe. "Courage is a full-time *job!*"

Netherite crashed into wood, splintering the posts between me and the imprisoned golem. "Don't worry, buddy," I said, taking down the second-to-last obstacle. "I'll have you out in ju—"

WHP!

An arrow smacked into my back. Its owner must have seen the ghostly flying axe, and calculated where the rest of me should be.

"Nice shot," I wheezed, chopping out the final post.

"Harr, harr, harr!" came the alarmed chorus as the clanking warrior lumbered free.

"Take 'em down!" I said, and hid the axe back in my belt. I turned for the tower but found myself nose to big droopy gray nose with an archer cocking their weapon. Maybe I was too close for the invisibility to work. Be it smell, sound, or just intuition, the crossbow followed me as I dove to the side. But before the shot flew, a pair of steel fists came crashing down.

"Hargh!" growled the wounded guard, either in pain or calling for backup.

More arrows were loosed, but not at me. The chrome colossus blinked red like a signal light for me to get moving! Timing was still critical, and now it was working against me. Just as I took off for the tower, the last drops of speed potion sputtered out. How long before the other potions waned? How long before my chrome partner gave out?

The tower doorway! Right in front of me! I almost missed the unmarked, me-height hole. Just a few more steps.

"Harr!" Another egghead, standing in the opening, crossbow raised!

No time to stop, or even dodge. Into my belt, I reached for my sword. Diamond flashed. The archer retreated. I sliced like a chef. The door guard evaporated. I spun just in time to slice their buddy back outside. Sword to logs. Too slow. An outside arrow, right in the nose! I couldn't pause. I had to seal myself in. First the doorway, then the windows. Finally, a moment to breathe! Out came the clock, which told me to keep that moment short.

Time to start setting up Summer's package for what she'd dubbed "Operation First House." If you haven't already figured out what we'd had in mind, you will when I tell you what the core of that package was.

TNT.

Tons of it! Hoarded from Summer's mountain stash, the desert temple, and all the loose gunpowder bought from our wandering merchant. That last part, if you're wondering, was why my mission had to be delayed. The missing ingredient to make TNT had been sand, which Summer shoveled out from the bottom of the river. When added to the others, it was enough to build an explosive column that stretched right to the tower's ceiling.

I started stacking the charges, wrapping the core column in a spiral wooden staircase. After each step, I paused to sprinkle a pinch of redstone fuse so that they would all detonate simultaneously. Hopefully there'd be enough to reach the top. Quickly, carefully, I stacked my way to the ceiling, then used Summer's axe to chop my way to the second floor.

From this open-air story, I was able to see the battle below. One golem taking on the entire horde. I don't know if these machines have any emotion, so I can't accurately call this one brave, but when I saw how much damage it was taking, how its cracked, pockmarked armor was so close to collapse, I couldn't help but get a lump in my throat.

"Thank you," I whispered, just as it happened to look up at me.

"If you want to thank me, don't squander the precious seconds I'm buying you."

No, it didn't say that, but it might as well have, because I jumped right back to building my bomb.

With clanking combat ringing in my ears, I worked as mechanically as my ally. TNT, wood planks, redstone. Slow and steady, up to the third, and obviously safer, floor. I say safer because this room was entirely closed in. No chance of an outside raider shooting me.

Unless it wasn't outside.

Thnk! A crossbow arrow in my leg, knocking me forward as I turned to face angry, narrowed eyes!

Another barbarian! How? From where? They had to be spontaneously spawning, around and inside the tower! And wouldn't ya know it, just at that moment, my night vision potion went kaput! "Awe, c'mo—"

An arrow sunk into my shoulder. Reaching for Summer's axe, I swung at open air. The room was almost pitch dark, and until my opponent crossed the small square of light made by the stairway opening, I'd have no way to spot them. No windows!

"Where are you?" I shouted desperately, only to take another arrow in the leg. I swung again, missed, then heard the crossbow cock, and jumped away to avoid a hit. Why did my potion have to quit now?! How could I find the attacker? This world's sound had no direction! All I could do was keep moving! But I couldn't do that forever.

Tickety-tock, taunted the clock, *you're falling way behind!*

Another dodged shot, another blind swing.

Oh, for just another couple of minutes, just a few more seconds . . . which I had!

Stew!

Ignoring the next arrow in the stomach, I filled that stomach with suspicious but night-vision enhancing gruel.

One second . . .

There they were! Off to my left!

Two seconds . . .

Netherite axe smashing them back.

Three seconds . . .

Chopping like mad, pinning them against the wall.

Time's up.

Darkness returned, but the smell of smoke told me the job was done.

Tick-tock!

Back to building, groping in the darkness. Memory and luck were with me as I piled explosives to the ceiling and chopped up into gloomy fresh air. The open deck, lit by torches on the columns.

I saw a chest against one of them, forced myself to ignore it. No time for loot.

Tick-tock!

I worked like a demon, fast and focused. But this story was twice as high! Halfway up, I heard a sickening sound: grinding metal, screeching, then silence.

The golem was gone, finally succumbing to the cruel math of overwhelming odds. *You won't have died in vain!* I swore, rushing to reach the roof. But now that they'd smote the iron guardian, all the gloating, harr-ing monsters focused their crossed eyes on me. The air whistled with missiles, thickened by the arrival of spawning skeletons.

In moments I was a porcupine, my armored body bristling with feather-tipped quills. No time for potions, no time to dodge. *Ignore the pain. Keep going!*

More hits, puncturing diamond, piercing flesh.

One more block!

I broke up through the final ceiling into open stars. The moon, nearly at its height! Confirmed by the last few day-specks on the clock! I put the axe away, reached for the remaining bomb parts.

"Harr!" Another one? Spawned on the roof!

An arrow knocked me back, almost off the edge. If I fell . . .

Steadying myself, I regained balance.

The cocking crossbow creaked.

"I do *not* have time for this!" I bellowed, charging my foe. I didn't have a weapon. I didn't need one.

"Harr!" Red, pain. Thorns!

"You tell 'em, pokey pants!" I pushed forward, Thorns helped by fists.

A final "harr" sent him tumbling over the side.

Back to work! I placed the final TNT block, then topped it off with what Summer called her "insurance policy."

I put down the layer of four glass blocks, then the raised glass around them, then four buckets of lava from our hot tub. This was why we'd chosen to call this operation "First House." Just like my island mansion, these civilization breakers would be facing a double whammy of explosives and fire.

Placing the last piece of this payback puzzle, a simple wooden button, I made a final check of the clock. One blue dot left! I gulped down the creamy, fizzy Potion of Feather Falling, pressed the button, then ran off the edge of the roof with a rousing "Bing! Bang! Booooooom!"

The blast—blasts—tossed me like a human cannonball.

Boom! Boom! Boom!

Multiple explosions. Multiple shockwaves. But feather fall landed me safely on my feet, and far from the danger zone. "Aw yeeeeeaaaah!"

I was victorious! I'd beaten the Dark Tower! If only this world had let me craft a camera, because this was quite a sight! The once imposing edifice was little more than a gutted ruin under a slowly descending, stone-covered, wood-burning, night-illuminating fountain of lava.

And the pillagers, they just stood there. No panic, no acknowledgment of their total defeat. There was even one guy, standing at the bottom of what was now a blasted-out crater, waiting passively for the slowly falling lava. I couldn't believe it. Were they idiots, or so crazy that they didn't notice anything except enemies? No, I realized, recalling a term from my world. They were shocked and awed!

All except one, who had been far enough from the inferno, and close enough to my landing spot, to try to exact some small measure of revenge. "Not gonna happen!" I taunted, knocking him back with a crossbow shot. "You might as well just sign the surrender terms"—I checked my clock—"'cause right about now my buddy is taking out the last of your raiders!" Cocking back for another shot, I gloated, "And ya know what they call that back in my world?"

I pulled the trigger, and yelled at the smoke, "Mission accomplished!"

I would have stayed to finish off the rest, but other night mobs were starting to converge on me. "Good luck cleaning up your mess," I jeered and popped my Potion of Speed.

Flying home felt like a victory parade. The war was over! I'd saved the village! And could it have ended any cooler? A risky, courageous mission with an explosive, movie-worthy climax.

Even as mobs wandered or spawned right in my path, I slid past them with elated greetings. "Sorry, dance card's full. Wish I had time to kill ya, but that medal of honor's not gonna award itself!"

Can't wait to tell Summer, I thought as the welcoming glow of the village came into view. *She is gonna be so jeal . . .*

I stopped. Squinting at the gray mass. Something was wrong, different. The wall! The section facing me had a giant hole. And past it, movement? Figures. Most small, one large. Fast and frantic.

Oh, no!

Running again, sweating, feeling like I was going to throw up.

What happened? Had Summer missed her cue? Killed the last raider too soon? Did another wave show up before I could destroy the tower? That had to be it. I didn't want to think about the other options, but at the same time, I couldn't stop.

What if the attacking pillagers were a completely different group than the ones in the Dark Tower? It would explain why the raiding parties never came from the desert. And that feeling . . . the curse. I'd been too drunk on my success to notice. But now I realized it was still there, laughing at my worst mistake! I'd been right the first time, talking Summer into leaving the tower alone. If they're not bothering you, don't bother them! But all that had gone out the window when the other barbarians attacked. I'd been so angry at their treachery, so eager to keep the village safe, that I'd lumped both groups together, simply because they looked alike, and ended up making everything worse!

Were people like that back in my world? Did they make similar mistakes? Had some world leaders, grownups with the power of life and death in their hands, been so weak and flawed that they'd attacked the wrong people? Yes. It was true. Otherwise I wouldn't have had this phrase from that world hammering my brain, as well as the new Vesson it formed:

Nothing is more destructive than the wrong war, in the wrong place, at the wrong time.

All these thoughts flew through me as I raced to the river. No point using the underwater tunnel now. "Summer!" I called, thrashing to the other side, then scrabbling up and through the six-by-six breach in the wall.

A madhouse greeted me. Raiders were everywhere, mixed with the mobs of the night.

"Ghugh!" groaned a zombie, blocking me, punching me in the eye. I ran past, barely feeling the blow. "Summer, where are you?" A skeleton, in front of me, its bow raised. My shield was still packed away! I dodged, just in time, reaching for the board. Left hand up. Block! A golem, its iron punches turning the skeleton to fertilizer.

I looked frantically around, straining for a hint of diamond armor.

"Eeeeyahahaha!"

What the . . .

I looked up to see a grayish creature flying at me on pale ghostly wings. I guess you could call it an angel, but aren't angels supposed to be good? This one wasn't. I could tell by the raised sword. As red veins spread across its pale body, I swiped the air with my own blade. It must have connected, because this new airborne creature flew back with a high-pitched squeal.

"What are you?!" I shouted as it flew in for another strike. I swung again, but took a painful cut in the side. This evil pixie had a wingman. I pivoted, crossbow replacing sword. Backing up, I hoped to get both of them into multishot range. They swooped up, spun around, then dove at me like angry bees. I pulled the trigger. Three arrows flew. One hit! Only one hit from me, but both died, as the second blow came from an approaching golem.

"Thanks, Officer!" I said, then rushed past it to look for Summer.

There she was, across the village, facing what I thought at first was an axeman. But the clothes were wrong; a long, dark robe with gold cuffs and a broad gold stripe down the middle. No weapon, just wide, raised arms.

"Summer!" I was running, pushing past my own shock as, right before my eyes, a line of what looked like metal jaws extended from this raider all the way to my friend. Summer tried to shoot, but the arrow went wild as metal teeth clamped around her legs. "Get away from her!" I shouted, smashing its face with my crossbow.

The robed wretch uttered an annoyed "Huh!" and turned to me with open arms. A new spell? Maybe, but that spell was interrupted by a tri-shot from me and a flaming arrow from Summer.

"Guy!" Her voice, scratchy and quivering. "Did you . . ."

"It's gone!" I panted back. "I took out the tower, but . . ."

"I know." She shook her head, repeated her insectoid curses, then spat, "It didn't bloody work!"

"The wall?!" I asked, gesturing to the breach. "What happened?"

CHAPTER 20

Right then, this is Summer. I told you I'd be back. This time, it's to write about what happened to me when Guy was off playing the gallant hero.

My separate tale began as he entered the pond. I took my station at the northern wall, so I could see the river. I waited patiently for what seemed like an eternity, but when I saw his head surface, so did the baddies below me. As they converged on the riverbank, I let go with a barrage of slowpokes. I think I shouted something encouraging to Guy as he just stood there on the opposite bank. I know he was just trying to find the right speed potion, but, honestly, wouldn't you have had it in hand, ready to go? Oh, Guy!

He finally found it, and shouted something I couldn't make out. Then he sped out of sight, like that bird in the old cartoon. I said something to the effect of "Moving on," and continued my sniping of the horde. Keep in mind, I couldn't snuff them all. That would just bring more. I had to wait till my clock told me that Guy had done in the Dark Tower. It was the only way for the operation to succeed.

That didn't mean I couldn't start trimming away the bulk of them, and witches were top of the naughty list. I found one at the east wall, amidst a gaggle of archers and a bannered leader. This was a great spot of luck, because my plan would muller them all. I hit the cackler with a flaming slowpoke, then reached for my "surprise."

Before meeting Guy, in my early brewing days, I'd managed to accidentally stir together my one and only poisoned potion. Don't forget, I didn't have a book to guide me. It was all trial and error, and so after quaffing it, and almost dying, I swore never to mix those ingredients again. Then came this battle and the witches' toxic grenades. And when that cackler splashed all her mates, I saw the value in chemical warfare. That's why, after brewing some potions for Guy's trip, I went back to the old recipe and cooked up a poison bomb of my own.

Now it was in my hand, all bubbling and noxious and ready to be hurled into history. "Fancy a taste?" I teased, and tossed it over the wall.

But it didn't break! It just hovered, mockingly, right at the foot of the witch! I understand, now, that there must be another step in the process, and, as I think back to being on the receiving end of all those grenades, I'm reasonably sure that the bottles had a slightly different shape. Still, judge if you must. I would. I did.

I uttered something that Guy would never allow me to write

(he is rather stiff with keeping our language clean), then rushed back down to the trading post. The potential fix was already in my head, and it had to do with my metaphor of calling them "grenades." I assumed that gunpowder must be the missing ingredient and, this time around, that assumption paid off handsomely.

"Second time lucky," I called a few minutes later, and thank our lucky stars for the extra gray pinches that hadn't been enough to make Guy's TNT. The hurled orb broke right in the middle of their tight formation, and as green bubbles rose, I followed up with a firestorm of arrows. The blighters burned, but repaid my shots with a few of their own. And as much as I'd liked to indulge in a little shot-and-shield switch, I had to keep firing to prevent the witch from healing. It wasn't easy, or painless, but I finally smoked the pointy-hatted potioneer.

By this point I was in quite a state, and had to duck back below the wall for a quick rabbit stew (Guy doesn't know what he's missing). After repairing my body, I popped into the trading post to repair my armor. I'd like to say that it was a nice respite from combat, but not having a life-or-death task allowed me to worry about Guy.

Yes, of course, I believed in him! I wouldn't have let him go otherwise, but the thought of my mate alone, in the enemies' lair, gave me the kind of tension headache that starts at the back and works its way forward to my eyes. I tried to blink it off, ignored it as I always do, and set about whittling down the rest of the horde. I smoked the next witch, then a few archers, then got down to the serious work of the battle bison.

It was a good deal harder without Guy for added support,

especially when you're taking hits from crossbow archers and (now that night had fallen) newly spawned skeletons. Even if I'd wanted to use my shield, I couldn't, because I had to keep the clock in my left hand. My head must have looked like a proper pin cushion. I kept telling myself "just another shot," which I must have said three or four times.

I probably would have had to retreat and regroup, when a couple of villagers rode to the unexpected rescue. All right, I'm not saying they knew what they were doing. It was probably just a coincidence of location. As I happened to be shooting from the hotel roof, the civilians inside decided to magically summon another golem, which just happened to appear right outside the wall!

I recall cheering it on with a rousing "ten out of ten!" but after it battered the burning buffalo and started working its way through the others, I suddenly worried about mucking everything up. I know it was silly, but I blurted out, "Wait a moment! Don't smoke them all or you'll set off the next wave!"

I wasn't sure what to do. It couldn't understand me. It was just doing its job. The only way to stop it was to shoot it, but that would automatically set all its mates on me. I probably would have taken the risk if the clock hadn't saved us both. Before I could raise my bow, I saw that its spinning dial has just buried that hint of the blue. That meant it was midnight and Guy has just blown the tower to smithereens.

I chuckled, "There we go," and let fly. Not at the golem, but at the axeman it was knocking about. Together, we puffed our way through a couple more archers, then on to the last bannered leader. As it vapored off, I called down, "Thanks, old boy," then strode casually over to the north wall. I remember thinking, *It won't be long before I see Guy, strutting across the desert, ready to regale me with tales of his heroic deeds.*

I'd just made it to my welcoming position when the worst sound in the world assaulted my ears.

"Bubuhbuhbuhbuhbuuuuhhhhh!"

That horrid horn! Another wave! I dashed back to the south wall, the headache now feeling like a proper hurricane behind my neck.

There were just too many to count. But I could see the pointed hats of the witches, the banners of multiple leaders, the mass of a demon bull. And someone new. Two of them, with those gold-cuffed robes Guy's already warned you of.

I was so vexed, so angry that our plan hadn't worked! All that preparing, all those risks Guy had taken! It was all for naught! And now there I was, all alone, facing the greatest force yet! Not that I was scared, mind you! I'll never cop to that.

I shouted "Tallyho!" and I tilted my bow for the highest, longest shot. Lobbing arrows like a mortar, I reasoned that their volume ensured at least some hits. I torched one, then two, then lowered my bow to match the decreasing range. Two more lit up like birthday candles before their archers got close enough to respond.

I tried to stay on the move, never shooting from the same spot. It worked to keep the hits away, but not enough to thin their ranks. The problem, as always, were the combat medics. I'd set an archer smoldering, duck and run to my next firing position, then look up to see a witch's infuriating pink bubbles swirling around it. I tried to shift fire to the cacklers, but they were too close to the wall. And the newly forged constable, well, it didn't last very long. Too much force, too little help from me. I can't rightly remember exactly what the Victoria Cross is, but I'm pretty sure that metal bobby deserved one.

Now I was really in for it, because all their attention locked on me, including three of those conjured, winged frights! I shot one right away, then shifted to its mate, but got hit so hard it knocked me off the walkway and into the village.

I fell hard, cut, bruised, but also, somehow, on fire! There was no time for a healing brew. The blighters were still on me! I squinted through the flames (and the pain!) to return the favor. But these little buzzing (expletive deleted) were too difficult to get a bead on. They flitted about so erratically, like devilish mosquitos. Flaming arrows flew everywhere as I ducked and dodged their sword swipes, but I managed to finally hit Pixie 2, then turn to see Pixie 3 coming at me right through the bleeding wall! Just like a ghost, with the red veins and horrid scream. Cheeky little . . . well . . . you know. I stood my ground, snuffed it with a couple of burners, then popped a healer and the fire-proof potion Guy demanded I keep. I realized these new wizards had to be eliminated first, otherwise their fire fairies would make our wall obsolete.

I ran back up to the walkway and poked my head around a peg. I spotted a flash of gold thread, and shot "from the hip," as they say. The shaft hit, but not with enough damage to stop him from invoking more sparkers. This time I was ready, though. I zapped the first one before it even got halfway. And as its wingman touched me, I growled, "Not this time, Tinker Bell." I knocked it back with a fast shot, then into smoke with a quick follow-up. I think I was halfway through a gloating "Turnabout is fair play," when, suddenly, something struck me from behind.

I'll never forget that sound, the thin, piercing shriek. It was a phantom. They were back! Three nights without sleep had given our attackers new allies. I didn't have time to shoot it, or even look up. I fell right over the wall! Right out into the whole dark monster mess! And who do I see first, of all the nasties old and new?

The flash. The hiss. I jump back with no time to raise my shield.

The distance probably saved my life—that and this wonderful, glorious chest plate which, if you recall, I'd once enchanted with Blast Protection. Still alive, but barely, I flew through the air, and as I landed all crashed and smashed, my barely working eyes took in something worse than any wound.

The creeper had blown a hole in the wall!

Barbarians were pouring through, along with all the nearby night mobs!

You know I'm not one to complain, but that run back to the village, on fractured legs, with all those burnt and burst bits of me trying to stitch themselves together . . . well . . . I can only hope you never experience anything so utterly dreadful. I ran, or rather stumbled, up into the village, took an arrow in the bum (can I say that? Bum? Sorry, Guy), but since my eyes were fixed on the wall's breach, I completely missed the crater right in front of it. I fell into hovering dirt and cobblestone, heard them pop into my pack, then scrambled up the opposite slope into pitched battle.

Bless those golems, doing all they could, and not just to stop the invaders, but to buy me time to try to secure the villagers' homes. How ironic that I'd once argued with Guy about blocking up the doors. Now it was their only hope! Using debris from the breach, I limped to the first house. I shouted, "Stay away from the walls!" to the cowering cartographer inside, and clicked two cobblestones into the entrance. One down. How many to go?

I moved to the next house, but saw that it was empty, and shuffled achingly to the third just as Weaver and Nitwit rushed out. I thundered, "Get back inside, you idiots!" But did they listen?

"Hrrh-hrrh-hrrh!" Running this way and that like headless chickens! I rushed over, pushing and shoving them in the general direction of the library. Thankfully, they took the hint and skittered inside.

Two dirt blocks sealed the doorway just as an axe blade struck my back. I turned, hissed an impolite version of "Please, go away," then knocked the gray-face in their face with my fist. Chopper stumbled back, tried for another axe blow, but I ended our row with a couple of torchy shafts.

Through the death smoke, I could see one of the wizards approaching. Arms raised a shaved second before my bow. The shot went wild as that magic, shark-tooth line reached out to gnash my barely half-healed feet. I muttered another unmentionable phrase and nocked another arrow to my bowstring, when I heard . . .

"Get away from her!"

Guy!

He was on the wizard, clubbing them with his crossbow. The gray head turned, raising their invoking arms up. But we both put a stop to that.

As I was running up to him, he babbled that the tower was gone. I shook my head and babbled back something about it not bloody working.

He then looked down, held out his arms and said, "You're right, Summer, you're always right about everything."

Okay, it's Guy again, and, first of all, I *never* said that! And why would I!? Taking out the tower was her idea!

Anywayz, I'm back to finish the chapter, which I'll start off with me asking, "What happened?"

"No time!" She tossed me a handful of cobblestones. "Plug the hole!" Then she took off again for the nearest house. I didn't have to ask or wonder what she was up to. I just galloped like a gazelle to the breach.

There were only enough cobblestones for one across. Nothing for above, or below! The crater also ran well under the wall, with more than enough space for mobs to fit through. Logs? I still had a few in my pack. I started laying them in the ditch, right up to where they met the stone line. Just enough! But no more! Part of the hole was still there, but since it opened up above the deepest part of the crater, I figured, hoped, that no mob could climb it.

"It'll have to do," I breathed, then, reaching for my sword, I turned to look for Summer.

A rotting fist connected with my jaw. I staggered back, raising my blade. "You're so—" I was gonna say dead, or toast, or something like that, but what came out was . . .

"Smith!"

Green skin. Crossed red eyes.

"Aw, buddy," I whined, backing up to avoid another blow. "Not you."

"Gogh," gargled the newly zombified villager, reaching out with putrid hands. I jerked my head back, retreating slowly. "Don't worry!" I said, staying one step ahead of the blows. "We can change you back, we found a recipe to cure you, but . . ." I didn't have a weakness potion, or a golden apple. Both would have to wait. But I couldn't leave Smith out here now. While being zombified was protection against mobs, it was also a target stamp for the golems.

And one was clanking over now! Arms out, ready to obey its programming.

"Follow me!" I begged Smith, a desperate plan starting to take shape. The nearest building was Weaver's workshop. It was empty, with an unblocked door. I made for it slowly, resisting the urge to run. "Keep after me!" I said, praying we'd both make it. Smith was just ahead of the golem, and I was just ahead of Smith. Not much farther, another few paces.

The screech. Above me.

Not now!

A dive-bombing phantom hit me from the side, driving me diagonally next to Smith. "Huuugggghhh," it growled over a sideswipe to the face.

Resisting the instinct to hit back, I grunted, "Just stay with me!" and drove on toward Weaver's hut. I made it inside, withdrew to the back wall, and waited for Smith to enter.

Those horrible few seconds, trapped in a tiny box, trying to squeeze past the snarling, snapping cadaver. Punches. Bites. *I know you're in there,* I thought through the gauntlet of punishment, *trapped somewhere deep under dead flesh. I promise, we'll free you!*

The last blow, clocking my eye, right before reaching the door. Slamming it behind me, thinking to dig up dirt for a barrier.

Green eyes, on their way down!

No time for my crossbow. Sword! I reached for my bladed weapon, praying that Smith hadn't hurt me badly enough that I couldn't survive another hit.

"Hhhahhhh!"

Turning to look up, I saw green eyes growing larger.

Fists! Large, metallic, batting the bat monster away.

"Protect and serve!" I said, repeating what I think is a slogan for cops, then turned to finish sealing up Smith. First the door, then the windows, just in case the sunlight fried him.

"Sit tight," I told the muffled gurgles, then plunged back into the maelstrom. There was Summer, outside one of the houses, dirt blocks in hand. But behind her . . .

Huge, dark, charging with lowered horns.

"Buffalo!" I shouted, and jumped the last few squares. My sword sliced down, into a wall of flashing red flesh.

The bio-tank lurched sideways with a snorting "Hrroarrr!" then turned its battering ram of a head toward me.

Yikes!

I turned and fled, trying to lead the monster away from Summer.

"Run, rabbit!" she called over the THWP of a missed arrow. "Lure the beggar back to me!"

I did my best, but the danger wasn't only behind me. I dodged a spider, ducked a phantom, then hopped ahead of a raider's crossbow shot. I looped around Weaver's shop, heard Smith's comforting groan, then weaved back toward my waiting partner. She was ready, bow raised, straining for her chance to get the right shot. Hot breath on my back, angry snorts in my ears. I glanced back for just a second, then looked forward again to see a creeper. Right between us!

"Get clear!" Summer called. "I've no shot!"

Stuck! Pinned.

If I ran to the side, they'd both converge from either side. But if I kept going . . .

This might have been the craziest, dumbest thing I'd ever done. Maybe it was experience talking, the countless times I'd dealt with creepers. But unless they'd changed recently, unless their fuse time had shortened . . .

"Guy! No!"

I ran right at the living landmine, close enough to trip the timer. It stopped, flashing as I zoomed past. Shouting to Summer, "Get back!"

Boom!

I spun to see the bull flashing red, lifted a block or so off the ground, crashed down into the newly formed crater, then climbing right back up at us!

Fifteen squares. That's how much space we had to live. Her bow, my crossbow. Shooting as fast as we could. It was burning now, loping at us like living lava. Ten squares. Five squares! The heat of the flames. The smell. Cooking meat! One square!

"Hrroarrr!"

POOF.

For a second, I just stood there, shaking and hyperventilating at what had almost happened.

"The villagers are safe," huffed Summer toward me, "I locked up the last hou—"

CRACK.

Broken glass. Burning pain. And the sickening, green bubbles of poison.

"Hahahahaha!"

The last witch! Approaching from behind the nearest building.

"The trading post!" I gagged on the taste of poison in my mouth. "Get inside!" Pushing her into our nearby shack, I slammed the door, then sealed it with earth cubes for good measure.

"Milk!" I burped, throwing her one of my pails. Lifting the other, I drank deep, and realized a second later that it hadn't only nullified the poison.

"The curse," I exclaimed, "it's gone!" I took a few deep breaths, walked around the room. "That was it! All this time!" I started taking apart the dirt barrier. "Not the raider's banner, not the Dark Tower. All we needed to end this war was just a regular old slug of fresh milk!"

I opened the door, expecting to see the town square cleared.

"Harr!"

An axeman, right in front of me, and the disappointment hurt worse than its chop.

"I wish you were right"—Summer was reaching past me now, re-blocking the doorway with dirt—"and that might have worked a while ago." A heavy, resigned sigh. "But I don't think there's any quick fix now. The only way to stop this war is to win it."

"But how . . ." I swallowed, fighting back tears. "How do we win?" From mind to heart, top to toes, I suddenly felt like all was lost. "If they just keep coming . . ."

"Then we keep fighting." Summer's voice was low, steady. She stepped into my face, locking her eyes to mine as she announced, "We shall defend our village, whatever the cost may be. We shall fight in the fields, and in the streets. We shall fight in the hills. We shall not flag or fail. We shall go on to the end. We shall *never* surrender!"

"Summer," I said, feeling a sudden rush of hope, "did you just make that up?"

"Why . . . yes," she answered, seemingly surprised at her own words. "I believe I did."

"Well, it sure did the trick," I said, raising my chipped sword for battle. I peered outside, just in time to see a golem smash the witch that attacked us.

"Ready then?" asked Summer.

I nodded, adding, "Hey, for what it's worth, I just want you to know that whatever happens, I wouldn't trade this short time I've had with you for a lifetime of safety back on my island."

"Likewise, Guy." Summer raised her fist to mine. "As a wise man once said, growth doesn't come from a comfort zone, but from leaving it."

"Wasn't that E-mop?" I said, and after a much-needed laugh, I asked, "Ready to leave this safe space?"

Summer raised her bow. "Let us go forward together."

I peeled off the earth cubes, opened the door, and rushed out into the swinging blade of the axemen . . . two of them. An equal match, with no room for ranged weapons. Give and take. Sword and shield, but, in my case, the latter broke after two hits. I'd forgotten to repair it! Now my armor was my only protection! *No problem*, I thought, as the demonic lumberjack puffed away after a jab from my Thorns enchantment.

"Eeeeyahahaha!"

Another angel of death! And, behind it, another conjuror with raised arms.

"I've got the sky!" said Summer, switching from sword to bow. "You take the ground!"

Ignoring the battle above me, I switched to my own arrow launcher. Three arrows flew, the center one striking the wizard. Reloading quickly, I shot again, just as a second winged wailer faded in. I aimed high, hoping that my triple shot might get them both. Instead, I got a double miss! The pixie flew away, no doubt toward Summer, as its creator raised their arms again. "Uh-uh!" I barked, shooting once more as the living, magical aircraft carrier finally wafted into dust. But when it vanished, I noticed something strange hit the ground.

"What are you?" I asked, rushing over to pick up the hovering loot. It was a small, gold statuette, the same type I thought I'd find way back in the jungle temple.

"Huh," I mused, holding up the idol. "Now this is kinda interesti—"

"Eeeeyahahaha!"

A sword to my head. The pain pixie had doubled back! I staggered forward, twisting to counter. I swung, missed, and took another brutally unfair stab. Agony. Injury. No time to hyper-heal!

"Eeeeyahahaha!" Diving again, red veins growing.

Battered and bashed, my poor body was nearly broken. Between the battle with the axemen and now this latest airstrike, the next solid blow might be my last!

I raised my shield to block, forgetting it was gone . . . but the gold idol was there in my left hand. Of course!

Idols have magical powers, right?

"Behold!" I bellowed, brandishing the glittering totem. "I smite thee!"

What was I expecting, lightning from the heavens or the sprite to spontaneously combust? Maybe I was too punchy from my beating, or just desperate for a miracle, but the timing, the luck of finding this treasure . . .

C'mon, world, gimme a break!

"Eeeeyahahaha!"

Please!

No lightning, no smiting. Just a falling sword in my face!

Jolting anguish, darkening vision. Cold. Fading.

Is this what if feels like to die?

But I didn't!

I should have, but I didn't!

"What the Neth . . . ?" I started to say, but took another, lethal stab.

Nothing . . . well, not exactly nothing. I felt the impact, the puncture that pierced my heart. How was it still beating?

The idol! It was magical, just not the way I'd assumed!

Never assume anything.

"Now," I snarled, as the floating screamer bobbed toward me, "we end this."

My crossbow gave a WHP, and the winged horror howled a tortured, final, "Geehhuh!"

At the same time, my partner shouted, "Got 'im!" Her last arrow erased the other sprite.

"S-Summer," I rasped, hobbling toward her with the idol. "This statue the wizard dropped, I think . . . I think it keeps you from dying!"

"We'll need it," Summer said matter-of-factly, as she pressed her comforting back against mine, "because who knows what's coming next!"

"Got that right," I said, downing my last healer, "but . . . where are they?"

Our combined, 360-degree field of vision didn't show one single raider.

"Come out!" I howled to empty ground. "Don't be shy!"

All we got back was silence, then strange sounds. Whistling, popping. "What the Nether are those?" asked Summer, stepping up next to me and pointing skyward.

Rockets.

Small red and white missiles were shooting up into the air, where they popped into tiny puffs of smoke.

"Fireworks?" I asked, but I saw that Summer was nowhere close. She'd run over to the breach and sealed the last open square with dirt.

"The next wave!" she called back. "Has to be! The bull was a tank, the pixies were aeroplanes, and now they've upgraded to bloody heavy artillery!"

"But," I argued, tracing their upward arcs, "why are they coming from our houses?"

She looked to see I was right, then added, "And where's that horrid horn?"

Something was wrong . . . or . . . right? We couldn't dare get our hopes up. But there weren't any more raiders, and the night mobs had all burned away.

Summer rushed up to the wall, scanning the field with her spyglass. "Clear," she reported, swinging it in a full circle, "on all sides."

I probably shouldn't have done this. Not my smartest move. But curiosity drove me to punch up the dirt blocking the hotel. Instantly, Fletcher, Weaver, and Mason came out to greet me. None were sweating or flailing around in panic. They just looked at me, hrrh-ed calmly, and, to my forever shock and awe, started chucking stuff at me. Blocks of wool, new crossbows, and colored cubes of clay.

"Whoa there," I said, backing up with raised fists, "what's goin' on?"

"Check the others!" said Summer, who'd run down to un-block another house. Out came Junior and Librarian, who immediately showered her in cookies and blank books. "What's all this about?"

"They're celebrating," I said, feeling my heart take wing. "I think we won."

EPILOGUE

That was two months ago, and a lot has happened since then. Nothing that exciting or dangerous. Well, one thing. Okay, call me crazy if you want. Summer sure did. But destroying the Dark Tower left me feeling really guilty—so guilty that I couldn't move on until I'd tried my darndest to rebuild it.

You read that right. "You break it, you own it." Didn't someone once say that about a war in my world? Didn't a much wiser man than me once warn his boss that if they invaded a country, they would end up owning it, and therefore be responsible for whatever it took to put that country back together? This is what took so much time, even with Summer helping.

Every day we'd set out, armed with potions and building materials. Summer would try to distract the new raiders (who were still spawning in the lava-soaked ruins). And once they were far enough away, I'd run in to fix a little bit more of what I'd broken.

It definitely wasn't easy, especially when you think about what it took to jump-build a temporary sand column up to the suspended lava cubes. Just thinking about that still gives me the shakes.

And the memory only gets shakier when I think about the barbarians spawning in the middle of my work. That happened every day. I'd hear "Harr!" and pop an invisi-brew, which is why I worked armorless, making it all the more perilous. "Time to go," I'd call and, together, we'd head back to the village. We did that day after day, and it wasn't cheap—and using up our initial emerald cache to buy the gold melons from Junior was what set us back another month. I don't regret it, though, not even when we finished and the locals responded by chasing us away. It wasn't about gratitude. It was about setting things right.

And speaking of postwar messes, the first to be cleaned up was Smith! The last of our gold went into gilding an apple, and the last of our gunpowder created a grenade of weakness (shout-out to Summer for discovering the latter).

We headed over to the temporary prison, removed the top earth cube, and opened the door. Smith of the Living Dead instinctively came at us, arms raised and throat gurgling with hunger. "Stand back," Summer warned me, then whipped the potion ball through the doorway.

Glass broke. Gray bubbles rose.

Now came the hard part. Apple in hand, I stepped as close as I could. Would they bite me? Would it even work? I probably should have said something profoundly poetic like "Apples were the first food to keep me alive in this world, and now one will bring you back to life." But instead, I blurted the bad joke, "Take one of these and call me in the morning."

Smith snatched the shining fruit from me, crunched down, then started shaking as pink bubbles mixed with gray.

"It's gotta be working," I said hopefully. "Don't pink bubbles mean healing?"

They did. Smith shook for a long while, then, before our eyes, they transformed back into their old hrrh-ing self.

"Well, that's lucky," Summer breathed, as we let Smith out to join the crowd, "and a cheating reminder of what we lose in war."

I nodded, thinking about that loss. Back on our world, you could rebuild stuff, like the Dark Tower, but you couldn't bring back people. Summer was right about being lucky. We hadn't lost anyone, but that couldn't happen on our world. One more reason to make sure war was a last resort and not the first choice to solve any problem.

After that happy moment, and the scary, obligatory month of rebuilding the Dark Tower, we got back to the daily grind of re-stocking enough emeralds to buy all those Ender pearls. That's what took the next month, which also gave us time to prepare for moving on. I don't just mean physical preparation, getting "kitted out" and all that. I also mean saying our goodbyes.

Mason, Junior, Librarian, the Smiths. I took my time with each one, telling them how much they had meant to me. I fol-lowed them on their morning walks, or talked to them during work time. I reminisced about all we'd been through, and warned them against the dangers of wandering outside the walls after dark. They all just hrrh'd politely back. Not the most emotional culture. Oh, well, that's their way.

And speaking of sentimentality, Summer surprised me with her farewells to the axolotls. One morning I found her down by the river, breaking the dams she'd built for her fish farms. "You're free now," she said, waving as the amphibious family swam out into open water, "and if you ever want to return to that lush cave, it's just down the river a bit." She sniffed hard, clearly fighting her feelings. "Take care, all of you. And thank you"—but as she saw me approaching, her quivering voice hardened—"thank you for a very profitable business relationship."

I didn't tease her. It would have been too easy to poke fun at my warrior pal's softer side. I just asked innocently, "You ready to go?"

That was yesterday. Today we tossed the pearl.

We stood in the middle of Flower Valley, facing the breezy west. Summer did the honors, holding up our newly crafted Ender eye. "Luck with rainbows," she breathed and chucked it into the air. And wouldn't you know it, the cat's eye–looking thing shot right between us and into the air on a pink, sparkly trail.

"Back the way we came?!" I chuckled, as the eye fell back to earth.

"Who knows how far," Summer said, collecting it. "With our luck, the ruddy portal's right underneath my mountain."

"Or my island." I shook my head. "Which would be kinda cool, since you'd get to meet all my animal friends."

"Sounds delicious."

"Summer!"

"Just winding you up."

We shared a laugh, then headed back to Slate House. It would only take a few minutes to pack up our gear and for me to write these last few sentences.

And right before writing them, Summer asked, "You think the End is really the end?" She gestured to the path before us. "You think we're headed in the right direction?"

I nodded. "You asked me the same thing when we left your mountain."

"Really?" She blinked, clearly not remembering. "What was your answer?"

"I didn't have one," I said. "But I do now."

"Which is?"

I told her what I'm telling you now, and it's an answer that comes from another book. I know, typical me, always referencing books and movies and other people's stories. But you sure can learn a lot from stories. I hope you've learned from ours.

Anyway, this book I once read (or someone read to me) was about a family that adopted some kind of rodent. A squirrel or a guinea pig? Doesn't matter. What matters is that he befriends a bird, and when the bird flies away, he heads out to find her. I can't remember if he does or not, but I can't forget this one line, which suddenly popped into my head the moment the Ender eye popped into the sky. It kinda sums up all the lessons we've learned along our journey, and why some journeys can matter more than the destination. That line simply read:

"He somehow felt he was headed in the right direction."

THE WORLD OF MINECRAFT

(AS WRITTEN BY SUMMER)

1. When meeting a new community, come in peace, but don't let your guard down just yet.

2. Specialization moves everyone forward.

3. Trade is a universal language (and money can be a very efficient translator).

4. It's not the money that's evil, just what people might do for it.

5. The key to good business is supply and demand.

6. The police should never punish anyone just because they *look* like a criminal.

7. When shopping, always have a budget.

8. The punishment should never be harsher than the crime.

9. The way to tell people who won't work from people who can't work is to give everyone an equal opportunity.

10. When making an investment, consider all the hidden costs.

11. It's okay to depend on others, but always be ready to depend on yourself.

12. It might take more time and effort, but there's always a way to shop responsibly.

13. Immigrants make a village stronger.

14. Every member of a community should provide for the common defense.

15. Even a good king is a bad idea.

16. No matter how hard you try to make peace, some people just want a war.

17. It's a lot easier to start a war than to end one.

18. Adaptation is a key element of war.

19. When the community is threatened, everyone has a role to play.

20. Nothing is more destructive than the wrong war, in the wrong place, at the wrong time.

21. War should always be a last resort.

22. And finally . . . a shoutout to Guy's first story: growth doesn't come from a comfort zone, but from leaving it.

ACKNOWLEDGMENTS

Thank you to all the kids who've written to me asking for more adventures of Summer and Guy, and to everyone who helped me make this adventure possible: the teams at Mojang and Del Rey, my wife, Michelle (always!), and the late author E. B. White for the last line in his novel *Stuart Little*, which is also the last line of this book. Like Stuart, Summer, and Guy, we're hopefully all headed in the right direction.

ABOUT THE AUTHOR

MAX BROOKS is a senior nonresident fellow at the Modern War Institute at West Point and the Atlantic Council's Snowcroft Center for Strategy and Security. His bestselling books include: *Minecraft: The Island*, *Minecraft: The Mountain*, *Devolution*, *The Zombie Survival Guide*, and *World War Z*, which was adapted into a 2013 movie starring Brad Pitt. His graphic novels include *The Extinction Parade*, *G.I. Joe: Hearts & Minds*, and the #1 *New York Times* bestseller *The Harlem Hellfighters*.

maxbrooks.com
Facebook.com/AuthorMaxBrooks
Twitter: @maxbrooksauthor